About the Author

JEAN-LOUIS DUBUT DE LAFOREST (1853–1902) was the *belle epoque*'s most popular and prolific writer of thrillers. Born in the rural Dordogne area of central France, he took his law degree in the southern city of Bordeaux, then became a police prosecutor, a job he left in 1882 to join the newspaper *Le Figaro*. He soon earned more fame and money writing sensational novels, exploiting crime, sex, and drugs, which he turned out at breakneck speed. In the last fourteen years of his life, he wrote dozens, including *Le Gaga* (1886), which was prosecuted as an offense against morals. His best-known novel was, and remains, *Morphine* (1891).

About the Translator

JOHN BAXTER is the author of the memoirs *Immoveable Feast: A Paris Christmas* and *We'll Always Have Paris* and the erotic reference *Carnal Knowledge*. An acclaimed film critic and biographer whose subjects have included Woody Allen, Steven Spielberg, Stanley Kubrick, and Robert De Niro, Baxter also is the co-director of the Paris Writers Workshop. He lives in Paris, France, with his wife and daughter.

MORPHINE

Selected Works by Jean-Louis Dubut de Laforest

Les dames de Lamète (1880)
Le Gaga (1886)
Rabelais (1893)

Also by John Baxter

Carnal Knowledge: Baxter's Concise Encyclopedia of Modern Sex
Immoveable Feast: A Paris Christmas
We'll Always Have Paris: Sex and Love in the City of Light
A Pound of Paper: Confessions of a Book Addict
Science Fiction in the Cinema
The Cinema of Josef von Sternberg
Luis Buñuel
Fellini
Stanley Kubrick
Steven Spielberg
Woody Allen
George Lucas
Robert De Niro

Also Translated by John Baxter

My Lady Opium, by Claude Farrère
The Diary of a Chambermaid, by Octave Mirbeau
Gamiani, or Two Nights of Excess, by Alfred de Musset

MORPHINE

Jean-Louis
Dubut de Laforest

Translated by John Baxter

HARPER ⬤ PERENNIAL

NEW YORK ● LONDON ● TORONTO ● SYDNEY

The photographs that appear on pages xiii and xv are courtesy of the author's collection.

HarperCollins books may be purchased for educational, business, or sales promotional use. For information please write: Special Markets Department, HarperCollins Publishers, 10 East 53rd Street, New York, NY 10022.

FIRST HARPER PERENNIAL EDITION PUBLISHED 2010.

Library of Congress Cataloging-in-Publication Data is available upon request.

ISBN 978-0-06-196534-0

10 11 12 13 14   OV/RRD   10 9 8 7 6 5 4 3 2 1

To Professor Cesare Lombroso, the teacher who, by commenting on my books during his admirable lessons on criminal anthropology, gave me the greatest fortune that can come to any writer, I dedicate this novel.

Jean-Louis Dubut de Laforest, 1891

CONTENTS

Penny Dreadful

The *brocante*, or flea market, is a French institution. During the warmer months, you can depend on finding one every weekend, if not spreading along a few blocks in your own Parisian suburb, then taking over the central square of the town where you are spending your holidays.

In this case, the sellers—hundreds of them—had set up their stalls around a lake in the middle of a camping ground deep in the countryside. From battered kitchen implements to children's toys, rusted wrenches to unplayable vinyl discs, everything had been hauled out of the attic in hopes of a sale. I expected this. But I wasn't prepared for a carton filled with scores of ancient paperbacks, all from the early 1900s.

Uniform in size, they mostly belonged to a series called *Les derniers scandales de Paris—The Latest Paris Scandals*. All were written by the same two authors, Jean-Louis Dubut de Laforest and Oscar Metenier, and boasted covers by the same two or three artists. But what covers! Bombs exploding; a maid running amok with a hatchet; men in flowing beards guzzling champagne with half-naked chorus girls; a terrified citizen cowering back from a severed hand just received in the morning post. Who could resist such a treasury of trash? For a few euros, I bought the whole lot, and carried them back to Paris to do some research.

I soon realized I had stumbled on the French equivalent of the "penny dreadful."

British publishers coined the term "penny dreadful" or "penny blood" in the late nineteenth century to describe cheap serial stories, published in weekly episodes, each one costing a penny. The "bloods" usually featured tales of highwaymen who, when not robbing coaches, were rescuing beautiful heiresses from their evil guardians. Others earned their "dreadful" label with tales of gore, among them the legend of Sweeney Todd, the Demon Barber of Fleet Street, who butchered his customers and sold their flesh for pies. Todd proved such a crowd-pleaser that he remains alive and bloody today in the musical by Stephen Sondheim.

French bloods began where the English stories left off. Uninterested in anything as humdrum as armed robbery, *Les derniers scandales de Paris* dealt in sex, drugs, madness, terrorism, and wholesale slaughter. Metenier and Laforest had been police prosecutors, and so knew crime fighting at first hand—although their brand of criminology would not sit well with modern investigators. *Morphine* is dedicated very warmly to Cesare Lombroso, the psychologist who believed criminal tendencies were hereditary, and could be detected from the shape of the head. Women, he decreed, were too stupid to make effective criminals. The few who did were immedi-

The original cover design for *Morphine*. Christine Stradowska is horrified as her lover, Raymond de Pontaillac, hallucinates under the influence of the drug.

ately identifiable by excessive body hair, wrinkles, and certain bumps on the skull.

As writers, Metenier and Laforest clashed with the world of law enforcement they left behind. In each case, the problem was prostitution. Brothels flourished openly but unacknowledged in every French town, but in 1896 Metenier had the temerity to depict a prostitute on stage in the play *Mademoiselle Fifi*, adapted from a story by Guy de Maupassant. It was promptly shut down. Laforest's brush with the law was more damaging. In 1886, he wrote *Le Gaga*, about a woman who, tired of her husband spending all his time and money with prostitutes, hires one to teach her the tricks of the trade. Accused of an offense against public morals, Laforest was fined a thousand francs and sentenced to two months in prison.

Though the men were friends, and even collaborated on a few plays, Metenier was the better showman. In 1897, he converted an abandoned chapel in Montmartre, Paris's bohemian quarter, into a theater for dramatized versions of the crimes described in *Derniers scandales*. His *Theatre de Grand Guignol* became infamous—and hugely popular—for stories of rape, torture, and violent death. Its grisly stage effects included eyes gouged out, hands and fingers severed, faces burned with acid or pressed to red-hot stove tops. Leading lady Paula Maxa, "the world's most assassinated woman," estimated that, over twenty years, she was murdered more than ten thousand times in at least sixty different ways, and suffered three thousand rapes. The term "Grand Guignol" even passed into the language as a synonym for any scene of bloody horror.

Among the scores of novelettes turned out by Laforest, *Morphine* has a special interest to us because of its theme of addictive drugs. Not only are the dashing cavalry officer Raymond de Pontaillac and his lover, the Marquise Blanche de

Luce and Therese, courtesans and fellow addicts, try without
success to excite Raymond de Pontaillac.

Montreu, destroyed by morphine, but abuse of the drug, like
an infection, spreads to everyone around them.

In describing this, Laforest exposes the secret Paris that lay
just below the glamour of the so-called *belle epoque.* The "beautiful age" emerges as anything but a paradise, its inhabitants
driven almost exclusively by lust or greed, though always with
a distinctively Gallic twist. Madame Xavier, typical of the numerous abortionists who flourished in France, disguises her
trade under the poetic term *"faiseur d'anges"*—literally "angel
maker," since her innocent victims went directly to heaven.
Hornuch, the crooked pharmacist, sets up a basement morphine factory where, in a curiously domestic detail, he puts his
three daughters to work earning the dowries that will attract
suitable husbands. And two of the most sympathetic charac-

ters are Luce and Therese, high-class prostitutes—although Laforest, having learned the lesson of *Le Gaga*, obliquely calls them *"horizontales."*

In making his addict hero a military officer, Dubut de Laforest took a greater risk. France's army was regarded as the backbone of the state, and ruthlessly suppressed any threat to its integrity. In 1915, France would ban absinthe because it supposedly sapped the energy of potential recruits. How much more controversial the damage done by morphine, a drug that, because of its cost, attacked the elite officer class? In 1895, France had condemned Captain Alfred Dreyfus to incarceration on Devil's Island for supposedly leaking secrets to the Germans. When his innocence was revealed, the high command argued the error should be hushed up, rather than undermine public confidence.

Morphine isn't high literature. But *Les derniers scandales de Paris* stands in relation to the novels of Zola and Balzac as Daumier's caricatures of the law courts and Toulouse-Lautrec's sketches of brothel life do to the paintings of Manet and Renoir. It's not in those great canvases but in the jagged line and smear of paint that we see how death was truly encountered and life, however briefly, was lived.

John Baxter
PARIS
JUNE 2009

MORPHINE

{ 1 }

That night in November 1889, at the Café de la Paix, the clock had just struck eleven in one of the small, stuffy rooms whose doors open onto the Place de l'Opera as young Jean de Fayolle, of the 15th regiment of Cuirassiers, leaned forward from the red velvet banquette and clacked down his last tile on the marble table in front of him.

"Domino!"

Winning brought a flush to his boyish face that for a moment made his skin match the bushy red mustache he'd grown in hopes of attaining an impression of military toughness. But nobody looking at his two opponents, Major Edgard Lapouge, a medical surgeon, tall and blond, his blue eyes glinting behind a gold monocle, and portly, gray-haired Arnould-Castellier, director of the prestigious *Military Review*, would have been fooled for a moment.

Lapouge, glad the game was over, didn't even bother to tote up the points on his remaining tiles.

"Is Pontaillac coming," he asked the group, "yes or no?"

"He'll be here," said Fayolle.

"Pontaillac?" Lieutenant Léon Darcy looked up from where he was lolling at a nearby table, listening to the stories murmured in his ear by two evidently amusing young women. "Not tonight."

"You know something Fayolle doesn't?" demanded the major. He made it seem a foregone conclusion. Fayolle flushed a deeper red.

Darcy gestured out the window at the façade of the Opera, with its gaslit arcade, flanked by angels soaring on wings of song.

"Pontaillac's at the Opera—and for a change he's not enjoying it from the dressing room. Tonight he's in a box—with the Marquise de Montreu."

The eyes of Arnould-Castellier narrowed. "Where is her husband?"

"I have no idea. But she's there only with Pontaillac."

"You're crazy, Darcy!" said Fayolle. "Young Olivier de Montreu is one of Pontaillac's oldest friends. I'm sure it's all perfectly innocent. Anyway, Raymond has eyes and ears only for Stradowska."

"And do you wonder?" said Darcy respectfully. "A beauty like that—and such a voice!"

"All the same," observed Arnould-Castellier thoughtfully, "I wouldn't put it past Pontaillac to have two loves at the same time."

"Three," growled Lapouge. "You forget, gentlemen, the most expensive of his mistresses, as well as the most perfidious and dangerous. Morphine."

At the mention of the drug, the girls pricked up their ears. They'd have liked to hear more, but Darcy shushed them. As the others went back to their dominoes, Luce, the blond, asked, "This Stradowska. She's a singer?"

Darcy reached for the latest issue of *Rabelais*, a popular picture weekly, and opened it to a full-page illustration of a slim but well-formed young woman on stage.

"*Voilà*. La Stradowska. She hadn't been in Saint Petersburg for more than a season before she had princes and moguls flinging jewels at her. She ruined a grand duke. Then she gathered up all her gifts, and moved to Paris. Her home, Villa Said, is legendary."

"And Captain de Pontaillac is her lover?" inquired Therese, the brunette. "So he's rich too?"

"Two hundred thousand louis a year—at least!"

Luce's eyes narrowed. "Good-looking?"

Darcy glanced over her shoulder. "See for yourself, my darling."

Captain Raymond de Pontaillac was sufficiently handsome even to startle the two courtesans, who surreptitiously pulled down their bodices a little to better expose their décolletages, and pinched their cheeks to give an additional flush.

At thirty, he was tall, broad-shouldered, and tanned, with a fine mustache. Under the ankle-length fur coat, he wore a simple black suit as impeccably cut as the uniform he normally boasted as a captain of the 15th Cuirassiers, a crack regiment of heavy cavalry.

Ignoring the wine and liqueurs, he called for a waiter and demanded a glass of water, which he downed in a long swallow.

"I'm dying of thirst tonight."

The major indicated the half-finished game of dominoes. "Care to play? One louis a point."

But Pontaillac brushed aside the suggestion. "I won't take your money. I shouldn't have come at all. I'm in a black mood, and I have no idea why."

"We all know why," Darcy said. "Morphine. That stuff will kill you, Pontaillac."

"Don't be absurd. I can stop any time."

More iced champagne arrived, and more water for Pontaillac, who could never get enough. Yet though he drank no alcohol, it was he who, heading for the screens that hid the chamber pots, lurched against the table and scattered the dominoes.

"For God's sake, Pontaillac!"

But the young count ignored him. Luce, who had been idly studying the portrait of Stradowska, put down the magazine and followed him behind the screen. She found him with his back turned and his trousers pulled down over his hips to reveal a pair of silk underwear. Instead of urinating into one of the chamber pots, however, he was injecting himself in the thigh. As he straightened and began to button his trousers, Luce said, "Oh, what a pretty little syringe."

Raymond turned hurriedly. "Give me that!"

But Luce was too quick. She ducked out from behind the screen, and almost ran into Lapouge. By the time Pontaillac emerged, he was examining the little implement of silver.

"A Pravaz," he said, with grudging admiration. "Only the best for you, Pontaillac, as always."

The syringe developed by Charles Pravaz was as elegant as a piece of jewelry. Barely the length of a finger, it was made entirely of silver and glass, and, unlike cruder British implements, operated with a screw, not a plunger, allowing the most precise measurements.

"If you please!" The count held out his hand.

"I should crush this under my heel," said the doctor. "Like a deadly snake."

"Too late, my friend. I've already injected myself. Anyway, I have another one in my pocket and fourteen more at home."

Pontaillac spoke casually, but Lapouge noted with a professional's eye how his voice, a little throaty when he arrived, now rang crystal clear, and his eyes, formerly weary, had a fixed, even manic glint—all signs of the morphine user.

Now it was the turn of the other woman of the party, the voluptuous brunette Therese de Roselmont, to examine the Pravaz.

"It doesn't look so dangerous," she said, running her thumb over the gleaming silver.

"It isn't—when used correctly," Lapouge said. "During the Tonkin wars, it relieved the pain of hundreds of wounded men."

"Including myself," said Raymond.

"Except in your case, you received your cut in a duel!"

"It hurt just as much," said the count carelessly. "And with morphine, I found I could regulate my life. I hadn't been able to eat, to sleep, to drink. One injection—and I eat, sleep, and drink without a care. I had been sad—suddenly, I was happy."

"And . . . love?" inquired Luce coquettishly.

"Oh, my dear, with love it's exactly like everything else. Don't believe those lies they tell you."

Taking a black velvet pouch from his pocket, he slipped the Pravaz into its place beside its sister, and next to a tiny flask, the size of a perfume bottle, filled with morphine solution.

Luce looked at it speculatively. "And the needle . . . it doesn't hurt?"

In answer, the count refilled the syringe he had just used, rolled up his sleeve, and, as the young women watched in fascination, slid the needle into his muscular arm. As he withdrew it, a bead of blood stood out on his skin. With a silk handkerchief, he wiped it away.

"See. As expert as any dentist." Looking at the girls, he said, a glint in his eye, "Want to try?"

"Not for a hundred louis!" said Therese.

"You're mad. It's heaven." He looked at Luce. "And you, my dear?"

"Well . . . if it really does no harm. And if it's even half as good as you say . . ."

An hour later, when they left the café, the lights on the façade of the Opera had been extinguished, and the Place de l'Opera was almost empty.

The three officers hailed a cab and helped the girls into it. "Come and have supper with us, Raymond," said Fayolle, but Pontaillac waved them away.

"Thanks, but I have another appointment."

As the count hailed another cab, Lapouge smiled to himself. No doubt he was off to meet his other mistress— Stradowska.

But the address Raymond de Pontaillac gave to the cab driver was not the Villa Said of Stradowska but his own town house on Rue Boissy d'Anglas. Nor were his thoughts filled with the beautiful diva or the dreams induced by morphine. Rather, he thought only of the woman with whom he had shared a box at the opera, the lovely, aristocratic, but, sadly, unavailable Blanche de Montreu.

{ 2 }

During the fifteen months Pontaillac had been under the influence of morphine, he had lived in a mental state somewhere between reality and dream. Far from reducing his capacities, the drug seemed to double them—to create, in fact, two different Raymonds.

To his fellow officers in the barracks of his regiment, this member of the landed gentry of Limousin, a graduate of the Military College at Saint Cyr, was the best sort of soldier, respected by his commanders, admired by his men as a brilliant officer with, at the same time, a generous heart.

Off the parade ground, in his magnificent town house, with his mistress, or his friends the Montreus in their mansion on Boulevard Malesherbes, a different Raymond emerged.

Almost none of them noticed the mischief the Pravaz played with his character, and the inexorable signs of progressive deterioration typical of the addict.

Initially, he had offered pretexts for its use. First, the effects of the wound received in the duel—no doubt painful, but not as bad as he claimed. After that came insomnia, palpitations of the heart, stomach problems—for all of which he diagnosed a reviving injection of morphine.

At first, the results had been a miraculous sense of well-being and beatitude, a delicious intoxication, a Buddhist Nirvana, ecstasy, a revival of the spirit, and acceleration of the mental processes—a double life. Increased use of the drug, however, led to a fragmentation of the personality, an inability to concentrate on anything for a long period, an impatience that could only briefly be calmed by another injection.

And then there was . . . love.

At the café, Raymond had claimed that morphine heightened his sexual abilities. His mistress had a different view. For some months, she'd noticed his waning potency, and blamed the drug. She could not know that, at this point at least, morphine had not reduced his ardor but rather channeled it in another direction, toward the beautiful Marquise Blanche de Montreu.

That afternoon, Pontaillac passed through the foyer of the Montreu mansion, its marble floors illuminated by the gleam of bronze and gold, and found the marquis in his library, surrounded by shelves of books, all richly bound in Cordoba leather, embossed in gilt with the double crests of his own family and that of his wife, the La Crozes.

"So how are you, Olivier?" Pontaillac demanded, shaking his hand. "You look pale."

His friend wore a simple black velvet dressing gown that accentuated his pallor and frail figure, an effect augmented by a silky blond beard and the blue eyes of a dreamer.

"I'm worried. My wife is in pain."

"Nothing serious, I trust."

"I hope not." He glanced upward to her private apartments. "Aubertot is with her now."

"Last night, at the opera, she was gay, smiling."

"Yes, but this morning, at breakfast, she suffered a violent headache, and since then the pain has been intolerable."

At that moment, the door opened and a servant ushered in a man whose high forehead and gray hair suggested the intelligence of a great thinker or an artist. Raymond recognized Dr. Etienne Aubertot, a member of the Faculty at the Academy of Medicine.

"Well?" demanded Olivier and Raymond at almost the same moment, the latter doing his best not to show his excessively deep concern for his friend's wife.

"The marquise is not in danger," said Aubertot, "but she is suffering atrociously from suborbital neuralgia, which I am going to combat with Antipyrine."

"And you believe this will cure her, Doctor?"

"It will relieve the pain, my dear marquis. Suborbital neuralgia is one of the most agonizing of afflictions. As to a cure . . ." He pursed his lips. "We know so little of the human nervous system. Perhaps, in time . . . But at least we can reduce the symptoms. In half an hour . . ."

"She must suffer for another half hour?" Raymond said urgently.

Aubertot shrugged. "Antipyrine takes time. And there is no other remedy."

"I beg to differ, Doctor," said Pontaillac. "There is something far stronger, and quite infallible."

Aubertot frowned. "And how do I not know of this panacea?"

"It's morphine, my dear doctor. Morphine!"

Reaching into his pocket, he took out the pouch containing the two silver Pravazes and the phial of morphine solution, and thrust it into the doctor's hands.

"Just give her this, and the pain will disappear."

Aubertot regarded the instruments cautiously, then took them.

"Of course you're quite correct, my dear captain. Your presence is providential." He seemed about to query Pontaillac on why he should be carrying the drug and syringes, but one look at the concerned eyes of both men persuaded him to silence. "Tell me, what is the strength of this solution?"

"Ten percent."

The doctor raised his eyebrows. Seven percent was regarded as strong. Most doctors used five.

"Give me a moment to mix a weaker one."

A few minutes later, the three men stood beside the bed of the ailing marquise.

On the vast bed, in a froth of lace, Blanche de Montreu, née de La Croze, tossed agitatedly, whimpering, her white hands clutching her head under the mass of red hair. Raymond de Pontaillac feasted his eyes on her bare arms, her pale throat, beneath the skin of which the blood coursed. Under her thin robe, her body, slim as a girl's, writhed, every movement an exercise in voluptuousness.

"Madame, we have brought you relief," said Aubertot.

But as he bent over her, Pravaz in hand, Olivier grabbed the doctor's arm.

"No, stop!"

"But . . . why?"

"I'm afraid—for her."

"No need. There is no danger."

"You swear?"

"Monsieur le Marquis, I swear."

In the silence, Blanche said faintly, "I'm not afraid, Olivier," and held out her arm. She watched the doctor empty the syringe into a pale blue vein running on the inside of her elbow.

"That didn't hurt, did it?"

"No," said Blanche. "But the pain in my head . . ."

"Just wait."

Olivier and Raymond retired to the other end of the chamber, leaving Aubertot by the bed.

Swiftly, Blanche felt herself fall under the domination of the drug. Immobile, with eyes already half closed, she stared at the objects that filled her room; the silver crucifix set in black velvet, the ivory font of holy water, the stool where she knelt to make her devotions; and beyond, the Venetian glass, the stained glass of the windows, her precious objects, the boxes and figurines of silver and gold.

Raymond and her husband approached, noting that her breath, so agitated a few moments ago, was now steady and calm.

Blanche herself did not sleep; she no longer suffered; she heard nothing of the words Olivier addressed to her. Or, rather, she saw his lips move and heard his voice, but the sound fell on her ears as a succession of harmonies that, though not unpleasant, conveyed nothing to her. She felt only a sweet blessedness. Her lips curved in a smile as the drug carried her outside herself, into a region where her body was swept by secret and incomparable ecstasies.

When her calm had persisted for an hour, the doctor prepared to leave.

"You must call me again," he said in parting, "if her breathing slows unnaturally."

"Is that likely?" asked Olivier anxiously.

Jean-Louis Dubut de Laforest

"With this drug, you cannot always tell." He glanced over his shoulder, to where Raymond de Pontaillac stood by the bed of the sleeping woman—more like the husband, thought Aubertot, than the anxious boy to whom he spoke. "There have been cases where people have fallen into a comatose state from which it proved impossible to arouse them."

{ 3 }

As the night came on, Olivier remained close to the bedroom of his marquise, until a new arrival called him to the door.

"Come in, my good Catissou," he said, standing back to let the visitor enter.

Despite the streaks of white in her hair and the deep wrinkles in her face, the woman who stepped into the foyer stood erect, notwithstanding her great age. Her black dress, with a collar of red silk, identified her as a native of the area around Bordeaux. Though she addressed the marquis with respect, there was nothing servile in her manner.

As nurse to the parents of the marquis, Catissou had seen the marquis born and grow up in the great château in Limousin. When his parents died, it was she who took him to his uncle, with whom he completed his education. And when, in time, he came into his fortune and moved to the Paris mansion of Boulevard Malesherbes, she had accompanied him as honorary housekeeper. No longer required to cook or manage the household, she was content to sit by the big stove in the kitchen and, on the pretext of knitting an apparently infinite succession of stockings, keep an eye on the comings and goings of the maids, cooks, and myriad servants demanded by a fashionable Parisian house.

Regarding her as a friend, Olivier allowed her to address him in the familiar *"tu"* rather than the more formal *"vous,"* but she never did so without discomfort, and if others were present, invariably reverted to a deferential "Monsieur le Marquis."

"I've come to put little Jeanne to bed, monsieur. How is madame?"

Olivier briefly ceased his nervous pacing. "Much better."

"Then there's no point in staying by her side all night. Go to bed."

But Olivier shook his head, and led her to the next room, where the pretty blond four-year-old Jeanne already slept. Then he installed himself in the big armchair by his wife's bed, determined to keep watch all night for the feared signs of an incipient coma.

Not that there were any indications of that. Blanche's beautiful face looked relaxed. Her smile was positively beatific.

Gone was the agony of the neuralgia. In its place were a sense of languorous pleasure in her own body, and a sensual awareness of her desirability. She retained some memory of the pain, but under the spell of the morphine, in the easing of her suffering, it was transformed into something different—a perverse pleasure. It was as if the drug made her into another woman.

As she was transformed, so were her surroundings. She was back in the château where she had spent her childhood. She looked around in wonder at the gardens that, in her imagination, were as vivid as in a painting. Even better, she was not alone, but with her two best friends, as close and intimate as they had been back in those days and not, as now, separated by distance and the inevitable parting that accompanied marriage.

Mathilde de Chastenet, a cousin with little money, was now Madame Gouilléras, the wife of a prosperous timber merchant, and permanently exiled to the provinces. The other, Geneviève de Saint-Phar, had never married, but had, in her way, also set herself apart from the life of the marquise by electing to become a doctor. In the first agony of the neuralgia, Blanche had proposed calling her old friend, but Olivier firmly overruled her in favor of the more distinguished Maître Aubertot.

A cloud passed over the perfect landscape in which Blanche wandered in her drugged dream. It was her fate, it seemed, to be overruled. Even her husband was not of her choosing. As she reached her teens, two men had competed for her hand. One was Olivier—the son of the family whose estate adjoined that of the La Crozes. The other, though wellborn, lacked the wealth of the Montreus, nor were his prospects so promising, since he had elected, rather than managing his estates and increasing their value, to pursue a career as a serving officer in the army. To Blanche's parents, the choice was clear. Their daughter must marry the highly eligible Olivier de Montreu, and suppress forever her infatuation for that handsome, dashing, but altogether too risky young lieutenant of the cavalry— Raymond de Pontaillac.

As if, belatedly, to repair the deficiency that made him a less attractive prospect than Olivier de Montreu, Raymond had acquired, because of his heroic behavior in the Indochinese campaigns, not to mention a number of notorious duels over matters of honor, a redoubtable reputation in the army; he had also, through some equally audacious coups of investment and innovation, become rich. It was this Raymond de Pontaillac, trailing clouds of glory and wealth, who had re-entered the life of Blanche de Montreu shortly after the birth of little Jeanne, and become thereafter a friend of the family so valued and intimate that to accompany the lovely onetime object of his desire to the opera without her husband aroused no more than a slight raising of the eyebrow among those of an earlier generation who still adhered to the standards of the old empire.

As for Raymond, he was punctilious in treating Blanche as no more than a good friend, an impression he reinforced by speaking frankly to Olivier about his many mistresses, and sharing the most intimate details of their activities together. Secretly, however, he harbored a love for the lost Blanche that was as powerful as ever—a love that, ever the skilled tactician, he disguised with an ostentatious passion for the beautiful and exotic Christine Stradowska.

{ 4 }

In a vast room with a mirrored ceiling, hung with red satin tapestries, and decorated with exotic objects—daggers, guns, lances, hatchets, hunting whips, the horns and heads of animals, Chinese masks and parasols—Christine Stradowska reclined on a pile of animal skins and tenderly caressed her two greyhounds, Bog and Tolgo.

Her opulent body was draped in a cashmere robe, under which she wore a satin chemise embroidered with chrysanthemums. Taking a mirror, she contemplated her tumble of blond hair, a pair of eyes as blue as sapphires, an aristocratic nose, ruby lips, and fine white teeth, and smiled a smile that expressed at the same time pride in finding herself so beautiful and sorrow of a love that was not returned.

Beside her, a dais, draped in old rose silk decorated with white daisies, supported two lamps that terminated in the heads of dragons. They cast soft light on a phantasmagoria of exotic fabrics, plumes, and flowers; palms and vines; baskets of white lilac; fans from the feathers of ostriches, peacocks, and eagles; mimosa, Spanish jasmine, camellias, rhododendrons, an orgy of roses . . . a Sardanapalus of vegetation, while everywhere in this temple to sensuality animal skins created the illusion of a sanctuary guarded by lions, tigers, jaguars, buffalo, beaver, foxes, wolves, bears, hyenas, and crocodiles.

Her ebony dressing table supported an infinity of artistic riches, of curios of all ages and peoples; enamels, ivories, items of lacquer, of serpentine marble, bronze, silver, and gold.

Opposite a monumental granite fireplace, gilded bars enclosed a huge aviary within which multicolored cascades flowed, illuminated like the fountains which had astonished all Paris at the great Exposition. The cage sheltered a world of birds, which the trickling of the spray and the rustle of plumage, blending with the odors from bowls of fragrant herbs and dried flowers, exalted into constant song.

Beyond this, its walls draped in imperial purple, extended a gallery of all that was greatest in ancient and modern art. From Rubens and Benvenuto Cellini to Carpeaux, Falguière, and Meissonier; a head by Ribot stood before a landscape by Guillemet; a study by Puvis de Chavannes had to its left a watercolor by Forain, while below, on a dais of white velvet, stood a grand piano by Erard. To complete the collection, a cabinet glittered with jewels, necklaces, bracelets, miniatures, cameos, flowers of rubies and crowns of gold—souvenirs of the princes, kings, and emperors who had surrendered to her.

But Christine had no eyes for her treasures. She thought only of the letter in her hand—a letter from Raymond de Pontaillac, offering some banal excuses to justify his absence. A sick friend! How feeble.

"Liar!" she snarled. "Liar! Liar!" She crumpled the paper savagely.

On the small table at her elbow were piled other letters, many of them accompanying articles or pieces of music she had inspired. The heap held manuscripts dedicated to her by the most famous of composers—Gounod, Massenet, and Saint-Saëns among the French, but Russians as well—Cui, Rimsky-Korsakoff, Glazounov, Liadov, Lavroff, Beleff. Truly a harvest of glory. But to Christine it was all worthless, and with one sweep of her arm she dashed every last item to the floor.

The daughter of a Russian officer who died before she really knew him, Christine had shown even at school in Moscow's Music Institute that she possessed the soul of an artist. She charmed the teachers with her warm, vibrant voice, and soon had a career on the concert stage, first in Moscow and Saint Petersburg, where she discovered that beauty could win her as much as, if not more than, her voice, then to Milan, Vienna, London, and finally Paris. There she had captured the heart of the French capital from the stage of the Opera, just as a young captain of cavalry had captured her heart in her dressing room with the first words of love ever to touch her heart.

She loved Raymond; loved him with all the passion of her youth, with her very blood. She had given herself to him completely. Those other lovers were forgotten. She was reborn in a new faith.

Why then had he abandoned her? At first, she attributed it to that nervous temperament that he calmed with the sinister fluid which, without success, she had so often tried to persuade him to abandon. However, two nights ago, seeing him alone in her box with the lovely Marquise de Montreu, she suspected a rival. Onstage, she had sung only for him, deaf to the applause and bravos of the packed house, desiring only that he should cease to cast looks at the young woman next to him and instead turn the same gaze of love on her, her, her!

Her thoughts were interrupted by a servant.

"Monsieur Rajileff is here, madame."

Loris Rajileff, gray-haired and solemn, had been her accompanist in Moscow, but now acted not only as her pianist but also as personal secretary and manager. Even though he had known her almost from infancy, he formally kissed her hand and remained standing while they spoke.

"The conductor has asked for a rehearsal this afternoon at four . . ." he began.

"Oh, I can't sing today." From a box emblazoned with the double eagle of the Russian monarchy, its eyes set with tiny rubies, she took a cigarette and lit it. "In fact, I'm wondering if I will ever sing again."

The old man was accustomed to her moods. "You know that is impossible, madame."

Christine drew on the dark Turkish tobacco, and expelled the smoke toward the ceiling.

"Loris?"

"Madame?"

"Am I as beautiful as Parisian women?"

"More so. The city is unanimous in celebrating your loveliness and talent. Haven't you seen this morning's papers?"

"Oh, they don't mean it. They make fun of me."

"Not at all. *Rabelais* has even announced a cover article about you for its next issue."

Christine crushed the cigarette savagely. "Well, they can think again."

Rajileff said nothing, but sat down at the piano. The song he played had no name, but in it was the sense of the Russia that, however far they traveled, never left their hearts. It evoked the endless steppes, the mighty rivers, the dark, brooding forests of their faraway home. Gradually, under the spell of the music, Christine relaxed . . .

. . . but only until a maid nervously tapped on the door.

"Madame, a gentleman insists on seeing you. Here is his card."

Christine snatched the pasteboard.

César Houdrequin,
Redacteur en chef,
Rabelais.

Her first impulse was to refuse to see him. But *Rabelais* was the most widely read picture magazine in France, and notorious for its interest in the private lives of the famous. Perhaps here was a way to reignite Raymond de Pontaillac's dwindling interest.

"I'll see him," she told the maid. "Loris, why don't you wait in the next room?"

The old man gestured toward the peignoir clinging to her body, and the way it revealed the deep valley between her breasts.

"You're going to receive him . . . like that?"

"And why not? If he wants a picture for his cover, I'll give him one he won't forget in a hurry."

To her disappointment, César Houdrequin wasn't particularly flustered to be confronted by a beautiful woman in the costume of her boudoir. A young man with a monocle screwed into his left eye, a fashionably curly haircut, and a little beard which, though he hoped for the effect of a man of the world, just made him look like the desk clerk of a chic hotel, he barely raised his eyebrows before bending over her hand.

"Madame, *Rabelais* has the honor to present its compliments."

"I know your magazine, of course," said Christine, "and always enjoy it. Take a seat, please."

She opened the gold cigarette box and presented it. "*Papirosy?*"

She expected Houdrequin to be unfamiliar with the relatively new innovation of cigarettes, and particularly the Russian variety, but he disappointed her. He took one, expertly pinched the hollow tube of white card that served as a filter, and leaned forward to light the tobacco, enclosed in black paper, from the candle she offered.

"My dear madame," he said, "we have already written much about you; your talent, your charm, your artistic genius. I know that you have refused many requests from American impresarios to sing in the United States, and also from opera houses in Germany. If I may say so, you have given your heart to France as it has given its heart to you."

"You're very kind."

"But, my dear madame, the French, having had their interest aroused, are anxious to know more about you. Not simply your talent and your professional life, but the *real* Stradowska—the woman behind the voice."

He took another puff of the cigarette, then put it out in the ashtray that sat between them on the table.

"For example, our readers would be interested to know if it's true that you entertained a certain grand duke at lunch yesterday."

"Monsieur!"

But the journalist was unfazed. "My informant tells me His Grace arrived in a closed carriage at noon, and was shown into the house through the back garden." He nodded to the riot of greenery dimly glimpsed beyond the fountains at the end of the salon.

In fact Christine had entertained no grand duke yesterday, nor any day since her infatuation with Raymond de Pontaillac. But there were ways of denying such things that would inevitably confirm a suspicion rather than eradicate it.

"Your informant has misled you, monsieur. There was no closed carriage, no assignation with the grand duke, yesterday or any other day since I left Saint Petersburg."

Had she felt herself libeled, any woman, particularly one as mercurial as Stradowska, would have lost her temper, called the servants to throw him out. Such calm denials amounted almost to confirmation. She could see him writing the article in his head as they spoke. *While denying any intimate rendezvous, the beautiful diva admitted that she remained "close" to the man who, in Saint Petersburg, was widely acknowledged as her benefactor and protector . . .*

"But in Saint Petersburg, you and the duke were . . . close?"

"I had many good friends in Saint Petersburg, monsieur. They remain just that . . . good friends."

"And . . . the Prince of Wales?"

The Prince of Wales!? Where did he get this nonsense? As if she would have anything to do with that fat old fool—so fat, in fact, that the whores at his favorite brothel, Le Chabanais, refused to fuck him, in case his belly crushed them to death. The management had a special table made. The girl lay on top of it with open legs, and the heir to the British throne stood to enter her. Afterward, the girl bathed in a bath of champagne while the prince and his cronies sat naked around it, dipping out the wine.

But if Houdrequin thought she was enjoying regal patronage . . .

"What about His Royal Highness?" Christine asked.

"Is it true that you had supper with him in the Pavilion Chinois last Friday?"

At such times, Christine's sense of theater was invaluable. She allowed a long moment to pass before she replied—a pause during which the journalist was free to imagine anything he cared to about her mental processes.

"You would not expect me to discuss anything connected with the private activities of His Royal Highness," she said evenly at last. "Such matters are not for publication."

Houdrequin leaned forward eagerly. "But you don't deny you and Prince Albert are acquainted?"

"I do not discuss it in any way, monsieur. Whatever conclusions you draw are your own. Nor do I need to remind you, I'm sure, that both the courts and our diplomatic service have remedies against the publication of slander and libel. And now . . ." She tugged the bellpull to summon the maid.

"Of course," said Houdrequin. "And *Rabelais* thanks you for giving so much of your time."

After he'd left, Rajileff emerged from the inner room.

"You know what he's going to write."

"More or less. But don't concern yourself, Loris. I have my reasons . . ." She rose and stretched. "You know, I think I might manage a little rehearsing."

{ 5 }

About four in the afternoon on a day of the following week, with *Rabelais* being read all over Paris, and the cafés of the Faubourg Saint Honore buzzing with gossip about Strad-owska, a carriage pulled by a wonderful pair of Orloffs drew up in front of the Villa Said, and Raymond stepped down.

He had barely handed his hat and cane to the servant when Christine burst into the foyer. Ever since his valet had come round the previous day, bearing his note suggesting that "if it might be convenient," he would call on her, she had existed in an agony of anticipation. All night, sleep had eluded her, and for an hour before the appointed time of their rendezvous, she had tried on costume after costume, and summoned her maid a dozen times to brush and arrange her hair.

"Ah! You are finally here!" she moaned, throwing herself into his arms.

Drawing him into her salon, she pushed the doors shut behind her, then, before he could begin his invented apology for having neglected her, closed his mouth with an urgent kiss.

"You must let me explain, *ma chere* . . ." he began finally.

"Do not lie! You love someone else, I know."

It was true. The vision of Blanche de Montreu on her bed, drowsing in the drug dreams of morphine, refused to leave his brain. Any lie! Just to drive her from his mind.

"I swear to you . . ."

She held up her hand in a theatrical gesture. "Please. Between us, there is no need of oaths—or of lies. I know you as you really are, and I accept that."

But then, with no less contrivance, she stepped away from him, moving into the light from the window to show that, beneath her thin silk gown, her magnificent body, heavy-breasted and wide-hipped, was completely nude.

"But you do love me a little, don't you?" she wheedled.

Almost as intimately as the music she sang, Christine understood men. She shrugged the robe from her shoulders, letting it slip to the floor. At the same time, Raymond felt her hands expertly undoing the buttons of his trousers. In an instant, her insinuating fingers were fondling deliciously his swelling manhood.

Roughly, he pushed her back onto one of her ridiculous animal skins, and thrust brutally into her accommodating wetness.

How she loved it! How she writhed and moaned, her hips meeting his, thrust for thrust, the repeated spasms of her climaxes shaking even his powerful body.

"Je t'adore! Je t'adore!"

If only it were Blanche's voice! The thought finally tipped Raymond into a spasm of his own, and though he spent his desire deep within the wide hips of his mistress, it was the tight and discreet loins of the marquise that, in imagination, he flooded.

• • •

At the end of the day, they took Christine's car for a leisurely drive in the Bois de Boulogne, then returned to a dinner for two, served under the disapproving eyes of the Old Masters in her private gallery.

Over a glass of Imperial Tokay, Christine played her trump card. "What if," she asked with calculated casualness, "I left the theater?"

"Why would you?"

"So that we could be together always."

"You'd do that?" Even in the depths of his duplicity and lust for the married woman he could never have, Raymond was moved. "What about the fame? The glory?"

She grasped his hand across the table. "You are the glory, my dear. You, and nothing but you!"

In an instant, a sense of despair and helplessness overwhelmed Raymond. When life confronted him with complex judgments and warring emotions, only one thing could alleviate his sense of panic and confusion. Springing up from the table, he hurried to where his coat was draped over a chair, and fumbled in the pocket.

Knowing what he looked for, Christine grabbed his arm. "Darling, please . . ."

He shook her off. "Let me alone!"

Opening the pouch, he feasted his eyes on the phials of morphine solution, the delicate Pravazes.

"Morphine kills you!" she hissed.

"No, it makes me live."

"Tomorrow, Raymond," she pleaded, but without hope.

"No! Now. And quickly."

Back home the next morning, he found a note from the Marquis de Montreu, and a small package. It contained the syringe he had lent to the marquis for Blanche's use.

"My very dear Pontaillac," the marquis wrote. "Thanks to the morphine, my dear wife's neuralgia disappeared. We proclaim you the best doctor in France, and trust you will celebrate with us on Monday evening, at seven. Hunting has been good, so there will be partridge, snipe, and a Limousin hare. Your friend, Olivier."

Even though to be in Blanche's presence would be agony, he could not refuse the invitation. As panic overwhelmed him again, he reached for the Pravaz.

{ 6 }

Stealthily, like an insidious infection, the specter of morphine invaded the great houses of Paris, unacknowledged except in the most secret conversations of the rich and powerful. Only a few men, because of their privileged position, saw the problem in all its sinister dimensions.

One was Professor Aubertot, the doctor called to minister to the Marquise de Montreu.

In February, and again in March and April, Blanche de Montreu suffered further attacks of her neuralgia. Olivier called Professor Aubertot once again, but he refused to prescribe morphine, warning the young couple of the grave dangers of addiction. Unwilling to see his wife suffering, the marquis found a more obliging doctor, and the injections recommenced, with the familiar eradication of pain. The use of morphine became so much a part of their life that, as a birthday gift, Olivier commissioned the best jeweler on Place Vendome to create for his wife her own unique private Pravaz. Made of silver, enamel, and gold, studded with precious stones, it carried, defiantly engraved, the Montreu crest.

• • •

"Dr. Aubertot?" inquired Luce Molday at the door of the consulting room in a building on the Avenue de l'Opera.

"Please come in, mademoiselle." The servant, severely dressed in black dress and white cravat, showed her into a salon, where a dozen men and women waited. Some sat at a central table, reading or leafing through albums of illustrations. Others, isolated, slumped in deep armchairs, barely visible in the shadowy corners.

The beautiful girl, more subdued and pale than she had been in the private room of the Café de la Paix only a few months earlier, took a seat, and watched as, one by one, the patients before her were called into the surgery.

Aubertot's hours of consultation were almost finished when the servant opened the door to a young man whom he recognized instantly.

"It's very late, Monsieur Lagneau," he murmured. "I don't believe the doctor will have time to see you tonight."

"Come on, Baptiste!" A two-franc piece changed hands, and Luce and the remaining patients looked up resentfully as the newcomer was ushered across the waiting room and into the inner sanctum.

The consultation didn't take long. Aubertot was known as the doctor to whom you could speak frankly about all nervous disease, including your use of drugs, and who was familiar with the methods of treatment.

"I'm continuing the same prescription," he said, scribbling. "Potassium bromide, electrical baths . . ." He looked up. "And remember—don't tire yourself, and stay calm. No agitation."

Luce watched the young man leave, conducted out by the servant, both of them studiously avoiding her eye and those of the two men and three women ahead of her.

On a suspicion, she followed them and watched Baptiste show the young man out.

"How long will I have to wait?" she asked.

The servant looked solemn. "I fear, mademoiselle, that the doctor may not be able to see you today. There is a ball tonight at his house."

Luce took a silver coin from her purse and accorded him her most seductive smile. "Will this improve my chances, monsieur?"

Baptiste winked. "I believe the professor might squeeze in just one more patient."

Luce was shown in to the surgery just before Baptiste announced to the remaining patients that there would be no more consultations that day.

Aubertot wasted no time on polite amenities. In French, the term "bedside manner" doesn't exist.

"I'm listening, mademoiselle."

"For some months," Luce said, "I've been injecting myself with morphine."

The doctor's face betrayed no emotion. "Why?"

"Initially, for amusement. Later . . ."

". . . you came to need the injections."

"Yes."

"Was it a doctor who gave you the drug?"

"No, sir. It was a soldier—a captain of cavalry, and a good friend, Raymond de Pontaillac."

Aubertot recalled that evening at the bedside of Blanche de Montreu, but betrayed nothing of his acquaintance with the count.

"I see."

"I bought a little syringe, and a pharmacist named Hornuch on Rue de Gomorrhe supplied me with morphine."

"In unlimited quantities?"

Luce smiled grimly. "Limited only by the amount of money I could afford."

"But you've stopped injecting yourself, you say."

"Three days ago."

"And the effects?"

"I feel better, but I still long for morphine." She frowned. "It was delicious, but I know it wasn't good for me."

"It certainly was not," said Aubertot. "Do you wish me to cure you?"

"Yes! Oh, yes!"

"Very well. To do that, you must begin the injections again." When Luce looked startled, he continued, "It's dangerous to cease abruptly. Since you are not yet completely addicted, we will reduce the doses gradually. But it's entirely up to you how quickly you regain your energy and health."

{ 7 }

That night, a succession of carriages drew up at the home of Professor Aubertot on Place des Etats-Unis. Their owners, the men dressed in black and the women in the finest ball gowns from Worth and Poiret, ascended in a steady stream the white marble stairs to the first floor, where Aubertot and his wife, he as solemn as the profile on a Greek medal, in his customary plain black, she gracious in a gown of lilac silk, waited to greet the cream of Parisian society, its intellectuals and clubmen, scientists and military officers, writers and artists.

The three main chambers of the Aubertot mansion provided something for every taste. A buffet had been set in the main dining room, which opened onto a winter garden roofed in glass. In the sitting room, a small stage had been erected, on which Coquelin Jr., brother of the great performer who had created on stage the role of Cyrano de Bergerac, and himself no mean actor, was declaiming a monologue. Seated in front of him, the ladies who made up his devoted following hung on his every word, giggling at his jokes, closing their eyes in ecstasy at his flights of poetry, and all the time cooling their passion for the handsome young man with a fluttering of their lace or feathered fans, an action which—purely by chance, of course—drew attention to their bare shoulders and breasts, not to mention the diamonds that dangled from their ears or decorated their throats.

Behind them, only half listening, their men, a line of somber black, enlivened by the occasional brilliant military uniform, held themselves aloof while indulging, no less than their women, in the favorite Parisian sport of gossip.

Since no city, however cosmopolitan, has more than a few score of people who Really Matter, it is not particularly remarkable that almost everyone at the soiree knew everyone else, and that they expected to run into one another at least once a week at some event. So it was that among the women watching Coquelin was Blanche de Montreu, and that the men grouped at the back of the salon included Blanche's husband Olivier, Raymond de Pontaillac's friends Arnould-Castellier, Lapouge, Jean de Fayolle, and Léon Darcy, not to mention César Houdrequin of *Rabelais*, who, however, was taking the opportunity to conduct an interview with Professor Emile Pascal on the recent discoveries by Robert Koch of the bacillus that carried tuberculosis.

Inevitably, in such a parade of familiar faces, a newcomer stood out. Once Houdrequin turned from the professor, he moved immediately to the side of Olivier de Montreu. "May I inquire, Monsieur le Marquis, as to the identity of the lady seated with your wife?"

The woman did indeed appear out of place. Though her face radiated intelligence, her simple, old-fashioned brown dress and lack of jewelry made her seem a sparrow among birds of paradise.

"A childhood friend of the marquise," Olivier explained. "Geneviève de Saint-Phar."

"Of the Breton Saint-Phars?"

"I have no idea. She has no time for matters of family and society. By profession, she is a medical doctor."

A woman doctor! Such a rarity clearly deserved an interview, or at least a reference in his coverage of the event, but Houdrequin was prevented from approaching her by the almost immediate appearance, after the conclusion of Coquelin's performance, of the true star of the evening.

The moment Christine Stradowska stepped onto the stage in her white satin robe and long black gloves, with the beautiful bareness of her shoulders emphasized by her necklace of sapphires, the room fell under her spell. At the piano, Loris Rajileff paused until the applause died, then caressed the keys in the first delicate notes of an old Russian song. Though her voice filled every corner of the salon, its power never overwhelmed the tenderness of her words, nor the warmth that brought to every listener an echo of her distant homeland, and made them feel lifted and transformed.

So riveted was the audience by her performance that almost nobody noticed Blanche de Montreu become pale and abruptly slump in her chair. Nor did it excite more than passing interest as, leaving her friend to listen to the recital, she slipped away into the side chamber reserved for the *toilette* of ladies alone. Only one person had eyes exclusively for the marquise—and ironically it was the person whom Christine most wanted to be paying attention to her. The diva watched in despair as Raymond passed along the line of standing men, moving as close as possible to the curtained doorway behind which the object of his love had disappeared.

As he did so, his friend Lapouge caught his sleeve. Nodding toward Christine, he said, "Marvelous, isn't she?"

"Tremendous," added Darcy. "You can be proud, old boy!"

But Raymond brushed them off. "Let me alone, dammit!"

Watching his departing back, Lapouge shook his head. "It's the morphine talking."

"It's poisoned him," Darcy agreed.

"He's crazy," agreed Jean de Fayolle. "It will kill him."

"Such a fine boy," said Lapouge.

Arnould-Castellier, older and wiser, shook his gray-haired head. "And all the more dangerous for that. How many people has he introduced to that evil drug? He even offered some to me for a toothache!"

Finding the ladies' room too crowded for her purposes, Blanche made her way to the glassed-in winter garden, which was almost empty. At the very back, a single copper lamp with a dim electric bulb illuminated a rocky grotto. The sounds of conversation and music from the party faded to a murmur.

Hidden by the greenery, Blanche urgently pulled up her skirt to expose, above the pearl-gray silk stocking, a zone of soft pink flesh. The same garter that supported the stocking also held in place her personal jeweled Pravaz.

The goldsmith who created this beautiful object had, for a few hundred francs extra, adapted one of her bracelets so that, if one turned the catch counter-clockwise, a jewel sprang back, revealing a tiny reservoir of morphine solution, sufficient for one injection. With the unhesitating expertise of experience, Blanche filled the syringe and plunged the needle into her thigh.

At that instant, a shadow passed over her, and she looked up in guilty terror, to see Raymond de Pontaillac watching her.

Flushing, she fell back on a pose of offended prudery.

"Monsieur, by what right do you spy on me?"

But the insult expired on her lips. What secrets could she have from this man, who had introduced her to morphine in the first place?

"I saw you leave," said Raymond. "You were obviously suffering."

"And what is that to you?"

Kneeling before her, Raymond took her hands.

"Blanche, Blanche, I love you . . ."

Not for the first time under the drug's mysterious influence, Blanche felt herself to be two creatures. One was the chaste and dutiful wife, the loving mother; the body of the other, the morphine addict, trembled with desire.

"Monsieur . . ." she said tentatively.

"Blanche, since your marriage, since your refusal to marry me, I've struggled with my passion . . ." He looked around wildly at the rocky walls of the grotto, as if seeing them for the first time. "Where are we? I have no idea. I see only your eyes."

Blanche too sensed a dizzying confusion as the two aspects of her character battled within her. She was like a traveler, who, confronted by an abyss, feels both terrified by it but drawn to it as well, and driven by an eager hunger to plunge over the edge.

{ 8 }

Blanche had no idea of how she left the winter garden. When her senses returned, she was standing on the edge of the dance floor, with her solicitous husband at her side.

"Are you in pain?"

"A small headache . . ."

"Do you want to leave?"

"No . . . not yet . . ." She stared at the waltzing couples, swirling to the sound of a Roumanian orchestra. Among them was Christine Stradowska, in the arms of Léon Darcy. "I want to dance."

Olivier looked uncomfortable. Expert enough at the prim dances of polite society, he disliked the waltz. He was saved by Jean de Fayolle, who extended his hand.

After the first few turns, however, Blanche felt the floor floating away from under her.

"You're holding me too tight!" she protested. "Your hand is as hard as iron."

But the moment he loosened his grip, the marquise sagged in his arms, then fell backward to the floor, insensible.

With the help of servants, a path was cleared through the crowd of guests, and Blanche conveyed to the small surgery Aubertot maintained in his home. She did not lack for medical expertise. In addition to Aubertot, she was attended by her friend Geneviève de Saint-Phar, Major Lapouge, and Emile Pascal, another professorial colleague of Aubertot.

But it did not take four doctors to note the wildly beating heart, the breathing that changed from far above the normal to well below it, nor the spasms that shook her body.

"Is it the first time madame has exhibited symptoms of nervous illness?" asked Pascal.

"The first time," replied Aubertot.

"Normally spasms of this sort don't persist," he said thoughtfully. "You've been struck, I'm sure, by the dilation of the pupils."

"Obviously."

"Let us take a look at the arms and legs."

As the three male doctors retreated to the far side of the room, Geneviève de Saint-Phar, assisted by a servant, removed every stitch of Blanche's clothing, and covered her with a sheet. Aubertot, watching closely his female colleague, once his student, was struck with the delicacy, even tenderness with which she unbuttoned and unclipped every garment, laying each aside before continuing with the next. No lover could have been more considerate. He searched for the correct word to describe her manner, encountered "erotic," but discarded it as he would a piece of fruit that proved, when he bit it, to be rotten at the core. Bad enough for such a relationship to exist between a male doctor and his patient, but between woman and woman, it was unthinkable.

Once the naked Blanche was modestly covered, they approached her again. At a nod from Aubertot, Geneviève de Saint-Phar pulled the sheet back from her legs. On the white skin of her slim and lovely thighs and calves, the marks of numerous injections were vividly evident.

"We see here an extreme case of morphine intoxication," said Pascal. He looked around at his three colleagues. "You concur?"

All of them nodded. Aubertot sighed. "I must reveal," he said, "that last December, I administered an injection of morphine to the marquise to fight an attack of suborbital neuralgia. A number of times since, she and the marquis asked me to prescribe additional injections, but I refused."

"Plenty of doctors are less scrupulous," observed Saint-Phar.

"It's not doctors who did this," Lapouge growled. "It's Pontaillac who's behind it."

"This isn't the time to fix blame," said Aubertot. "Our first duty is to this poor young woman."

For thirty minutes, they applied every test to establish the progress of the addiction. Blanche made no protest. The drug had reduced her sensitivity to all stimuli. A light blow to the kneecap produced no result. She didn't react to a pin jabbed into her flesh, nor did her pupils react to bright light.

However, under the influence of tannin and numerous cups of coffee, her breathing became less shallow, her heart, little by little, beat more steadily, and, with rubbing and massage, her temperature rose.

Courteously refusing Madame Aubertot's offer of hospitality, the marquise returned with her maid to the family mansion while Olivier joined the doctors in the winter garden for an urgent conference.

He listened to them with growing disbelief. "But you must be wrong! My wife uses morphine only during a neuralgia attack."

"All addicts know how to lie," said Geneviève, "particularly women."

● ● ●

To reduce her reliance on the drug, Pascal, Aubertot, and Mademoiselle de Saint-Phar advised the system devised by doctors Ball, Zambacco, and Lancereaux, based on continuing injections of progressively diminishing strength. Lapouge, however, preferred immediate and radical termination, as proposed by the German Levinstein.

Once Olivier accepted the reality of Blanche's condition, he agreed to follow the majority opinion and adopt the method of gradually smaller doses, strictly supervised—a treatment for which Dr. de Saint-Phar accepted the responsibility of explaining to Blanche.

Terrified by her near encounter with death, the marquise listened to the advice of her old friend. She showed her the bracelet with its cache of the drug, and swore to obey the orders of the doctors and her beloved husband. A few days later, the family left Paris to stay at the estate of her parents, the Château des Tuilières—far from the temptations of Paris, morphine, and Raymond de Pontaillac.

{ 9 }

It was spring, and all was green in the valley of Saint Martin l'Eglise that held the Château des Tuilières, from which Monsieur and Madame de La Croze exercised a beneficent influence over everyone in the area, rich and poor.

Visitors, after admiring the noble façade of the château, passed into an inner courtyard, dominated by an ancient chestnut tree, famed in the region. To one side were the stables, to the other an arch that led to the gardens, the park, and a lake that bathed the walls of the castle. From the commanding heights of the château, one could see in the distance the village of Saint Martin l'Eglise, and in the other direction, the château of their closest neighbors, the Pontaillacs.

Sensibly, Blanche's protectors severely limited the number of visitors. The Abbe Boussarie, their parish priest, came every Sunday to say Mass, and, during the week, to counsel Blanche. Her cousin Mathilde de Chastenet visited with her *nouveau riche* husband, the timber merchant Adolphe Gouilléras. The Pontaillacs too made a number of courtesy visits, but though Olivier and his parents-in-law received them politely, Blanche was always "too ill" to be seen, lest the sight of them revive memories of their son, who, though they could not know it, was the cause of all her suffering.

For Blanche, there could be no better place in which to recover her strength and escape from the influence of morphine. The birds sang, the air was rich with the scent of thyme and lavender, and in the waters of the lake the lilies bloomed. From time to time, when her need for the drug was at its most extreme, she remembered the garden as it appeared in winter. At such times, the sky became gray, the trees shed their leaves, and from the distant forest floated the howls of wolves.

But then Olivier was at her elbow, to soothe her and administer a sufficiently weak solution of morphine to calm her terrors.

The process had been anything but easy, so deeply embedded in Blanche was the need for the drug. On their arrival at Tuilières, her parents had imposed a gradual diminution, and its replacement with other stimulants that were less addictive. During the first days, Blanche had revolted, brushing aside the ether, chloroform, and alcohol. She must have morphine, and nothing but! She wept, wailed, threatened, then, abruptly, became calm, agreeing to renounce the drug and all its replacements. At such times, she would be most self-critical, speaking with disgust of her addiction, finding the former passion ridiculous. She once again began to play the piano and the harp, to sing, laugh, even go horseback riding. Olivier sent enthusiastic letters to Dr. Aubertot—who responded, "Very good. But be on your guard. Watch her every minute."

A few days later, Olivier de Montreu and his father-in-law were enjoying a cigar in the avenue of lime trees running along the edge of the park, while little Jeanne played under the supervision of her grandmother.

Blanche wandered out, abruptly grabbed Jeanne, hugged her hard, and covered her in manic kisses.

"My dear, take care!" warned Madame de La Croze. "You're hurting her. She's crying."

And indeed the child was in tears. Struggling, she said, "Naughty mummy!"

Blanche dropped her daughter as if in horror, turned and ran back toward the house. Alarmed, the marquis called, "My dear, where are you going?"

"To my room. I need to cry."

They followed her, but she ran so swiftly that, before they could catch up, she had slammed the door behind her and locked it.

Each day, the marquise spent some time in prayer in a tiny chapel in a grove at the edge of the garden. Inside the metal gate, watched over by a Virgin of white marble, the light of golden candlesticks played on a line of four velvet-upholstered *prie-dieux*, while vases of fresh flowers and two magnificent stained glass windows added to the atmosphere of peace and piety.

One morning, Olivier and Jeanne accompanied Blanche to the chapel, waiting for her outside while she prayed. Jeanne, playing among the flower beds, suddenly said, "Oh, look, Papa. What a pretty jewel."

She held up what she had found. The sunlight glittered from a Pravaz syringe.

Olivier took the syringe, remembering how they had encountered his wife here earlier in the week, and how extreme had been her treatment of their child.

"Jeanne, darling, you must not tell your mother you found this."

She pouted. "But . . . why not? It's pretty."

"She would be very upset. I'll buy you another toy. I promise."

They walked back round to the other side of the chapel, to find a demure Blanche drawing on her gloves and waiting for them.

"What a beautiful day," she said.

Aubertot's words came back to Olivier. *Watch her every instant.*

{ 10 }

That afternoon, the marquis and marquise, accompanied by the Gouilléras, visited the village of Saint Martin l'Eglise. Slipping away, Olivier strolled to the pharmacy, in the doorway of which the pharmacist, Monsieur Teissier, was enjoying a cigarette.

"Could I have a moment of your time, monsieur?"

"Naturally, Monsieur le Marquis. Please come in."

Inside the tiny shop, Olivier came straight to the point. "You know that my wife is specifically forbidden to have morphine, under orders of her doctor. And yet you have been supplying her secretly with the drug."

"But this is untrue, monsieur! I have never supplied her with the drug except by prescription."

"You swear?"

"Of course. Monsieur le Marquis, we have very little call for morphine in this locality. When you arrived, I received fifty grams, which I have dispensed in small doses of between two and five grams on prescription of your doctor, Monsieur

Thavet of Labrousse. Forty-three grams remain. Allow me to show you."

From a locked cabinet, Teissier removed a small bottle and placed it on the scale.

"But . . . it's impossible!" he said. "Only fourteen grams. In God's name, who has stolen it?" Turning, he called "Victor! Victor!"

A young boy with red hair hurried from the dispensary.

"Is it you who took the morphine from this bottle? Don't lie or I'll strangle you."

"Yes," said the boy defensively. "I have the money."

"I don't care about the money! Who did you sell it to?"

"To my aunt."

"Madame Gouilléras?" demanded Teissier. "What would she want with morphine?"

Olivier said, "You're the nephew of Mathilde de Chastenet . . . Mathilde Gouilléras, that is?"

"Yes, monsieur. Did I do wrong?"

The story quickly emerged. The Chastenets had always been the poor relatives of the much richer La Crozes, who had done all they could to help them. After providing the dowry for Mathilde to marry Adolphe Gouilléras, they had discreetly aided her brother, Abel, by setting him up in business, and finding his son a job with the village pharmacy, where he could learn a useful trade.

"You idiot!" said Teissier. "You may have poisoned the very person who has been your benefactress."

"Leave the boy alone!" ordered Olivier. "The drug was not for her. Was it, Victor?"

"I don't know, monsieur. My aunt only told me to keep it secret. That's why I didn't put the money in the *caisse*. But I have it hidden. I can show you."

"I'm sure you do," he said kindly. "Don't punish the boy, Teissier." He sighed. "The bonds of family are the strongest ties of all."

After that, Olivier paid minute attention to any item entering the château. He was soon rewarded when the postman, arriving one morning, handed over a parcel addressed to Blanche from Madame Gouilléras.

Retiring to his study, the marquis, obliged by his love and by his role as guardian, and completely against his habits and tastes, opened the packet addressed to his wife. Inside he found a letter and two bundles of blue wool. One contained a bottle of morphine, the other a Pravaz.

He read the accompanying letter.

My dear Blanche,

At Limoges, in the school of Sacre-Coeur, you shared with your poor cousin the delicacies sent to you from the Château Tuilières. Now, I have the pleasure of sending you half of the treasure which we both so much enjoy and which you have entrusted to me.

Mathilde an addict as well? The insidious spread of the affliction astonished him, not only in the number of people affected but in their variety, which encompassed every level of society. It seemed nobody was safe.

He read on.

Excuse the Pravaz, which is less elegant than the one you lost, though somewhat larger. As for the divine fluid, guard it well, because it is increasingly difficult to acquire. Unfortunately, my nephew informed me yesterday that he will no longer be able to supply it from your local pharmacy, since his employer has forbidden him, for reasons he will not reveal. I suspect your husband has discovered from which source you have been obtaining morphine.

Be careful. He will be even more watchful. There will be no drawer too private for a husband like yours, a man whom you adore and who does not see that to deprive you will be fatal. Continue to let your cute little Jeanne safeguard the Pravaz and solution. And angels protect you all.

> A thousand kisses from
> Mathilde.

P.S. Why don't you send a letter to your friend Geneviève de Saint-Phar? As a doctor, she could supply you direct. If she refuses, I know doctors in Limoges who might help, and perhaps an obliging pharmacist as well.

What did she mean "continue to let your cute little Jeanne safeguard the Pravaz and solution"? Was it meant symbolically, or did it disguise an actual fact?

The next time a servant gave Jeanne her bath, Olivier examined the child's bed. Under the mattress, he found a phial of morphine three-quarters empty.

That night, as they prepared for bed, Olivier confronted his wife.

"Despite all your sermons, you have begun to poison yourself once more with the horrible morphine."

"That's not true!"

"Blanche . . ."

"It's not, it's not, it's not . . ."

He showed her the two phials of morphine and the Pravaz Mathilde had sent.

"Why lie?"

"Where did you get those?"

"One of them, I found in the bed of our daughter. The others were sent by your cousin Mathilde."

"You opened a letter addressed to me?"

"Yes, I did."

"You're detestable." She held out her hand. "Give them to me."

"Never."

She flung herself at him, first in fury, then, more cunningly, as a lover. Letting her nightgown fall from her body, she groveled at his feet, offering herself flagrantly, in ways he had only dared imagine in his most lurid fantasies. She promised him pleasures of which he was astonished she had even the knowledge; delights reserved for the harems of Asiatic princes or the most accommodating of *maisons closes.*

"Olivier, the Pravaz, it's my life!"

"It will be your death."

Hoping to end her sobbing, he walked to the window and flung the two phials and the Pravaz into the darkness, where they fell into the lake that lapped against the château walls. As he closed the window, Blanche sobbed, "You have killed me. You have killed me."

Running to the window, she stared out at the midnight blue of the skies, scattered with constellations, then at the lake below, in which the stars were reflected. Its waters threw back a shimmer that, in her distress, seemed to mirror her need for the drug. In imagination, she saw the shattered phials and the syringe lying among water lilies and the fronds of plants, the edges of glass glinting points of light like those of diamonds. The swirling waters became a stream of morphine, a river, an ocean in which she longed to plunge, to drown. Nothing mattered but the drug. Without it, she did not wish to live.

She felt herself begin to sag. Olivier caught her in his arms.

"Blanche, my adored one . . ."

"I don't know you anymore," she hissed. "Get out of here. You horrify me."

{ II }

Captain de Pontaillac in those days found himself in a curious state.

To all outward appearances, he was in the best of health, and satisfyingly involved in a passionate affair with the beautiful Stradowska.

Beneath the surface, however, a different reality prevailed. As a bolt of lightning, striking a steel saber, can leave the exterior apparently untouched but the metal inside shattered like glass, or a predator can devour the flesh and bone of an animal yet the hide remain intact, so the morphine had consumed every part of his spirit, while leaving apparently untouched the organic envelope.

With Blanche gone, the young officer tried to forget her in his military labors with his comrades, Jean de Fayolle, Léon Darcy, and Arnould-Castellier. If Surgeon Major Lapouge joined them, he pretended to have given up morphine and repented of his days as an addict.

Outside of his military life, however, Pontaillac simply disappeared. He was no longer to be found at the Opera, nor at the Café de la Paix, the Cirque, nor even riding in the Bois de Boulogne. The letters and blue telegram forms directed at him by Christine Stradowska remained unanswered.

Instead, Pontaillac led a bizarre life of solitary and morbid introspection.

Having dismissed all his servants, he would wander his vast, empty house alone, revolver in hand, pausing occasionally before a mirror to put the weapon to his head and contemplate pulling the trigger. At such times, he took refuge in another injection, after which the desire for Blanche would overtake him once more. Then he would open the door to another room, dominated by a full-length portrait of his love, executed from a photograph, but with the most exacting attention to detail, supervised minutely by Pontaillac himself.

Next to the portrait, arranged as in a shrine, were intimate objects that had once been handled by, or, better, had once adorned the body of the beautiful marquise. Her maid Angèle had been more than happy to sell them. A broken fan, a satin dancing slipper, gloves, a bouquet, a delicate lace undergarment that he pressed to his face, inhaling the perfume of the body that had worn it.

At such times, he could imagine himself in her arms, and that the figure in the painting was indeed Blanche herself. But then the hallucination vanished, and he found himself once again before the mirror, pistol in hand.

So completely had the morphine consumed his soul that he barely heard the insistent knocking at his door. He opened it to find Christine on the doorstep.

"Raymond!"

"What do you want, madame? What are you doing here? Get out!"

But he didn't block her way, and Christine was able to slip past him, and push the door shut, so that nobody passing by could observe her humiliation or his deterioration.

"You don't love me anymore?" she asked piteously.

"I never loved you."

"Oh!"

Dragging her through the empty house, he brought her at last to the room with the portrait of Blanche.

"There is the woman I love, that I adore. It is to hide that criminal love from the world that I claimed to love you." Grabbing Christine by the shoulders, he shoved her forward until she almost touched the canvas. "Look at her! My God, she's beautiful . . . Now leave me alone."

He groped toward the painting, as if hoping to find, in the empty air, some corporeal manifestation of the real Blanche de Montreu.

"Blanche, Blanche," he moaned. "To taste your lips . . ."

But then the spasm passed briefly, and for a moment the real Raymond resurfaced from the ruin he had become. He looked at Christine as if seeing her for the first time.

"I am mad, my dear Christine."

"And I am here to console you," said Christine. "I want to heal you—and speak to you about her."

Even in his extremity of madness and addiction, Raymond recognized the heroism and compassion behind her acceptance of what he had become, and sank to his knees before her in silent gratitude.

"Would you like me from now on to be your sister?" she asked.

"Can you do that," he asked, without a sign that he understood the sacrifice it required, "without jealousy?"

"No jealousy."

"Really?"

"Really."

For the rest of the day, and well into the night, he spoke only of the absent Blanche.

After many hours, Christine said softly, "Why don't you ask for some leave? You could go down to Limousin, and perhaps see her. At least you would be close by."

"I'm frightened."

"You big baby!"

That night, Christine took him to the Gare d'Orleans, put him on the train, and then, in a state of anguish, returned to her home.

{ 12 }

At the Château des Tuilières, Blanche had entered the most extreme state in her addiction.

Dr. Vaussanges did his best to placate his noble client with trickery.

"Madame," he would say, producing a syringe, "I have brought you morphine."

Accustomed to these subterfuges, Blanche waved it away. "It's water."

"Well, there is water," he conceded, "but morphine as well."

"Liar. I don't want it."

Since the pharmacist in the village would no longer supply her, and her husband blocked all mail coming into the house, Blanche was reduced to bribing the servants—to no avail, since all had been sternly warned by Olivier that acceptance would result in instant dismissal.

From her old friend, Dr. de Saint-Phar, nothing was heard.

Between husband and wife, a state existed close to war.

Filled with hate, Blanche refused not only sex with her husband but the slightest embrace or indication of affection.
For his part, he had keys made of every cabinet, cupboard,
wardrobe, and box in the house, and tirelessly searched all
of them.

"You have no shame. You examine my underclothes, my
stockings." Trembling, she barely stopped herself from spit-
ting in his face.

Her entire nervous system was profoundly weakened by
the effect of morphine. The superficial signs of her earliest use
of the drug had, to some extent, disappeared. The abscesses
of the numerous punctures on her arms and legs had healed.
Her skin appeared fresh and her eyes clear.

Such changes, however, were merely cosmetic. Palpitations of the heart and a nervous cough betrayed the fact that
her body, for so long accustomed to morphine, was starving
for lack of it.

"Have pity, Olivier," she begged. "I'm dying."

The marquis steeled himself to resist her appeals. "Have
courage, my dear. You will be cured. You must stop thinking about the horrible stuff, and remember that we love
you."

"Never, never . . ."

Hoping to distract her, Olivier ordered the most extrava-
gant gifts, and, knowing Blanche would just throw them in his
face, gave them to Jeanne to give to her mother.

"Mama, it's from Papa. What a pretty bracelet! And such a
beautiful necklace—look at the flowers . . ."

Blanche hugged her blond head and lay back—without a
smile.

Blanche's parents tried to encourage their daughter with
news of others who had managed to fight off the effects of

the drug. Her old friend Mathilde Gouilléras, for instance, after long suffering, was no longer an addict, and bitterly regretted the way in which she had helped her cousin. Now the letters she sent contained no Pravaz or morphine—just exhortations to renounce the poison they had once so much enjoyed.

The day the latest letter arrived from the contrite Mathilde, Raymond de Pontaillac, having established himself in his parents' château, rode across to his neighbors at the Château des Tuilières.

He commenced at a gallop, presently reduced this to a trot, then, once he was under the avenue of chestnuts that led to the main entrance, he dawdled, as his desire to see Blanche was invaded by his shame at having been responsible for introducing her to morphine.

But, he consoled himself, she might not have been so susceptible to the drug as he. He had seen her only that one evening, at the ball of Dr. Aubertot, and while she appeared completely addicted, since then she'd been under the care of doctors, and sequestered here in the country. Perhaps she was completely cured.

His mind was made up for him when, as he rode up to the gate, Monsieur de La Croze saw him.

"Goodness! What a surprise, my boy. How long have you been at aux Ormes?"

"Since yesterday. I stopped in Limoges to see my uncle."

"You must say Monsignor," said La Croze, opening the gate. "And how is our bishop going?"

"Pontifically," joked Raymond, handing his horse to a servant. The two men walked up the drive to the house arm-in-arm.

"Captain, I'm delighted you've come. I'm dying of boredom here. How long is your leave? A month?"

"Two weeks only, I'm afraid."

"The devil! That's not long. Well, we must make the most of it. You know my daughter is here, and Olivier?"

"My father told me. I believe Blanche has been . . . unwell."

"Oh, somewhat. But she's on the mend. They'll both be glad to see you."

Pontaillac looked for any trace of irony or dissembling in the old man's manner, but found none. Apparently nobody had revealed his part in introducing Blanche to the needle.

The old gentleman conducted Raymond to the big salon, where he chatted with Madame de La Croze while a servant was sent to fetch Olivier, who was overseeing some new waterworks at the far side of the estate.

As he arrived and embraced his old friend, Blanche too descended from her room and joined them.

With an effort of will, Raymond controlled himself as he took Blanche's pale, cool hand. Though thinner, she appeared none the worse for her experience with the drug. (Someone more objective would have realized that people said the same of him; outwardly, he was in excellent health. In his case, as in that of Blanche, the damage wasn't visible.)

Leaning close, he said, in a voice inaudible to all but her, "Do you forgive me?"

She said nothing, just laid her hand softly on his arm. But only one thought filled her mind. *He introduced me to morphine. He can get me more!*

Sustained by this hope, Blanche was almost her old vivacious self as they chatted of Paris and its balls, its parties, its scandals. Nothing in voice or gesture betrayed her deep emotions.

Without being told, she knew that the man who had given her the first injection had come to relieve her terrible distress. She hadn't forgotten the confession of love blurted in the winter garden that night. Did he still feel the same way? He must—otherwise why make this bold assault on the castle that held her prisoner?

But how would he do it? How could he escape the ever-vigilant attention of Olivier? Should she write him a note, and send it via one of the servants? But nobody in the château dared accept such a commission. Well, she must leave it to him. Only he had the means to relieve her agony, and the desire to do it.

Olivier immediately saw how dangerous the presence of Pontaillac might be to his wife's fragile state, but Raymond intervened quickly to calm the doubts he saw gathering in his face.

"You know, Olivier, I finally gave up my stupid passion for morphine."

"Really?" said Olivier. "And you've broken it off with the Pravaz?"

"Broken it off, and definitively."

No hope, thought the marquise bitterly. *I will kill myself.*

But lifting her eyes, she saw that he lied, and recognized a promise in his gaze.

Daring to hope for the first time in weeks, Blanche dressed for dinner with particular care, putting on a light robe redolent of the spring, weaving a sprig of lilac into her red hair, and assuming a manner that was tranquil, even joyous. Her husband, having learned to be suspicious, attributed the transformation to morphine, and assumed their visitor had somehow conveyed a supply to her, but Blanche, skilled by long experience in lying, convinced him otherwise.

"Olivier, I know what you're thinking," she said. "You think

MORPHINE

I've somehow acquired some morphine. But you're wrong. Monsieur de Pontaillac has cured himself; why can't I do the same?"

The presence of Raymond had created a hope. With a little coaxing, Olivier took it for promise of a cure. Only Blanche knew what she truly hoped for, and what she intended to get, by whatever means.

{ 13 }

The next morning, Raymond left the Château des Ormes for his daily promenade. There was joy in his heart, now that he no longer felt guilt at what he planned—to seduce the wife of his best friend by trading on her desperate need for the drug to which he had introduced her.

This time, he arrived at the Château des Tuilières not by the main gate but through the woods, giving a wide berth to the marsh where Olivier was supervising new drainage works. He arrived at the private chapel at just the moment he knew he could depend on encountering Blanche.

A few moments later, she stepped out, and the two victims of the Pravaz confronted one another.

"Madame," Raymond began, "I gambled that I might meet you, and I'm delighted the gamble paid off, but you're so pale and trembling. And you've been crying."

"I cry because I suffer," she said, "because I'm dying!"

Distractedly, in a torrent of words, she described the agonies of her addiction; the subterfuges necessary to acquire the vital fluid; the scene when her husband had flung her morphine and Pravaz into the lake. The whole world had abandoned her; even her cousin Mathilde, who, more than anyone else, should have understood her desperate need.

"I understand," said Pontaillac. "I understand—and that is why I have come. Yesterday, it was necessary to disguise with a lie my desire to help you—because I, better than anyone, understand your illness. I too have suffered. I have wept. There are few tortures more terrible than the need for morphine. The doctors tell you that it will kill you. Imbeciles. The true death, far more hideous and terrifying, is to be deprived of it!"

He took from his pocket a small pouch of blue silk in which he carried his morphine, and an aristocratic Pravaz.

"Take this, madame. Weep no more. Dry your beautiful eyes. For you, hell is over."

"Thank you, Monsieur de Pontaillac," sobbed the marquise. "You have saved me."

Raymond didn't linger. For the moment, he politely took his leave and continued on his morning promenade.

The moment she returned to her boudoir, Blanche threw off her dress and, lying down on the bed, injected herself in the thigh.

The result was swift, and unexpected. Instead of the gradual invasion of her senses by the luxurious pleasure of the drug, she felt a rush of pleasure such as she had never before experienced. Of course! As a longtime user, Pontaillac needed a stronger dose. She was accustomed to a solution of five or seven percent. What he had given her was ten or even twelve percent. Flooded with the drug, her brain launched a series of exhilarating fantasies which, in her overstimulated brain, assumed the clarity and vividness of enormous canvases. Her bedroom became a boat on which she embarked on a vast

lake. Her husband, so small, frail, almost effeminate, was rein-
carnated in the body of Raymond de Pontaillac, and Blanche
threw herself at the feet of his new incarnation as her severe
husband, more like her jailer, became a superb lover, a Prince
Charming, mounted proudly on his horse in the full uniform
of his regiment, silver breastplate polished to a mirror shine,
plumed helmet waving flamboyantly as he raised his mighty
saber and charged . . .

As a discreetly educated young woman and dutiful wife,
Blanche understood nothing of the orgasms that swept
through her. She knew only that, with the help of morphine,
she had experienced more pure pleasure than she had ever
known. Far from killing her, the drug had brought her to life,
and she fell into a languorous sleep so peaceful that she would
not have cared had it lasted for eternity.

But she did wake, with no idea how long she had slept.
And with waking came the cold, flat sense of the world that
she had come to regard as normal. Every impulse urged her
back to the Pravaz, but deprivation had made her cunning
as well as needy. The longer she could function without the
drug, the longer the supply would last. And just visualizing
the phial, almost full, gave her the courage to lengthen the
time between injections.

For the next few days, Blanche was punctiliously correct
with Raymond de Pontaillac but more than usually attentive
to her husband, in contrast to her coldness of the preceding
months. She even allowed him to penetrate her, and found the
experience, almost for the first time, enjoyable, though the
mechanical movements of Olivier and the brevity of the act
aroused in Blanche a consciousness of what pleasures might
be forthcoming were she to be partnered with someone more
athletic and attentive to her desires. Such unexpected pleasures dramatized one of the oddities of morphine addiction—

that the suppression of the nervous system, which in male addicts induced a lack of interest in sexual relations, led in women to the reverse, a state close to nymphomania.

Blanche was to learn how completely such a sense could possess her when, one afternoon in June, she injected herself with a new solution—a further gift from Raymond de Pontaillac.

Looking from her window, she saw the park and garden of the château transformed into the landscape of another time and place; surely she looked down on what had existed here centuries before—a Roman road along which chariots rolled, and groups of workers, olive-skinned men whose bare torsos were darkened by the sun, while the women, in homespun skirts and plain blouses, took shelter under the trees, and lounged there in amorous poses, awaiting any man who cared to possess them.

Although the marquise remained, externally, Madame de Montreu, within her lived another woman, dominated by thoughts of Raymond, whom she had agreed to meet this afternoon. Through the window, she saw him approaching on his horse from the direction of the Château aux Ormes. She watched him ride along the long dusty avenue of Italian poplars, and arrive at the main gate. There was nobody to receive him. Blanche had been careful to put all the domestics to work in remote corners of the house and grounds. One scrubbed the floor of the main salon, another cleaned out the henhouse, while a third, supposedly raking hay, dozed in a shadowy corner of the barn.

In her imagination, she reconstructed his movements. Raymond enters through the foyer into the dining room . . . He looks around for the men of the house, perhaps playing billiards . . . but there is nobody.

Wandering into the hall, he looks at the stairs . . . Somewhere up there, the beautiful addict sleeps . . . And then, not in imagination but in reality, she hears his steps ascending . . .

No longer sure which Blanche is controlling the body both of them inhabit, she opens the door of her bedroom and awaits him. Hurrying to her, he stands so close that the heat of his passion is almost palpable.

"Blanche, I love you. I adore you. I desire you with all my soul."

Without a word, she holds out her arms.

{ 14 }

Once Olivier de Montreu relaxed his rigorous surveillance of his wife, she embarked on a program of long walks and charitable visits to sick children, pregnant women, and the ill of the neighborhood.

In reality, each of her outings ended either in a small fishing cabin on the far side of the lake or in an isolated summerhouse on the grounds of the Château aux Ormes, where Raymond awaited her. In these two locations, so different, they exalted in satisfying the same desires, sometimes on a bed of leaves hastily heaped on the floor, at other times in luxury, on soft divans, and surrounded by the best interior decoration money could provide.

On each occasion, the lovers were joined by an even more seductive mistress, the Pravaz. However, instead of the furtive manner in which they had administered the poison before this, now they did so casually and at ease, the way Raymond might have smoked a Royal Havana, or Blanche powdered herself, or dabbed on a new *eau de toilette*. They even dressed for the occasion. How ravishing he looked, thought Blanche, in his royal-blue suit under a Panama hat, while he judged her adorable in a robe of pale linen, yellow slippers, and suede gloves, with wildflowers circling the crown of her straw hat.

They were young. They were beautiful. They were in love. That's all there was to say.

Of course, such an idyll could not last.

On the day of their next meeting, Blanche was about to leave the house when Jeanne grabbed at her skirts.

"Maman, take me with you!"

"No, darling."

"But I've been very good."

"I know, dear. But I have to visit some poor sad people—you know, that big lady, La Gire, and the old man, Le Guillot . . . You'd be frightened."

But the little girl held even more tightly to her skirts. "You *used* to take me with you," she wailed.

"Well, not today. I'm too busy. Now let go."

The cries of her child followed her down the steps, at the foot of which she stopped, then returned and gathered her little girl in her arms.

"Oh, my darling!"

Unfaithful mistress but dutiful mother, Blanche forgot her rendezvous.

At the end of the day, a letter from Raymond, carried by a servant, asked why she had not come. The next day, they met as planned in the summerhouse.

"Here you are at last!" said Raymond, aflame with desire. He tried to take her in his arms, but she evaded him.

"My dear, we must talk seriously."

But he didn't listen, and his passionate kisses stifled her protests.

"Raymond . . ."

"Your lips. I want your lips . . ."

"Darling, I beg you . . ."

"I beg you too. I want everything. There, a kiss on your eyes. And one on your mouth. Kisses forever . . . forever . . . forever . . ."

Blanche succumbed, but after the battle of love, she fled from the summerhouse, leaving behind a disconcerted Raymond.

She could think only of little Jeanne. Her agitated mind, further disturbed by the morphine, was prey to horrible imaginings. As she hurried across the fields toward the château, every tree, every path seemed to accuse her, *Your daughter is dead.* Hurrying by a group of farmers trudging toward their evening meal, she seemed to hear them agree, *Yes, yes, she is dead!*

"Don't tell me that!" she shouted in response to the words they had not said, and the men and women stopped and stared at her, then at one another, in uncertainty and confusion.

Bursting into the garden, she saw Jeanne not dead at all, but playing with a ball, and at that moment all her chimeras disappeared so completely that, had she been confronted with an account of them, she would have thought the teller insane.

"Oh Jeanne, my treasure, I will never abandon you again."

Thereafter, it was in vain that Pontaillac waited for his mistress in the cabin or the summerhouse, in vain that he sent letters to her, in vain that he loitered near the chapel. The rustle of her skirts, so light, so adored, were not to be heard.

He obtained a further two weeks' leave and remained at his parents' château, with a mixture of pleasure and despair, until his final night when, unexpectedly, he received an invitation to dine with the Montreus.

With Olivier present, there was no chance for more than a few whispered words.

"What has become of you?" he hissed when they were briefly alone.

"I've become an honest wife," she snapped.

These words, so haughty and glacial, made it clear to Raymond that their affair was at an end. The next day, he departed to Paris, where, in Villa Said, La Stradowska wept alone.

Still energized by the morphine with which her lover had left her abundantly supplied, Blanche made an effort to repair relations with her husband. One scruple prevented her. It seemed to her contemptible to throw herself, still hot from sex with Raymond, into the arms of Olivier, and she decided to spend a few days in repentance and purification. She was still doing so when, toward the end of the month, she was overcome with a strange malaise, of irresistible cravings and revulsions. When morning sickness followed, the reason was obvious.

"Well, Blanche," said her cousin Mathilde Gouilléras, "I'm going to start embroidering a pretty layette."

Blanche's heart fell. "Oh, you think so?"

"Well, what's wrong with that? You have only one little one; I have three."

"Oh shut up, shut up!"

"It will be a boy," Mathilde said complacently. "I see that in your beautiful eyes."

A horrible thought invaded Blanche's brain. If she was pregnant, it could only have been for a month, yet for six weeks her husband had been excluded from the marital bed. The father must be Pontaillac!

Blanche had to laugh at the disasters that appeared to follow inexorably in the wake of her encounter with the dashing Raymond. No less than a carrier of the plague, he seemed to spread a moral disease in his wake.

If only she had the courage to tell Mathilde the truth. *Dear cousin, there is no heir in prospect for the distinguished name of Montreu. Yes, I'm pregnant. But here is the horrible truth. The marquise, respected aristocrat and dutiful wife, the mother of little Jeanne, carries within her the fruit of adultery, the living crime of betrayal. What misery! What shame!*

But despite the progressive intoxication of morphine, Blanche said nothing to her cousin. Instead, she calculated every way out of her predicament. There was, she decided, one obvious remedy—make peace with her husband, and admit him again to his legitimate place in her bed.

"My exile is over?" demanded Olivier when he was permitted one night to enter the conjugal bedroom.

"Yes," responded Blanche tenderly. Their lips touched, and a ray of moonlight penetrating the tinted glass of the window bathed them both in a lambent glow.

Oh Blanche. Oh noble victim of the delicious poison. Just a few minutes more, a few seconds, and your sacrifice will be accomplished. Your husband will know nothing of your adultery, and you may live in peace as a mother until the baby arrives.

But then, abruptly, the marquise struggled out of the arms of her husband. Revolted by the ignoble lie she was about to impose, she cried, "Never, no, never!"

Olivier recoiled, his sensitive nature distraught at her evident loathing. "Why do you hate me so much? What have I done? What is there about me that you find so disgusting?"

"It's not you," moaned Blanche. "You are the best of men. It's just . . ."

"But I'm your husband. I have my rights."

She slumped back onto the bed, drained by the drug and by her failure to carry through her plan. What now?

"Later, Olivier . . . please, later . . . Look at me. I'm exhausted. You will kill me."

Each subsequent night, Olivier came to her door, and each night his wife refused his embraces, destroyed and vanquished as she was by the memory of her sin.

It seemed to Blanche de Montreu that no woman had ever been so unfortunate, so confronted with a dreadful dilemma, and so poorly equipped to deal with it.

She desired desperately to seek advice. If only she had a sister, a close friend. But of the women near her, Mathilde was too much of a gossip and her mother too pious. Making matters more urgent, it was now an open secret among the servants of the château, particularly those who washed her intimate linen, that the marquise was pregnant.

There came a moment one morning when Blanche felt all her resolve evaporate like the dew from the grass of the garden outside. Below her window stretched the lake into which Olivier had flung her drug and her Pravaz. Why not throw herself after them, finding release in the cool depths? Or, better still, let the drug itself release her. Taking her phial of morphine, she removed the stopper and raised it to her lips, determined to drink it all, and die in the extremity of intoxication.

It was at that moment she saw, on the far side of the lake, Father Boussarie, the parish priest of Saint Martin l'Eglise, tricorne hat under his arm, apparently heading toward the château. Replacing the morphine in its hiding place, she hurried to meet him in the garden before he reached the house.

"Your humble servant, Madame la Marquise," he said formally. "Are you feeling better?"

Blanche groped for words. "Father . . . listen to me . . . I need to speak with you . . . privately."

"If you wish me to hear your confession, it would be better if you came to the church. However, if you prefer, we can go to your chapel."

But at the last moment Blanche's nerve failed. "No, no, it's not a matter of confession. I just wished to pass on some money for one of your parishioners . . ."

Unexpectedly, her mother finally provided a solution to her dilemma.

"Blanche, you seem sad these days," she said, after they had spent an hour together during which her daughter said almost nothing. "Are you bored out here in the country?"

"Not at all."

"Is there something you would like? Some little personal item Olivier could buy for you?"

"No. Olivier is very generous, as you know."

"Well, you seem distressed at times. If you like, we could spend a little time in Limoges together."

Raymond's uncle, His Reverence Aymard de Pontaillac, was assistant to the bishop of Limoges . . .

"That might be very pleasant, Mother."

Two days later, a stately Panhard limousine stopped at the door of the bishop's residence in Limoges. Blanche descended, leaving her mother in the car.

"Don't worry, Mother," Blanche said. "It's just a charity thing. Some money I want to give. But it needs to be done with discretion."

Monsignor Aymard was working with the bishop when Blanche was announced. She was not unknown in the episcopal palace. During one of his evangelical tours, the bishop had visited the La Crozes and bestowed his blessing on the children about to receive their first Communion. He had no hesitation in interrupting his work to see her.

Even attired in her least fashionable dress, Blanche made a startling contrast to the austerity and simplicity of the monsignor's office. Genuflecting before the gray-haired gentleman in the violet soutane, she kissed his hand, then took the seat offered. Almost before he could take his seat on the other side of the desk, her reserve cracked.

"Oh, Monsignor, Monsignor, have pity on me. I've come to confess a terrible sin. A crime!"

Startled, the monsignor said, "My dear marquise . . . of course . . . speak. Speak without fear or shame. God's forgiveness is infinite."

"Monsignor . . . Father . . . I have sinned . . . I have sinned . . ."

Without revealing the identity of her lover, or the contributing effect of morphine, she poured out the story of her infidelity and the pregnancy that resulted.

"The bastard that I carry within me I can never love, do you understand, Monsignor, never! It has already made me suffer far more than I suffered when I gave birth to my little Jeanne. It burns me, tears me, it is like a poison within me. It defiles our house . . . What should I do, Father? Must I carry my secret to the grave? Oh, I'm ready to die, to destroy this living proof of my dreadful fault. No matter what punishment you may inflict, I will obey . . . Monsignor, will you permit me to destroy this seed of my shame? May I arrange an accident, at risk of my life? I swear to you; with this abhorrent seed within me, under the burden of misery, I will die."

Aymard's conscience battled with his instincts as a man.

The new law of divorce, which the Church condemned, nevertheless offered a solution. But there was the question of the child. What would become of it? He could advise a reconciliation with the husband, but to do so and not to admit that the child was fathered by someone else . . . didn't this merely prolong the lie and widen the treason?

"I see only one path to follow, my dear," said the monsignor. "You must confess all to your husband, and rely on the mercy of the Lord."

"Tell him everything?"

"Yes."

"Even the name of my lover?"

"That's not necessary. Confession of the crime is enough."

"I am happier thus," said Blanche, "since I have forgiven him—as I hope you will, since he is of your family, a Pontaillac."

"My nephew Raymond?" said the astonished priest.

"Yes, Father."

Agitated, Aymard rose and paced around the room, troubled and humiliated by the news.

"Madame," he said finally, "any personal feelings I may have toward my nephew are insignificant beside your moral duty. I repeat. You must confess your fault to your husband. By all means withhold the name of Raymond if you wish. However, if the suspicions of your husband should fall on any other man, you must name Raymond as the father of your unborn child. You have no right to punish an innocent person."

"So I am the sole person to be punished," Blanche said bitterly.

"You may feel that," said Aymard sympathetically. "But if it is any consolation, be assured that I share your anguish. Your revelation not only falls on my affection for my nephew, but on my duties as his guardian. If I must, I will disown him, and give up my sacred charge."

Rising from his chair, he assumed the full dignity of his holy office.

"Address yourself to God, my child." His eyes wet with tears, he made the sign of the cross with trembling hands above the bowed head of the woman his nephew had wronged.

"Go in peace."

{ 15 }

After his return to his home on Rue Boissy d'Anglas, Raymond de Pontaillac passed the last days of his leave in isolation and suffering. When finally he admitted Christine, his mistress simply opened her arms and murmured, "I waited for you."

That exquisite creature didn't seek to penetrate his amorous secrets, nor did she interrogate him about what had passed at the Château aux Ormes or the manor of Montreu. The traveler had returned cold, broken, depressed, and she took care of him, wrapping him in a little of her own youth, warmth, and light.

But what good are the smiles and joys of a friend compared to the chaos of passion?

The young officer tolerated Christine, but he loved Blanche, and loved her with all the fury of his sickness.

First, he draped in black the portrait of the marquise, as if she had died. He removed from the chamber of love all those relics of the woman he adored, but soon he was again kneeling before the same objects, unable to forget the loved one from whom he was, it seemed, forever parted. Although he continued with his military duties, he doubled, tripled, quadrupled his morphine doses. Starting with twenty-five centigrams, he progressed to thirty, forty, sixty, and was soon injecting a gram and a half, and sometimes two grams a day.

One morning in August, Pontaillac had invited Stradowska and his friends Jean de Fayolle, Edgard Lapouge, Léon Darcy, and Arnould-Castellier to lunch. They had just reached dessert when his own orderly approached to inform Raymond that he was wanted in the hall.

"Who is it, Clement?" demanded the captain, in ill humor. "I told you I wasn't to be disturbed."

"Captain, it's a lady . . . She seems very upset. She demanded I call you, and added that she would be very annoyed if I disobeyed."

"Did she give you a name, or her card?"

"No, sir. But she's a very grand lady; I saw that right away."

Raymond knew who it must be, but pretended to be irritated.

"This is too much! But I think I know what it's about. Have her wait in the library." Turning to his guests, he said, "You must excuse me, my friends. Believe me, I would not be so inhospitable were it not a matter of the greatest urgency. Of honor, in fact."

As the party broke up, Christine, looking forlorn, said, "You're not even going to give me a kiss good-bye?"

As he embraced her, she murmured, "What is it? Not . . . a duel?"

"Not at all," he said, but the other officers, having had the hint, took it as fact.

"If it's a duel, we're ready to act for you," growled Fayolle. "Just say the word."

"There's no question of a duel, gentlemen," said Raymond, as if grudgingly admitting the truth, then continued, "at least, not yet . . ."

"Ah ha!" cried Darcy. "And who's the lucky man?"

"Why, Kaiser Wilhelm," said Raymond. "Or maybe Bismarck. I haven't decided. Maybe I'll let them toss for it."

They left laughing.

Blanche was waiting for him in the library, but as he tried to embrace her, she retreated.

"Sir, kindly let me come to the reason for my visit. It's not a skittish mistress you see before you, but an injured wife and a mother full of remorse. I am the unhappiest of women."

Raymond snorted in amusement. "I know exactly why you're here. I deprived you of your source of morphine; I left you to die. But I'm ready to save you again, if you want."

"Sir . . ." she began, but he didn't let her continue.

"Oh, Blanche, if that deprivation has given you the courage to come to me, I bless it. For you, for your eyes, your lips, I would make any sacrifice. For you, I would steal, I would kill! What would you have me do?"

Blanche sank into a chair, exhausted by the deprivation of morphine and by her terror.

"Raymond, I'm pregnant."

Startled, Raymond paced the room as Blanche poured out her account of having discovered her state, and her visit to Monsignor Aymard. But the fact that his uncle knew how he had seduced the wife of his friend was swept away by his joy at the news.

"Our baby! How wonderful. We'll adore it as we adore one another."

"You can't be serious!" said an agitated Blanche. "The child can never be ours. I will follow the advice of your uncle—confess everything to my husband, name you as the father, and pray that he accepts the child as his own."

"Well, do that!" said Raymond, stung. "Name me—but on the condition that you promise to marry me if I kill Olivier."

"I would never be so cowardly. You are no longer a part of this. I will face the anger of my husband alone, and accept whatever punishment may follow."

"I refuse to let you do that! I will defend you!"

Alarmed by his madness, the result of his intoxication, Blanche calmed him—only to have him suggest another possibility.

"Let's run away together. I'll resign my commission. Money isn't a problem. We can find someplace to raise our child together."

"But what about little Jeanne?"

"We can take her as well," he said carelessly.

"And Olivier?"

"What about him? If he protests, I'll insult him. Then he'll have to challenge me to a duel. Providing the outcome is favorable . . ." He didn't seem to imagine it would not be. ". . . we could be married in Austria, in Egypt, in Italy—before the pope, if you like. I'm so rich that my wife would live like a queen."

"Do you really think I would marry the man who had killed my husband, the father of my little Jeanne?"

Turning, she ran to the door.

"Blanche . . ."

But by the time he reached the street, he saw only the back of a fiacre receding down the avenue.

{ 16 }

The fiacre deposited Blanche at the home of her friend Geneviève de Saint-Phar. It was the consultation hour, and Geneviève was receiving her usual clients in her tasteful but severe office. Geneviève was careful not to reveal anything of her sexual tastes. Not for her the masculine clothing, the monocle, nothing audaciously virile. Her black dress was carefully chosen to show off her brunette hair, her high forehead, and her striking eyes, brilliant with intelligence.

Despite her fortune and her celebrity, Mademoiselle de Saint-Phar lived quietly and simply. Her old professors Aubertot and Pascal were proud of their student. But what courage! What a struggle, before she obtained her degree. And what efforts to overcome the general prejudice against women in medicine.

Orphaned at eight, she had been raised by the nuns of the Sacre-Coeur in Limoges, where an aunt, one of the nuns, hoped she might remain by taking the veil herself. Geneviève had other ambitions, however. As a girl, she had encountered the teachers of her richer friends. She began studying medicine at the local college, and after two years moved to the Faculty of Paris. After much discussion, it was decided to admit her on the same basis as male students, but not without an uproar from the press, which demanded, "Get back home! Learn to cook." Others supported her, however, most importantly her professors Aubertot and Pascal.

The closer she came to graduation, the more clearly she realized it would be almost impossible to find a hospital in which to complete her residency. "How is it," she demanded of the faculty, "that you allow women to register, take classes, pass examination, and then bar the doors of the profession?"

"But with male and female students thrown together," demanded her detractors, "what if there is . . . intimacy?"

To which her champions replied, "Well, what if there is? These are young men and women who know how to behave respectably, with discretion."

Resistance didn't cease once she had completed her residency and set up her surgery on Rue de Miromesnil. She took only women patients, and one day there appeared on the streets a handbill advertising her as MADEMOISELLE DE SAINT-PHAR. SECRET DISEASES OF BOTH SEXES. But her courage in the face of these attacks simply increased her reputation, and rich patients flocked to her.

Was there a lover? Perhaps. Geneviève was young, she was a woman. But, if she burned with the desire of all young people, she avoided scandal, and in France, a sin that doesn't become a scandal is no sin at all.

Geneviève cordially received her old friend Blanche.

"This is a nice break from patients. I assume you've come to visit me as a friend, not as a doctor?"

"Both, in fact, my dear Geneviève."

"All the better." She indicated a chair. "Is it the morphine?"

"No."

"Then . . . ?"

"Well, in part. Under the influence of the drug, I . . . well, I'm expecting a baby."

"Congratulations! The marquis must be delighted."

"He doesn't know . . . Geneviève, I'm pregnant by a man who is not my husband."

Geneviève couldn't hide her surprise. "You?"

"Yes, me. I've come to you as a friend. I want you to . . . deal with it."

"Well, of course, when the time comes, I'll be honored to . . ."

"No, I mean . . . immediately."

"Are you mad? How long . . . ?"

"Two months."

"And you want me to do what?"

"I beg you to help me dispose of the proof of my adultery."

"Do you realize, Blanche, what crime you're proposing?"

"Crime or not, I must get rid of it."

"I refuse."

"Not even for twenty thousand francs?"

"You insult me like that? In my own home?"

"It would be a greater dishonor to my body if I allowed it to be a source of anguish for one day longer. The law may forbid it, but my conscience tells me there is a higher justice."

"You've lost your head!"

"Geneviève," Blanche pleaded, "in the name of our friendship . . ."

"No! No!"

"You want me to die then?"

"Blanche, you will live. And you will come to love your child."

But all her prayers and all the threats left the marquise more determined than ever.

"Where do you wish to go, madame?" inquired the cabbie, who'd been waiting in the street. Blanche consulted a scrap of paper.

"Rue des Trois Frères, in Montmartre."

{ 17 }

As he negotiated the narrow cobbled streets leading up the steep hill of Montmartre, the driver wondered what a lady like his passenger, obviously wealthy and wellborn, could want in this rough and dangerous locality, the haunt of thieves, absinthe and opium users, and all the riffraff of *la vie de boheme.*

At Place d'Anvers, the marquise abandoned the car and, after many wrong turns, arrived at Rue des Trois Frères, where a crudely painted sign bore the words "Madame Xavier, Midwife" with the traditional symbol of a cabbage, the plant of the newborn.

About to enter, she was struck by a sudden qualm, and shrank back into the shadows.

Ideas of death seized her. She ran downhill, only to be stopped as she was about to cross Rue de Maubeuge. "Are you blind or crazy?" demanded the woman who grabbed her. She indicated the cars racing down the hill. "Any one of these would have killed you."

Blanche thanked her with a sad smile, and continued her

Jean-Louis Dubut de Laforest

flight. *Maybe better if she had been run down. Her problems would be at an end.*

The following morning, a young servant girl dressed in a simple tartan dress of black and violet checks, with a white apron and a linen bonnet, ascended the staircase of the midwife.

"Madame Xavier, please."

"That's me, miss," responded a fat, untidy woman with an amused look and a little mustache on her upper lip. "What can I do for you, dear?"

"I need . . . to talk to you."

"Then talk to me." She led her into a little salon furnished with tables and chairs of cheap varnished wood, with a threadbare Turkish carpet on the floor. There, with a series of encouraging smiles, she coaxed her visitor to confess her predicament.

"Two months gone? Bloody hell, you've come just in time. You did the right thing to come to me. If more people had your good sense, there would be far fewer . . . accidents."

The visitor explained that she worked as housemaid for a middle-class family, and that nobody knew of her state, except her master.

"So it was your employer who gave you this . . . little present?"

"Yes, madame."

"The pig! And he dismissed you?"

"Not yet, madame. But he gave me money."

"Well, that's better. In that case, you can board with me here, and when the baby arrives, we'll find a good wet nurse to take care of it while you find another position."

"That's just it, madame. Even though monsieur"—she touched her abdomen—"did this, I like my position. And if I left without explanation, madame, his wife, might suspect . . ."

"What are you saying, exactly?"

"Well, I thought . . . I hoped . . ."

"Stand up."

Blanche rose to her feet and stood, trembling, as Madame Xavier's fingers expertly probed and prodded her.

"Is your boss rich?"

"Yes."

"Three thousand francs."

"I . . . that is, he would pay you five, even ten . . . but it must be secret, you understand?"

Madame Xavier looked her over speculatively.

"You speak very well for a chambermaid."

"I was well educated."

"By the nuns?"

"Yes, by the nuns."

"What's your name, dear?"

"Antoinette Mathieu."

"Is it indeed? Well, Antoinette, how does a chambermaid come to be wearing a pair of earrings worth twenty thousand francs?"

Instinctively Blanche touched her ear. "These? Oh, they're not real. Just paste."

"Listen, dear. Let's drop all this pussyfooting. I know real diamonds when I see 'em. If I'm to do as you ask, I risk jail. I'm not doing that unless I know who I'm dealing with."

Blanche slumped. "I'm the . . . Marquise de Montreu."

After this revelation, Madame Xavier's manner changed for the better. It was with deference that she led her noble visitor to the door.

"We're agreed. Twenty thousand francs?"

"Yes, twenty thousand . . . tomorrow," said Blanche.

"Tomorrow . . ." Xavier opened the door. "Your servant . . . Madame la Marquise."

Twenty-four hours later, Blanche once again entered the door on Rue des Trois Frères.

"Lie down there, Madame la Marquise," Xavier said, indicating a divan, "and don't move."

She probed her again, this time more intimately.

"You're frightened," she said. "That's normal. You haven't lost your nerve."

"No, I'm ready. Kill me if you like. I don't care anymore."

"That won't happen. I've helped more than two hundred women, and never killed anyone . . . except the brats."

"You're a monster!"

"Madame la Marquise is too kind," said the woman ironically.

"Oh, don't look at me. Don't talk to me. You fill me with horror."

"Don't move!"

And throughout the terrible process, the marquise, defenseless, would only moan, "Kill me! Kill me!" Her poor eyes fluttered and she fainted, so saw nothing of the human butcher with the rolled-up sleeves, and only vaguely sensed the yellow light that fell across the table from the curtained windows, and the long glinting needles, the lint and sponges, the bottles of phenol and chloroform, all the modern yet still barbaric equipment of the criminal abortionist.

"Don't move!"

Madame de Montreu, deathly pale, descended unsteadily from her car and, leaning on the arm of her maid Angèle, walked slowly to her apartments.

"Tell Monsieur le Marquis I won't be dining tonight."

"Yes, madame."

The marquis found his wife on her knees, praying.

"You're in pain, my dear?"

"No."

"Then why do you refuse to eat with me?"

"I'm fasting."

"The doctors have warned you about anything that might damage your health."

"The doctors are not the guardians of my soul."

"You worry me, Blanche."

"Olivier, I just want to be left alone."

Thanks to the morphine Raymond smuggled to her, and which she hid about her bedroom—the ampoules of drug in her face powder boxes, the needles in bunches of silk—the days of Blanche's recuperation passed with far less pain than would have been the case with another sufferer. She spent the days on a chaise longue, amid flowers, reading novels, and toying with a fan until the book and fan fell from her hands, and sleep spread the sails of contentment. Nights she also spent alone, happy to have disposed of her difficulty without arousing the suspicions of her husband.

Once her energy returned, she suggested to Olivier that they take a trip. She needed to escape from Pontaillac, the father of her dead child; from Madame Xavier, who had killed it; from Mademoiselle de Saint-Phar, to whom she had confided her secret; she wanted to flee anyone, friend and enemy, who might have known or even suspected what she had done.

"Where would we go, my dear?" asked Olivier.

"A long way away."

While Catissou, the old servant, took little Jeanne to the Château des Tuilières, the Montreus set out for Sweden and

Norway. It took all Blanche de Montreu's energies to run the
risk of a long voyage so soon after having endured the agonies
of the Rue des Trois Frères, and to disguise her continuing
suffering under a false gaiety. Thanks to her arsenal of lies,
however, Olivier was still fooled.

"I'll devote myself to you every minute," promised the marquis, "and we'll love one another as we did before."

"I adore you," sighed Blanche.

"Relax. I'll take care of you."

In Stockholm, in Christiania, in Drontheim, on the glaciers
and fjords, the marquis rejoiced to see the color returning to
the cheeks of his wife. He could not know that, having come
well-supplied with morphine, Blanche continued to inject herself beneath the midnight sun as, at the same time, Raymond
was doing under the sun of Paris.

{ 18 }

Moving along parallel paths, the two addicts marched toward a collapse of body and brain, the effects altered by their difference in sex, but equally inevitable in terms of their destruction.

Painful abscesses covered the captain's body, and he was subject to lapses of memory. A cloud enveloped his brain. Sometimes luminous and flaming triangles obscured his vision. He forgot the names of his servants and his friends, would address Christine absently as "Louise," "Therese," or "Andree." On duty, he would give strange orders, and brutally punish his men, or praise them without reason.

Of the exceptional intelligence of this man, at once soldier, artist, and writer, enough survived to give a vivid and fantastic shape to his delusions. His deranged mind connected the contours of a battle map with those of a beautiful woman. The theory of the Symbolists, that each vowel had a distinctive color—that "e" was black, for instance, "i" blue, "o" red, and "u" yellow—preoccupied him. He adapted the idea to music, becoming convinced that the harp conveyed serenity, the organ doubt, the violin prayer, the flute a smile, while the trumpet—the divine instrument—was glory.

Thus deluded, Raymond de Pontaillac soon found a bizarre harmony in everything. He extended the theory of colors and letters to clothe the consonants as well in music, and allocated a musical tone to each. "H," he decided, was C sharp minor and violet; "m"—a gray letter, he proclaimed—was B flat. Exploring still further his eccentric theory, he created a physical alphabet, with movements of the body indicating the letters. Holding his head to one side indicated an "o," the right arm bent was "k." He also glimpsed a way to incorporate figures; a "w," for instance, represented eight inches, an "l" three inches, and so on. So accomplished did he become with his new and manic system of communication that he would give demonstrations, reading a magazine article as if it were a musical score.

But he soon came to despise these exercises as unworthy of a military officer. In hopes of forgetting Madame de Montreu and her pregnant condition, about which he had heard nothing, he ran to Christine and other women, though in his state of sexual enfeeblement they simply left him more depressed.

Searching for the euphoria of his first days on morphine, Raymond increased the doses, putting a tourniquet around his arm and massaging it to bring into relief his exhausted veins.

Sometimes he rediscovered the wonder of his earliest morphine "virginity."

"Everything is rose," he told Christine in wonder. "I see wonderful things."

Taking a flower, he placed it on the mantelpiece. Staring at it, he seemed to see it expand into a little bouquet, then a larger one, and still larger, until it attained enormous proportions, an entire garden. He stared at an artificial butterfly pinned at the corner of a mirror until it not only repeatedly changed color, but took flight, flitting around the room before coming to rest again in its original place, where Raymond, unable to believe what he had seen, tore it apart to convince himself it was just a creation of paper and wire.

These playful illusions were succeeded by real hallucinations, in which imaginary figures surrounded his bed. They advanced slowly on Raymond, hands extended, surrounded by a luminous aura—like the spirits that mediums claimed to be able to "call up" by an effort of will.

At one moment, Raymond would be violent, jealous, at the next apathetic. When he was not under the immediate influence of the Pravaz, an invincible torpor overcame him. "My head is lead," he would moan, "and my arms rubber."

He seldom went out, except to make an appearance at the Military School. Otherwise, he remained voluntarily imprisoned in his house, and closed the door to all but his oldest friends. When Jean de Fayolle, Léon Darcy, or Arnould-Castellier did manage to visit him, they were astonished to see dozens of medicine bottles scattered around a pharmacist's scales, on which Raymond liked to weigh out the drug and make up his own solutions.

Among the bottles, noticed his friends with alarm, were also bottles containing cocaine. Hoping to wean himself off morphine, or perhaps to explore new areas of addiction, Raymond had begun to abuse this drug as well, opening up a limitless series of psychosensual problems and terrifying hallucinations.

One night, Major Lapouge and his other friends invited Raymond to dinner at the Cercle Militaire, the exclusive military club, famous for its food and its collection of weapons and trophies captured in foreign wars.

From the start, Pontaillac was in a dangerous mood. Arnould-Castellier would have preferred one of the smaller side tables in the restaurant, but Raymond insisted on sharing one of the large tables with a number of other members. Most were in civilian clothes, though a captain of marines was in uniform, including the cross of the Legion d'Honneur. Another young officer of the Spahis also wore his medals.

"Look," Raymond whispered to Fayolle, indicating the young lieutenant. "That poor chap has no arms."

"He's in the 3rd. Wounded at Tonkin."

"Poor bastard."

Raymond tipped a sad, sweet salute to the young man, who bowed his blond head in acceptance.

While they waited to be served, a succession of soldiers in black uniforms with white cravats were entering and leaving one of the large private dining rooms. As the doors opened, the friends glimpsed two or three hundred people seated at small tables, in a blaze of electric light. The man with gray hair at the head of the largest table was apparently their host, holding a reunion dinner for old comrades.

"This is an admirable place," said Raymond sentimentally. "An *honorable* club. No gambling, no theft. Not like you see in those dives we usually frequent."

But Raymond was a millionaire, and seldom visited the Cercle except for some formal gala, when the rooms were full. For the rest of his friends, it was commonplace to see such events. They had attended many of them—serving officers sitting down to dinner with members of the territorial army and of the reserve, enjoying a meal in a spirit of brotherhood.

At their own table, the captain of marines started to leave the table, revealing that he had only one leg. As his friends helped him with his crutches, Raymond became angry.

"Another victim. One man with no arms. Now one with a wooden leg. War is disgusting!"

The officers glared as he continued to rave, cursing Germany and the problems of Alsace-Lorraine, until Jean de Fayolle lured him away to the library, then to visit some of the other rooms in the club where he would give less offense.

On the way, Raymond made an excuse and slipped into a toilet.

His friends waited outside. None of them wanted to observe what they all knew he was doing—giving himself another injection.

They moved on to the magnificent *salle d'armes*, a museum of weapons from every country and epoch.

Raymond grabbed a passing waiter. "Champagne! Champagne for everyone!"

"Are you sure . . . ?" Lapouge began, but Raymond stared him down.

"In Cologne and Berlin, I saw German officers guzzling our champagne, and I'd like to make sure there's a drop left for us."

The wine was served at a table just inside the enormous room, its walls covered in gleaming steel. Suits of armor stood along the walls, and overhead hung tattered and smoke-stained banners from a hundred skirmishes in which French soldiers had fought and died.

Drunk on alcohol as well as morphine and cocaine, Raymond stared in a daze at the deadly show towering above him. In the fragment of his intellect that remained intact, theories formed, but when he tried to articulate them, only nonsense emerged. Embarrassed by his incoherent phrases and bizarre gestures, his friends led him into a small empty side room and persuaded him to lie on a couch.

"Get a few minutes' rest," Lapouge said. "We'll come back in a little while."

He switched out the desk lamp that provided the room's only light, and closed the door. But Pontaillac didn't sleep. The instant it became silent and dark, he was completely awake, and afflicted by a terrible vision.

"Where am I? Has the bugle blown retreat?" He fumbled along the walls. "Where is my saber? My horse? My God, I'm a prisoner!"

His flailing hands overturned the lamp, knocking it to the floor and at the same time throwing the switch. Suddenly, on the far wall, he saw his shadow, grotesquely enlarged. To him, it seemed a monster, and he drew his service revolver and cocked it.

"Get back, you bastard!"

He advanced toward the shadow, which only made it more gigantic, more menacing.

"I warned you!"

Three shots blasted into the wall. Chunks of plaster and glass skittered across the floor.

When his friends burst in, fearing the worst, they found Raymond slumped in an armchair, gun drooping from his hand, and a foolish grin on his face.

"It was just my shadow!" he said. "Isn't it absurd?" Briefly restored to reason, he snorted in derision. "I shot myself. I wanted myself to disappear, so I shot at me."

He didn't protest as his friends helped him into a cab and returned him to Rue Boissy d'Anglas. Before they left the Cercle, Lapouge alerted Christine, so that when they arrived, Professor Aubertot was waiting. By then, Raymond was unconscious, and barely breathing.

Seeing his livid, almost crimson face, the pulsing of his carotid arteries, and noting the contracted pupils, the pulse of

ninety-two, the respiration of twenty-four, Aubertot administered a milligram and a half of atropine and, over the next few
hours, two more such doses. Raymond's pupils began to dilate
but the face remained flushed, and the eyes wild. In hopes of
restoring consciousness, Aubertot tried ice packs, and applied
leeches to his mastoid process and mucous membranes, but
without visible effect. At his orders, a bath was filled with ice
water, and Raymond immersed in it. This had some effect,
so Darcy and Fayolle took his arms and walked him up and
down. After half an hour, his pulse and respiration descended
to levels nearer normal.

Delving into his bag of instruments, Aubertot extracted
a morocco case and opened it to reveal a gleaming brass instrument. Oval, and the size of a small pear, it was shaped to
fit comfortably into the hand. Two spiked wheels, the points
studded with rubber, jutted from one end.

"Faradization?" asked Lapouge with professional interest,
examining the object with interest. "Levinstein's method? You
find it works?"

"In some cases," said Aubertot. "And at the moment, to be
honest, I'm ready to try anything."

He pressed a stud and the object hummed. Touching the
wheels to the side of Raymond's neck, he gently pressed the
instrument into his flesh. Raymond's face jerked into a lop-
sided grin as the battery delivered electric current to the
nerves controlling the muscles. He continued this treatment
for ten minutes, and gradually it began to have an effect. Raymond woke, and, though deathly pale, smiled at the friends
gathered round his bed before drifting back into sleep. The
next time he woke, it was to vomit, after which he clearly felt
better, and, to the relief of his comrades, became almost like
his old self.

{ 19 }

The Montreus arrived back in Paris on the fifteenth of October. The same day, Blanche left their town house and hurried to the pharmacy on Boulevard Malesherbes. But the pharmacist refused to give her morphine without a prescription, as did his colleagues on nearby streets, despite her mounting fury, and offers of greater and greater sums.

She returned home, and suffered through dinner with her husband, ignoring the food, taking only the occasional sip of water.

"Poor Pontaillac was almost killed," said Olivier casually.

Blanche paled. "An accident?"

"No, attempted suicide, apparently." He described how Raymond had fired at his own shadow at the Cercle Militaire.

Blanche was distracted. At one moment, she seemed terrified. Then she smiled. "You think you can frighten me with morphine stories?"

"Well, it does go to show, my dear."

"I'm cured," Blanche said shortly.

Pushing back her chair, she left the table and went to her apartments, where she threw herself down on her bed and wept with fury and frustration.

For the next five days, the young marquise tried without success to find a pharmacist sufficiently corrupt to sell her morphine.

On the sixth morning, she woke to Olivier knocking on the door.

"Your friend Geneviève is here."

Horrified by memories of her abortion, Blanche cried, "I don't want to see her. I don't want to see anybody!"

Thinking to send a note of explanation, she took a piece of paper, but the words eluded her. Instead she slumped back into bed, paper still in hand, and lay helpless, her eyes haggard, face pale. She hadn't eaten for forty-eight hours, and her breath exhaled the sweet odor of ketones as her body devoured its own substance. Delirious, she spoke of herself in the third person, imagining she was dead and had become a spectator at her own burial.

"Oh, the crypt is cold," she murmured. "It is so dark . . ."

She was only vaguely aware of someone at the bedside, and didn't immediately recognize Geneviève de Saint-Phar.

The doctor listened with growing horror as her friend, racked with bouts of uncontrollable shivering, babbled of what had happened after she refused her demand for an abortion.

"You know, the a . . . ab . . . abortionist Madame Xa . . . Xa . . . Xa . . . Xavier, in Montmartre . . ."

"That butcher!"

Blanche grasped her wrist with all her strength. "You mus . . . mus . . . mustn't tell . . ."

"Your secret is safe, my dear."

She caressed her clammy forehead, brushing back the wisps of hair glued with sweat. For the next hour, she sat with her friend as Blanche once more descended into the hell of morphine deprivation. It seemed to the marquise that her heart was pierced; that the sheets of her bed had become soaked in ice water. Yet while her limbs were chilled, her vagina burned with a desperate need.

Then the hallucinations came. She babbled of vampires, and a black bat with wings two meters across that perched at the end of the bed and waited to suck her blood.

Briefly lucid, she recognized her friend, and pleaded, "For pity's sake, Geneviève, morphine. Please. Morphine."

Early in the afternoon, the doctor injected forty-five centigrams of morphine solution. For a while, Blanche felt well enough to drink a little bouillon and a glass of port, but soon the muscle spasms returned, until her body was racked with convulsions that shook her from head to foot.

Geneviève sent for professors Aubertot and Pascal. They arrived in the evening, just as the patient, pale and jaundiced, became prey to the *delirium tremens morphinic*. She raised herself upright out of her bed, screamed, tried to shake off the hands of her doctors, uttered curses blaspheming Christ and the Virgin. Every attempt to have her take some nourishment was rejected. Grapes, oranges, even the air itself smelled to her of the pungent excretions of sex, of animal musk.

Faced by the doctors, she trembled, refused to answer their questions, and screamed, "I don't want to be examined! Let me alone, for God's sake." At one moment, she would be raving of cats clawing at her, of her stomach divided in a thousand pieces, of snakes and vultures that tore at her head and intestines. The next, she imagined herself sitting in the garden at Les Tuilières, watching the flight of the sparrows; then, abruptly, she was back in Scandinavia, being embraced by the Lapps; an instant later, she was Italian, singing at La Scala; and finally the Queen of England and Empress of India.

Her head slumped forward on her chest, her face cyanotic, foam on her lips, she complained of a sensation like a cord tightly wound round her body, and demanded they lift the wardrobe from the bed. Looking at Aubertot as if seeing him for the first time, she turned to Geneviève and asked, "Who is that man? He's so tall that his forehead reaches to the stars . . . And good morning, my dear princess; you honor me with your visit . . ."

Around midnight, she woke, looked around her, raised her hands as if to defend herself, and cried in an anxious voices, "What do you want? See the ghost?"

On orders from the professors and the marquis, Catissou, the old servant, and the maids carried Blanche to the bathroom, where Aubertot began a similar regime to the one that had recalled Raymond de Pontaillac from the edge of death. Calmed by cooling baths and twenty-five centigrams of morphine, Blanche slept for three hours. At dawn, she vomited, at the same time as diarrhea emptied her bowels. They administered another twenty-five centigrams of morphine, mustard plasters, injections of sulphuric ether, then cold compresses on her head, after which she was returned to bed.

"You must watch her every minute," Geneviève and the doctors warned Olivier and the servants.

Olivier took the first watch. Blanche hugged him, swore again that she was cured, begged forgiveness for the way she had treated him, wept with shame for the other dreadful things she had done. Fortunately for his peace of mind, he put these confessions down to drugged ravings, never imagining she might be speaking the simple truth.

He continued to sit with her every night, alert in an armchair by the bed, but one night in November, he dropped off, and woke to see the bed empty.

{ 20 }

On Boulevard Malesherbes, Blanche, barefoot, wearing only her nightgown, ran before the icy wind, a white phantom. In front of a pharmacy, she pounded on the door and rang the night bell.

"Wake up! Wake up! I'm dying."

Her beautiful red hair blew around her shoulders, the wind pressed the thin fabric of her gown to her lovely body as she fell to her knees and, raising her arms to heaven, pleaded, "Lord, pity me!"

Two policemen, emerging from the shadows, almost fell over her.

"My God, look at her!"

"Better get her to the station." He waved down a passing cab, and the two of them bundled the almost insensible Blanche inside.

"The police station on Rue d'Astorg. And hurry it up."

Inside the station, they seated Blanche on a bench. Someone draped a coat round her. The other officers crowded around.

"She's a good looker."

"You can say that again. Where's she from?"

"Whorehouse?"

"Maybe . . . or maybe she was with her boyfriend when the wife came home unexpectedly. Down the back stairs in her nightie. Or out the window?"

Another bent to take a closer look. "Here, I think I know her. Isn't it Tulipa—one of the girls from the new place? You know, Madame Clarisse's, around the back?"

"You think? Doesn't *look* like a whore."

"I tell you she is, though. A new one, just in from . . . I don't remember where. You'll see. Tomorrow, it'll cost you twenty louis to see her the way you're seeing her now for nothing."

"Tulipa, eh? Well, well. So . . . what's she doing out on a night like this with no clothes?"

"Who are you, miss?" demanded the officer in charge. "You Tulipa, eh? From Madame Clarisse's?"

Blanche didn't reply. Just stared at them.

"Crazy," murmured someone.

"No," said the chief, rolling up her sleeve. "Not crazy. Look at these marks . . ."

Just then, someone pounded on the door. A moment later, Olivier hurried in, with Geneviève de Saint-Phar close behind, and a maid with Blanche's clothes. Thirty minutes later, she was back in her bed, having been escorted to the house by a gang of ignorant bystanders.

In the state of calm that followed Blanche's flight, Pascal and Aubertot took Olivier aside for a serious conference.

"We feel the marquise would be better cared for in a . . . special clinic."

"You mean an institution? A madhouse?"

"No, no, not at all," said Aubertot hurriedly. "Nothing like that. These places specifically deal with what the Americans call the 'morphine-accustomed.' They're pioneers of techniques to reduce reliance on the drug."

Pascal said, "Unfortunately there are no such clinics in France, but in England and Germany . . ."

"I will keep my wife with me," Olivier said firmly, and no amount of persuasion would change his mind.

A few days later, he took his wife back to Les Tuilières. Though the pitiful state of her daughter horrified Madame de La Croze, she steadfastly refused to give in to Blanche's pleading.

"Mother, I need it . . . I'm in agony . . . You are heartless . . ."

The next minute, her manner changed to fury. Turning on her husband, she demanded, "Olivier, get me morphine! Get it, or I'll kill you!"

Geneviève de Saint-Phar did her best, calming her friend with all the means at her disposal, short of supplying her with more of the drug, but neither her efforts nor the lavish affection of her family, nor the hugs and kisses of little Jeanne, nor the horrors of greater addiction evoked by Geneviève could prevent the descent of dark misery onto the brain of the damned soul which the Marquise de Montreu had become.

In her despair, she continued to rave about her lost child and the lover she had renounced.

"I want to have my baby at Les Tuilières," she murmured one night. Geneviève de Saint-Phar shot a look at Madame de La Croze and the marquis.

"Blanche, you're dreaming," she said hurriedly. "You aren't pregnant."

"Shut up, you!" snapped Blanche, then continued, in an amused tone, "She's so funny, Geneviève. She doesn't want me to have my baby. Jealous bitch. You know, Olivier, the way the baby moves inside me, so energetic . . . I'm sure it will be a boy. I want to feed him myself, and not send him to a wet nurse. What shall we call him?"

"Don't mind her," Geneviève murmured. "She gets these obsessions."

"Good God!" sighed Olivier. "How I know it!"

{ 21 }

On convalescent leave, Raymond de Pontaillac lived like a prisoner in his house on Rue Boissy d'Anglas. Only Christine Stradowska dared spend any length of time there, and risk the madness of his addiction.

Poor Christine! She endured all the insanity of the man, without even a glimmer of hope that he might return to health, and love her. She had given up her engagement at the Opera, refusing the adulation of the public, and let her youth wither, like a flower deprived of water and sunlight.

Never a sign of her disgust, never a murmur.

As for Raymond, sometimes he was charming, but mostly he treated her like an old woman who, fallen on hard times, has been forced to take a job cleaning and catering to the whims of a middle-class master. Still smarting over his lost love for the Marquise de Montreu, he taunted her with humiliating comparisons.

"Come on, Christine, what do you think you're wearing? You must think you're still on stage at the Opera. You have no taste at all. Do you remember Madame de Montreu at the English ambassador's ball; such elegance, such distinction!"

From a forgotten closet, he raked out some ancient fancy dress, and appeared before her as a clown, with a wreath of roses on his head. Christine was forced to dress herself in a parody of the same costume.

Seeing her in this forlorn dress briefly excited his dormant lust. Thrusting her back on the couch, he tried to enter her, but the impulse passed as quickly as it had come.

His impotence drove Raymond into a rage which terrified the brave young artist.

"Who the devil taught you how to fuck? You'd freeze a bull with your clumsiness. Go and find me a whore. Roselmont, or Luce Molday. Now get going, or I'll take my sword, and cut off your head."

Christine fled to the Villa Said, swearing to never again go anywhere near a morphine addict. Her accompanist, Loris Rajileff, was astonished to see her, once so haughty, reduced to tears.

"He punishes me—yet I love him. I adore him. I want to save him."

"But . . . you can't go back there."

"I must. I have no choice."

She returned to the shuttered house, to find Raymond torpid with morphine.

The next day, a Friday, she woke to find all the windows closed and the curtains drawn, and Raymond wandering the house completely naked.

"Take off your clothes!" he ordered.

Numbly, she did as she was told, stepping out of her robe to stand naked, head bowed, in front of him.

"I am Adam," he cried. "You are Eve! The world begins here—a new world."

For the next hour, she followed him as he wandered, naked and raving, through the shadowed, stifling house.

Seized by the megalomania of a god, he imagined a new and grotesque world. Instead of arms, its men had wings. Women had horns in place of eyes. Then the sexes melted together, and he conceived a single androgynous creature, with the breasts of a virgin, the tail of a serpent, the paws of a dog, a single eye where its mouth should be, and human ears, tongue, and hands. But soon that monster too disappeared, swept away by an infinite variety of terrifying beasts—all the horrors of the Apocalypse, all the obscene dreams of a doddering erotomane.

So Raymond, wandering in what the poet Baudelaire had christened the "artificial paradise," fell headfirst into the hell of lust; and while the Pravaz—which he now utilized to the extent of two or three grams a day—deprived him of his potency, it ignited a curious cerebrality, close to that of genius.

Once again, he could think of himself as "me." He felt his intelligence expand and his memory increase. He became again the soldier and, fascinated by strategy, pored over maps and read military histories, filling the margins with annotations.

Thoughts of Madame de Montreu still dominated him, but they became somewhat subdued when he read in the newspapers the account of Blanche's nocturnal adventure, and her mad search for a pharmacist. The press disguised her identity by printing only her initials, but he instantly knew to whom they referred. He suppressed his urges to pass by the house on Boulevard Malesherbes, where he risked the legitimate reproaches of Olivier. Why expose himself, in the eyes of both the husband and the wife, as well as her doctor, as the apologist for morphine, the person responsible for that first fateful injection? Olivier would have every right to say, "You have brought disorder and unhappiness on our house."

On the other hand, Raymond was alarmed at knowing nothing of the pregnancy of his old lover. Was she mad, as her mother said? At his urging, one of his servants, Clement, put these questions to Angèle, the maid of the Montreus.

"I don't know what to think, monsieur," the orderly reported back. "Angèle told me that Madame la Marquise *imagines* that she's pregnant, but is not. She has never been pregnant since the birth of little Jeanne."

Dismissing him, Raymond wandered through the house. Why would she lie? Obviously, because of the morphine. "Well, all the better!" he shouted. If that was what she now believed, it meant one less thing for her to feel shame for. Such was the respect in which he held Blanche that any suspicion of the real explanation would never have crossed his mind.

From time to time, Pontaillac sent Clement to the pharmacy of Rue Boissy d'Anglas for a new supply of morphine. One day not long after, he returned with empty hands.

"Captain, the pharmacist refuses to give more morphine without a prescription."

"What an imbecile. Go and tell him . . . No, don't bother. I'll go myself."

Captain de Pontaillac put on his dress uniform, dripping with gold braid and medals, placed his plumed helmet on his head, and directed his coachman to take him to the nearest dispensary. After a number of cringing but defiant merchants had refused his demands, he found himself in the office of the director of one of the largest pharmacies in Paris, on Boulevard Haussmann.

"Monsieur," explained the man, "under the terms of the law of nineteenth July, 1845, and the royal proclamation of twenty-ninth October, 1846, pharmacists are required to keep a register in which they note every prescription filled, together with the date, the substance, the quantity, and the doctor who prescribed it. There are no exceptions. Nor are they permitted to alter the amount of any medication recorded on a prescription."

Raymond smiled. "All very interesting, my friend, but beside the point. I am Count de Pontaillac, captain of the 15th Cuirassiers. I have money, and I'm ready to pay a king's ransom for what I require."

The man glared. "Keep your money, Monsieur le Comte. And I pray, do not insist."

"What do you risk?"

"A fine—prison, perhaps, and a ban on conducting business. Last year, a pharmacist was convicted. And even if I didn't risk anything, I would not want to dishonor my profession simply for profit, and at the risk of your health and your sanity."

"Spare me the sermon!" Raymond snorted.

The next day, at his order, Clement acquired a list of every doctor in Paris. Servants were sent to visit them, and explain that their master was a former addict being weaned off the drug by the Erlenmayer method, being given smaller and smaller doses. How were the doctors to know better? And what harm could it do to give him a few grams? Some refused. But Paris boasted three thousand physicians. And Raymond's stable held twelve horses. The process was time-consuming and expensive. Grooms, maids, and footmen had to be paid to spend long, boring hours in waiting rooms, trudging up and down stairs, and parrying the questions of medicos, not to mention lying, but Raymond got what he wanted—enough morphine to last him, even at the rate he consumed it, for weeks.

{ 22 }

A few nights later, at the Café Americaine, Raymond was surprised to see two familiar faces. It had been months since that night at the Café de la Paix when he had offered Therese de Roselmont and Luce Molday their first taste of the Pravaz. He'd remembered them as beautiful. Now they looked almost ugly; their faces pale with makeup, their eyes outlined in vermilion.

They had taken a table far from the noisy supper parties, and Raymond joined them.

Supper was served. Oysters, a cold partridge, a lobster, all on a bed of ice, but none of them ate much, being content with tangerines and oranges, and a little tea.

The talk was entirely of morphine.

"I'm still using," Luce said casually.

"Me too," Therese confirmed. She looked around the busy café. "And so are plenty more here tonight."

"It's wonderful stuff," Luce said. "I don't know how I did without it. I don't know how anyone does. Listen. I was feeling under the weather, so I consulted the great Aubertot. He told me, 'Stop the morphine.' Well, I'd paid him a louis, plus having to bribe his servant, so I thought I might as well take his advice. So I stopped. It wasn't any great hardship. But then after a week, I started again. My lover, a big wheel at the Stock Exchange—don't worry, darling; he's out of town—suffers from rheumatoid arthritis. I gave him a shot, and he didn't suffer anymore. Therese had terrible headaches; eighty centigrams a day saw them off even quicker than my friend's rheumatism. Isn't that right, Therese?"

"Quite true."

"Our hairdresser, Felix, uses a gram a day," said Luce.

"And you?"

"Two."

The girls asked about their former lovers, Darcy and Fay-olle.

"I have no news," Raymond said. "I am on leave. I stay in my house, like a bear in its cave."

"And your beautiful marquise?" Roselmont asked.

"And Stradowska?" added Molday.

Raymond shrugged. "Old news."

Instantly the girls looked interested. "So you can come home with us tonight?"

"Maybe."

Therese laid her hand on his thigh and squeezed. "You won't be disappointed."

"Particularly not if you have brought your Pravaz."

"I have," Raymond said. "But . . . I find it . . . empties me."

"Not us," Therese said voluptuously. "Quite the contrary. We get very hot."

"Who's your pharmacist?"

"A seedy character named Hornuch—11 Rue de Gomorrhe, not far from you. He only takes cash, and he charges well over the odds. But it's good stuff. Refines it himself."

Raymond wrote down the address.

"My little Luce," he said. "You talk about your craving for sex. But I don't believe it."

"No, it's true. Really. We just can't do without it."

"Not for more than twenty-four hours anyway," said Therese.

They revealed that, if they tried to stop taking morphine for any length of time, they were seized by an irresistible need for a man.

"If I don't have one or the other," Luce said, "the weirdest things happen. I have chills, fever; I sweat. And my senses become deranged. I touch velvet, but it feels like brass or copper. And just touching my foot to the ground feels like needles. You should see me dance. I jump better than an electric eel. If it would amuse you, darling, I won't take any morphine tonight. Tomorrow morning, you can see the effect for yourself."

"It's worse with me," Therese said. "Abstinence drives me crazy. I eat coal. Ground glass! I burn. I let twenty men fuck me, and don't feel the least pleasure. But once I have a shot, I sleep; it's all I want to do. One night, at that club, the Mountains of Russia, I picked up this guy. When we got back to my place, we washed up, then, before we did the deed, I injected myself.

"This guy asked me, 'Why do you do that?'

"I said, 'It helps me sleep.'

"Well, he looked surprised, and said, 'And . . . before sleep?'

"So I kissed him, and said, 'Oh, before sleep, it makes me really hot!'

"Anyway, later in the night, he shook me, and said, 'Are you asleep?'

"But you know how it is when you've taken a shot. I could

see and hear, but I didn't know where I was, or who was talking. And do you know what that bastard did? He laughed, got dressed, and then he stole my watch, my money, and all my jewelry, and ran off. I wanted to yell, 'Thief!' but I just couldn't."

Raymond went home with Luce and Therese, but all their efforts couldn't revive his former potency. Dawn found the three of them entwined naked in the big bed. Raymond crawled out and struggled into his clothes. In despair, he scattered some gold louis and large-denomination banknotes over the sleeping women.

My poor beauties, he brooded. *You are so absurd, so pathetic. Forget what I, your teacher, showed you. Throw away the Pravaz.*

Profoundly depressed, he stepped out into chilly Rue de Moscou.

All I've done is spread pain and madness. Blanche, my adored one, forgive me.

Later in the day, he would visit the poison merchant Hornuch on Rue de Gomorrhe and buy as much morphine as the man would sell.

{ 23 }

Tended by Geneviève de Saint-Phar, with Aubertot and Pascal always on call, Blanche de Montreu lingered in the nightmare that was the final state of morphine intoxication.

Angèle, her maid, remained docile and respectful, ministering to every one of her mistress's needs, though not without a growing resentment of the expense and attention lavished on someone who, in her eyes, little deserved or appreciated it. A tall, slim blond, she had even lent her clothes to the marquise when she disappeared on one of her mysterious incognito journeys. And for what? A few sous tossed her as a tip.

If only people knew the kind of tasks she was set. Taking a note to the home of Count de Pontaillac, for instance, and being forced to wait for almost an hour while his valet Clement woke him, shaved him, and served his breakfast. Finally the valet handed her a letter for her mistress. As he let her out, he asked, "How is the marquise, by the way?"

It wasn't the first time he had quizzed her. People were anxious to know what only she could tell them. If information was valuable, why give it away?

"That's for me to know and you to find out," she said, and skipped down the front steps.

Back at Boulevard Malesherbes, she handed madame the letter, then lingered just outside the door, watching through the crack as she tore open the envelope.

"Madame," read Blanche,

> *I do not wish to deny you, but the poison is killing me, and, having been the cause of your suffering, I do not wish to become also the murderer of the one I love. Forgive me, and if my refusal costs me your love, it is no more than I deserve.*
>
> *Raymond*

Crumpling the note, the marquise threw it to the floor.

"Angèle!"

"Madame?"

"I want you to go to . . ." Feverishly she searched for a solution, and, fueled by desperation, found one. ". . . to go to Montmartre," she concluded. "Madame Xavier. Rue Trois Frères . . ." But the horror of what she was suggesting over-whelmed her, and she said hurriedly, "No, don't bother. Is Dr. de Saint-Phar here?"

Angèle found Geneviève and sent her to dose the marquise. Afterward, she considered what the morning had taught her.

Rue Trois Frères . . . What business would her mistress have in such a slum? Who was this Madame Xavier? Some kind of brothel keeper? Maybe the marquise and the count wanted to rent a room for their secret meetings.

That afternoon, Angèle trudged up the steep and slippery streets of Montmartre, and stopped beneath the sign of Madame Xavier.

A midwife? Stranger and stranger. No Parisian woman had to be told what such women did. They could deliver your

baby, of course. But they could also find a home in the country
for an unwanted child. And if you preferred the child never be
born . . . well, that could also be arranged.

A few minutes later, Angèle was seated opposite Madame
Xavier in her stuffy salon. Business was evidently good,
thought the maid. Madame's dress was new, if vulgarly over-
decorated with flounces, bows, and cascades of white lace at
the throat and cuffs. Angèle's well-trained eye also recognized
the glint of diamonds from a ring and a necklace.

"So, my dear," asked Xavier, "how many months?"

"Excuse me?"

The midwife pointed to Angèle's hips.

"That."

"You think I'm . . ." The girl snorted. "Don't make me laugh.
I'm more careful than that."

"Then what are you doing here? I'm a busy woman."

"Do you know the Marquise de Montreu?"

"No. Of course not. How would I know a marquise?"

"Really?"

"Really."

"Redheaded? About my build?"

"All right, I might. What about her?"

Angèle put two and two together, and began to understand
madame's ravings about being pregnant, those days when she
had suffered alone in the darkened bedroom, eating nothing,
dosing herself with morphine.

"I'm her maid. I lent her the clothes she wore when . . .
when she came to see you."

"So what?"

"Madame's very ill. She may die. You botched it."

"That's a lie!" said the old woman, her professionalism offended. "It was a good job. Nice and clean . . ."

Angèle's triumphant smile halted her in mid-sentence.

"Perhaps the police would like to know what happens here."

Xavier snorted. "You think they don't? The prefect is an old friend. Plenty of clients come my way from him."

"I wasn't serious," Angèle said placatingly. "It's just that . . . well, there might be something in this for both of us, if we handle it right."

"How do you figure that?"

"How much did she pay you?"

"Ten."

"More like twenty, from the look of those rocks. But that's just a drop in the bucket to them. They've got millions."

"So you're thinking . . . ?"

"Blackmail, obviously."

Madame Xavier shook her head in admiration. "You're frank, I'll say that for you. Why should they pay anything? There's no evidence. It'd be my . . . *our* word against hers."

"Oh, she'll pay. There's lots of stuff Madame la Marquise doesn't want known—particularly by Monsieur le Marquis."

"Such as . . . ?"

"Madame's on morphine."

"You mean addicted? Oh, now I think of it, I read something in the paper. An aristo morphine fiend running naked in the street . . . 'B de M,' was it?"

"Exactly! Blanche de Montreu!"

"How did that happen? Doesn't she have a doctor?"

"Three of them. Two professors, Aubertot and Pascal. And the doctoress, Saint-Phar. But they're keeping her off the stuff. They think she can be cured."

"From what I hear, the cure's worse than the disease. Anyway, come to that, I can lay my hands on plenty of that shit."

"Really? She'll pay almost anything."

"Is that a fact?" said the old woman thoughtfully. "What's your name, dear?"

"Angèle."

"Call me Ravida. Care for a drink, Angèle?"

And so it was, when Angèle returned to Boulevard Malesherbes, she brought with her a small packet from Montmartre, courtesy of her new friend Ravida Xavier.

Once the marquise's mother had taken little Jeanne for lunch, the maid tiptoed into the darkened bedroom carrying, to Blanche's delight, a silver salver with a Pravaz and a bottle of morphine.

After injecting herself, Blanche was suffused with joy. She hugged her maid. "Thank you! Thank you! You've saved my life."

"It's not me you should thank, madame, but Madame Xavier of Rue de Trois Frères."

"You . . . *know* her?"

"Quite well, madame."

"And . . . ?"

"Don't upset yourself, madame. I am as quiet as the tomb."

From her bureau, the marquise took a bundle of banknotes and handed them to the maid.

"Stay that way, and your fortune is made, my girl."

Angèle, at the service now of hell and of "artificial paradises," found a thousand pretexts to slip the marquise a syringe and a dose of morphine. Sometimes she administered the injections herself, relishing the chance to pull down her mistress's most intimate undergarments. It was no great chore, when she had done so, to satisfy her mistress's lusts with a probing tongue and criminal fingers. When the marquise babbled her gratitude, Angèle could whisper, quite honestly, "Really, it's a pleasure."

"Again! Again!" sighed Blanche.

"Whatever you say, madame. But it would be nice, don't you think, to remember your little Angèle?"

So Madame de Montreu lavished money on her maid, gave her jewels and, when there was no more, extracted further funds from the marquis, telling him, "It's for charity, darling. We mustn't forget the poor."

The marquise gave and gave—money for Angèle, but also for Madame Xavier. ("We need to keep her quiet—she's a greedy old cow.") And Angèle, taking advantage of those times when artificial voluptuousness drowned her mistress in pleasure, would whisper, "They convicted a woman who aborted her child . . . The sentence was two years, madame . . . She has you on a leash . . . Be nice, or you'll end up in a cell at Saint Lazare."

Memories of her adultery and of her obstetrical crime remained vivid and flaming in the blood of Blanche de Montreu—her poor blood, tainted and drained of color. She needed love and forgiveness. But the headsman of her guilt would not wait. Each night, she felt his horrible presence, each night nearer and nearer.

{ 24 }

Despite the location of his pharmacy in the Rue de Gom-orrhe, in an unfashionable district, Monsieur Sosthene Hornuch, pharmacist second class, attracted a considerable clientele.

Tall and thin, beardless, sallow-skinned, with a violet ribbon in his buttonhole, he gave all the appearance of a complete idiot. In his own eyes, however, he was a great philanthropist, member of a number of charitable societies, a few of which he had founded. Deserving charities could always expect a louis or two from Monsieur Hornuch, and his neighbors held him in high esteem.

Paris-born, Monsieur Hornuch, a widower for many years, had been left with three daughters, Annette, Irma, and Zelie, all blond, all plump, and all eager to marry—not easily achieved when any eligible gentleman would require a sub-stantial *dot* to take them off his hands.

As for his shop, it satisfied every expectation of a phar-macy. His window displayed two of those enormous bottles, each a meter high, filled with red and green liquid of no par-

ticular medicinal value but of considerable dramatic impact.
Inside, medical value was similarly sacrificed to superstition.
Clients could purchase cat skins to combat pain, rings and
medals that claimed to cure migraine and rheumatism, and
bottles containing every kind of potion the manufacturers of
patent medicines could concoct from colored water, bitter
herbs, and alcohol.

Hornuch brewed up many of these potions himself. He
maintained two dispensaries, one to fill legal prescriptions,
the other reserved for his more mysterious products.

At first, he confined his manufacture to syrups and pills
against colds, and ointments for common infections, but as
commercial medicines proved more effective than his ama-
teur efforts, and were better publicized besides, sales began
to fall.

"Oh, Papa," complained his daughters, "you're wasting your
time. At this rate, we'll never find husbands."

Above all a dutiful father, Sosthene applied his intelligence
to the problem, and had a brainwave. Perhaps it wasn't entirely legal, or ethical—but what did such things matter when
confronted with the demands of the family?

"My children," he said, "I'm going to relaunch our business—
and in a way we can continue to work together."

So it was that, some years before our story, Hornuch and
his three girls went into the business of manufacturing morphine, using the processes developed by Robertson, Robi-
quet, and Gregory. In the laboratory, at night, the Hornuch
girls earned their dowries by gaslight, and in the sinister glow
of the furnace. Annette installed the distillation equipment,
soaking the opium in water at 38 degrees Celsius to separate
the active compounds. Irma evaporated the liquid in a *bain-
marie*, adding calcium carbonate to neutralize the acids. Zelie
mixed the concentrate with calcium chlorate, while their papa

completed the process to extract the pure alkaloid of the opium.

Three blond girls in enormous black aprons, sweating and struggling all night in this cellar—a strange sight. And yet what pleasure, as they thought of their husbands-to-be. And what riches, thought their father, as the stock of morphine increased in his locked cupboard.

Almost all his colleagues, horrified by the suicides and murders committed by morphine addicts, refused to supply them, so their clientele flowed toward Rue de Gomorrhe. Without any mention of a prescription, Hornuch handed out any quantity of morphine they could pay for. He showed no curiosity about the use to which they proposed to put it, whether medicinal or recreational. He sold the Pravaz as well—and in due course brochures began to circulate clandestinely, celebrating the pleasures of the "artificial paradise" provided by morphine.

Zelie died, but Annette and Irma, helped by the generous dowries provided by Sosthene, both married well, and left Rue de Gomorrhe to set up homes for themselves, while their father, with the help of some apprentices, continued to make and sell the drug.

He knew a pharmacist had recently been fined two thousand francs for selling morphine. Two thousand francs? It was nothing to a man who earned three, four, even five hundred francs a day—and very often more, since he had developed a profitable sideline with Luce Molday, Therese de Roselmont, and other addicts of the *demi-mondaine*. If they had no money, he accepted jewels, even furniture, stolen from the homes of their lovers. Behind his store, Hornuch opened a sort of salon where clients could inject themselves, then relax and enjoy the effect. Nothing if not discreet, he had separate rooms for men and women. Hour after hour, people entered, faces pale, eyes dark, and left with sparkling eyes and a rosy complexion. From these people, the contagion spread to dressmakers, hair-dressers, and hatmakers, then their friends, pretty or plain, rich or poor, young or old.

Thus the drug flowed from a few corrupt persons into the very lifeblood of France.

Therese de Roselmont and Luce Molday created a fashion among the rich loafers and social climbers that hung around in the Bois, the Cirque, at theaters like the Elysee and the Moulin-Rouge, and anyone who had the money and wanted to try a forbidden sensation.

Their soirees became wilder, more depraved, until only the hungriest searchers after new sensations attended.

When the eating and drinking were done, the two women would retire to the inner bedroom, to which, after a few minutes, a golden gong struck by a maid would summon the guests.

At the center of the softly candlelit room was revealed a wide bed, shaped like a great boat, draped in sails of muslin and filled with cushions covered in the richest of Oriental silks. At the discreet pulling on a cord, the curtains slid back and up, revealing Therese and Luce, nude, and entwined in one another's arms.

Morphine had long since burned away any sense of prud-ery or restraint. Having licked, fingered, probed, and exhib-ited themselves in every imaginable pose, they invited their guests to join them, but not before the evening's most impor-tant guest was honored.

A handsome, hairless boy carried in a silver salver on which rested half a dozen syringes and phials of morphine.

"Here it is!" Luce would purr. "The Pravaz!"

Each woman took a syringe and, with lascivious slowness, plunged it into the flesh of her friend.

{ 25 }

Not long after, Raymond de Pontaillac read with incredulity in *Rabelais*:

> The radiance of the Grands Boulevards was dimmed this week by the extinguishing of two bright and scintillating lights. When their mortal remains were lowered into graves dug side by side in the earth of the Cimitiere de Saint-Anne, the light was that of common day—an illumination that these two lovelies seldom saw. Creatures of the limelight and the candle flame, Therese de Roselmont and Luce Molday . . .

Therese and Luce dead? He couldn't read any further. For an hour, he raged around his empty house, alternately weeping and staring in terror at his reflection. It was then he decided, once and for all, to give up morphine. Determined to remember every step of the process, he commenced an intimate journal.

MORPHINE

Paris, 4 December, 1890. Last night, I presented myself at the Montreu house on Boulevard Malesherbes. Angèle, the parlor maid, had gone to announce me to her mistress when Olivier entered the salon. "My wife is sick," he said, red-eyed. "Forgive us, Raymond. We are very unhappy . . ." I felt an urge to cut his throat.

5 December, 1890. Christine suggested all sorts of voluptuous diversions, but the *pot-au-feu* of the Villa Said didn't excite me. I must abandon the Pravaz, otherwise I will be too ashamed to renew my love for the one I adore the most . . . Blanche is going to recover, even more beautiful, and I will possess her again, damned if I won't!

16 December. Eleven days without food . . . Cold sweats all the time, and my teeth chatter convulsively . . . Impossible to write . . .

17 December. I struggle! I struggle! What torture!

The night of the same day. Thoughts of suicide invade me. Get out!

4 a.m. I return home from a gambling club where I broke the bank . . . My wallet bulges, my pockets are filled with gold louis . . . A humiliating and worthless triumph . . . I sent all the money to the Public Assistance . . .

18 December. No, no. No more poison! I will live. I will love . . .

19 December. What a liar, that Hornuch. He claims that it's superior beings alone who take morphine, to correct an inherent instability. He lies, I swear! Morphine addiction is a kind of drunkenness, and nothing else.

20 December. At the club, I lost everything I won, everything I gave to the poor, and a thousand louis more. What the hell!

21 December. What is it that I long for, that I dream of in my

madness? What is my ideal of happiness? I ask myself these things, and if I'm honest with myself, I must admit that, behind my poetry and the fantasies that obsess me, is a wish to kill myself, and to have Blanche die with me, in a way that allows our twin bodies to be consumed in flames, so that our spirits can live together for eternity.

22 December. I would like to have killed . . . and died . . .

23 December. Is it just that I've gone mad? I feel my head has shrunk and my brain has dilated . . .

24 December. My eyes are sunken, my face is pale . . . I look with horror on what I have become. I fear death. I think about death, and cannot understand the ideas that follow me everywhere, in the midst of my comrades and when I'm with Christine, and in the solitude of the night. I know I'm crazy, and I will not prolong that madness, even though I know it for what it is.

25 December. I hear the whistle of bullets—and I'm frightened. Me, a soldier!

26 December. The night terrors are less intense; they almost make me laugh . . . Just get onto the battlefield, and we'll see who thinks Monsieur de Pontaillac is a coward!

27 December. My orderly had to help me out of bed . . . I'd wet myself . . . in the night . . . I wept with shame.

28 December. I visited the catacombs. I touched the heads of the dead, and ever since I've dreamed of nothing but graves and cemeteries.

29 December. Driven by an irresistible impulse I can't understand, and without the power to resist, I threw myself into an open grave at the Saint Ouen cemetery. From the bottom of the hole, I cried out, "My God, pity me!" Rescued by a grave digger, I explained I'd fallen in by

accident, but I heard one of the guards say, "This man must be an Englishman, a madman . . ."

30 December. The voices ordered me to kill Blanche and then kill myself, and when I resisted, the voices repeated with the roar of a hurricane, "Kill! Kill! We must have hearts. We absolutely need hearts—get them for us." At dinner, the voices emerged from my plate; in bed, from my pillow. "Kill! Kill! We must have hearts . . ."

31 December. I'm interested in the progress of my madness. The products of my imagination seem real, so that memories of events assume the appearance of reality, but in forms completely different from the way they actually took place. I see now that Dr. Lasegue was right when he said, "Go back in the history of the patient, and if you search you will find the *ictus* which suddenly destroyed his mental balance. From then on, the brain is like a piano from which certain keys have been removed and which, therefore, produces only imperfect and dissonant chords."

My "imperfect and dissonant" brain tells me that the sound of the wind is the voice of Christine; clouds are ghosts; trees are phantoms; my dog, a montagnard, is transformed into a bull, a lion, an elephant; then the dog disappears, becoming an owl that rises above me on wings fifteen meters wide. Well aware that no owl ever attained this size, I look at the animal and hear it scream . . .

1 January, 1891. I'm having trouble seeing, and there is a marked difference between one eye and another. When I put a red glass in front of my eyes, it varies in its nature and intensity. To what should I attribute this phenomenon? Is it a sign of my weakness? Does it result from

my abstinence from morphine? I sense new sensation in my genitals. If I am to believe the pathologists, this is a precursor to recovery!

3 January. My stomach is struck by an intermittent paralysis. What will happen when I can no longer digest food? Claude Bernard has observed that, in dogs given morphine, the gland controlling digestion ceases to function.

4 January. Decided to make my own experiments with animals, on a smaller scale than Pasteur and Levinstein.

EXPERIMENTS

1. I injected a pigeon three times a day with five centigrams of morphine. On the tenth day, it died, fourteen minutes after the final injection.

2. For seven days, I injected my bitch Myrrha with twenty centigrams of morphine each. On the third day, she began to tremble, and on the seventh, she was dead.

3. I took a large rabbit and injected it with forty-five centigrams. After forty-five minutes, it rolled its eyes madly, and died.

In my disturbed state, I believed I had been condemned to death, and suffered the pangs of any man who feels the hour of the guillotine approaching ever nearer.

My agonies are not imagined but all too real. I feel like a piece of metal placed between the positive and negative poles of a magnet, flung from one to the other, utterly unable to control my situation.

23 January. All day, I hung about near the Montreu house. The very thought of Blanche is torture. I remember her as she was that night at the ball, in the winter garden

of Aubertot's house . . . She kissed me, and raised her beautiful embroidered skirt . . . Oh, the pearl-gray silk stockings . . . Oh, the garter with its diamond clip . . .

24 January. The hunger for morphine grips me tight . . . I feel I've been nailed in place, and that other forces tear at me, as if with red pointed claws, and shake my body.

25 January. I see now that Blanche has betrayed me, in telling me she was pregnant, and making me suffer. To numb myself, and to forget, I gambled three nights at the L'Etatant and the Deux-Mondes, and lost a total of four hundred thousand . . . I want to ruin myself.

26 January. Tonight, I went to a ball, and hung around, alone, and pathetic in a fake nose. The other guests, costumed as Pierrots and Columbines, passed me and said, "What an odd character. He has the eyes of a thief." I stared at my fingers . . .

27 January. Morphine is a bitch! I admit that Blanche lives, and that I love her. Would I have the resolve to tell her of my love? No, I'm empty, washed out, fucked! Ask Christine.

28 January. A car with blinds drawn delivers me to a place on the route to Versailles where a magnificent and expert girl does her best to excite me—without result.

11 p.m. Another car takes me to a brothel—again, nothing!

2 February. How much abstinence does it take to revive me? Three or four months, say the experts . . . I can't . . .

3 February. I must!

4 February. I went to refill a Pravaz . . . I hesitate . . .

The same day. 3 o'clock, Fayolle, Darcy, and Arnould-Castellier demand that I open the door. Major Lapouge is with them. I refuse. The colonel of the 15th, an intelligent and kindly commander, sends me a very friendly letter. But I write to nobody, I receive nobody . . . Oh, how boring life is!

7 February. I hate those physiologists who reduce love to a business of stamens and pistils, and thought to a simple movement of molecules . . . I find Platonic love absurd . . . Very well, if love will not wake naturally, there are other ways! Spanish fly or carbon sulphide—one to stimulate the sex urge, the other to numb it? Both!

8 February. A beautiful evening with the dancer Weg! . . . Oh Blanche! Oh my darling! Oh my treasure!

9 February. "Where are you going?" Christine demanded. And I replied, "To be with her."

At Boulevard Malesherbes, the concierge tells me that her masters have left for Nice.

I'll go there myself tonight.

Midnight. Clement tells me Madame de Montreu is in Paris, not Nice, and it was on the orders of the marquis that he has sent me away, like a servant.

10 February. Olivier, I'm going to kill you!

11 February. Why suffer all the horrors of abstinence when my cure hasn't blessed me with the love of my admired one?

I inject myself with a gram of morphine.

12 February. A gram and a half.

14 February. Two grams.

15 February. Two grams and a half . . . I wake with the needle stuck in my right pectoral.

16 February. Everything is red and yellow; everything is blood and gold, the colors of Spain . . . For an hour, I haven't been able to stop laughing . . .

17 February. I live in an atmosphere of light and fire . . . I dose myself with Spanish fly and carbon sulphide. Oh, what a duel! . . . Which will triumph, the aphrodisiac or the anti-aphrodisiac?

18 February. A fiasco with Christine. A fiasco with Weg. A fiasco even with twelve beautiful *horizontales* . . . Morphine triumphs, and that murderer Hornuch is king of the world.

19 February. I was going to continue my experiments with my horse. I stopped myself. I wasn't affected by the death of the pigeon or the rabbit, but the agony of my dog made me sad. The death of my horse would be even harder.

Here's what I'm thinking. I loved my dog and I love my horse. I had no particular feelings about the rabbit or the pigeon. But why do people have so little concern for the troubles of the morphine addict? They get indignant about beating a horse or killing a bull, when they think nothing of killing a hare, a deer, a boar, a wolf, of wounding a partridge, cutting the throat of a chicken or a sheep, or slaughtering a bull. It's as if we, the addicts, exist on a lower plane. Every animal, every insect, every living being feels sensations of joy and pain. Why is the life of the fly not sacrosanct? Why?

20 February. To hell with science. To hell with philosophy. From now on, sensation alone.

21 February. Returned home exhausted. My score—eight women, and eight flops. I'm going crazy.

22 February. I blush at having killed my dog, the rabbit, and the pigeon. Those experiences achieved nothing, because I'm incapable of conducting an autopsy and studying the effects of these drugs on animals or humans.

23 February. An autopsy! This gives me an idea.

Having abandoned the Spanish fly and the carbon sulphide, and restored his intellectual energy, thanks to morphine, Pontaillac ended his diary with an open letter.

Jean-Louis Dubut de Laforest

TO BE OPENED ON THE DAY OF MY DEATH.

To Professors Etienne Aubertot and Emile Pascal, members of the
Academy of Medicine,

Gentlemen,

The faculty of which you are distinguished members requires
human corpses to carry on its work. One sees, at each public
execution, the bizarre spectacle of an argument at the foot of the
guillotine between representatives of the various hospitals about who is
to have the trunk, who the limbs, and who the head of the deceased.

In this way, the profession deprives science and demeans his
position.

Generally, gentlemen, you operate on patients who have died in the
hospital, and sometimes on those who have drowned, shot themselves,
or chosen the numerous other methods of departing from this world.
But it is rare, I believe, that a living person offers his body, so I
hope you will accept mine, as a souvenir of our friendship, and in
appreciation of your high benevolence.

I desire that the autopsy take place in the great amphitheater, in the
presence of your colleagues, of Major Lapouge and all other doctors,
military or civilian, interns and students, whom you judge suitable
for this supreme task.

Gentlemen, let your studies be an example to the users of morphine!
Use me as an example to destroy forever this source of horrors—this
plague that's worse than war!

Your admirer and friend,
Count Raymond de Pontaillac. Captain of the 15th Regiment
of Cuirassiers
Written in Paris, 23 February 1891.

{ 26 }

While Raymond grappled with his demons, on Boulevard Malesherbes, the Marquise de Montreu was in no less agony.

No pharmacist would supply morphine without a prescription, and since Madame Xavier and Angèle were not aware of Monsieur Hornuch and his little factory, Blanche entered a new crisis.

She screamed, threw tantrums, fell out of bed, rolled on the carpet on her room, and, rising, stormed through the house, smashing anything she could grab—plates, lamps, even the mirrors. At such times, three servants were necessary to prevent her from battering her head against the wall.

During such fits, accompanied by palpitations of the heart, she collapsed; the burning sensations in her throat from her sobs and tears, and the pains in her lower abdomen, because excessive, taking on the character of labor before childbirth.

Despite her pallor, Blanche remained beautiful and desirable, even with her angry face, her pretty little teeth bared, her dark eyebrows, her sparkling eyes, and the voluptuous flame of her red hair. When she moped around the house, wearing nothing but a lace robe, there breathed from her, despite her fatigue, a sense of lust. When she crouched and put her arms around her dogs to cuddle them, one could imagine, from the nervous encircling of her arms and the pink tongue peeping from between her red lips, that she was possessed by the overpowering passion of a bacchante.

When at last she slept, she woke with a sense of being stifled. She felt her limbs were being ripped, her skin erupting, her blood pounding, her belly swelling, and was plagued— a phenomenon produced by the morphine, not by her abortion—by the horrible hallucination that she was, interminably, giving birth.

Unconcerned with the suffering of her mistress, her maid cared only for getting what she could from the marquise.

"Have we forgotten little Angèle?"

When Blanche had no more money to give, Angèle became more threatening. "Madame Xavier demands more money. A lot more! And so do I. I'm getting married. Fifty thousand, madame, or I report you to the public prosecutor."

"I don't have that much," said the marquise. "I will ask the marquis and my mother tonight, and tell them it's for charity."

"Ask for it now! You're on a high—and you may . . ."

"Die?"

"Could be!"

"I hope to God I do."

"The money . . . if you please?"

"I'll sell my jewels, and you will have a good dowry, but on one condition . . ."

"What's that?"

"That you go to Monsieur de Pontaillac for me."

"Him again! I don't want any part of your dirty affairs."

"I would like . . . I want morphine."

"There's none to be had."

"Monsieur de Pontaillac has some, I'm sure."

With the money from madame's jewels safely in her pocket, the servant carried to the captain a letter spotted with tears and impregnated with sensual perfume.

> *I love you, I adore you. You have let me suffer. You will let me die . . . Oh, Raymond, have pity on the sad state to which you have reduced me. I am so, so miserable . . . Give me the divine fluid . . .*
> *She who loves you, who adores you, who loves and adores you, Blanche.*

There was no reply.

On a Sunday not long after, Madame de La Croze, with Blanche, attended Mass at the church of Saint Augustin, but after the service could not find her. Vainly she questioned the coachman and footman of the carriage that had brought them from the house, then explored the deserted church, the confessionals, the sacristy. The priests and nuns helped the poor lady, but with no hope of success, since a car was already taking Madame de Montreu in the direction of Rue Boissy d'Anglas.

"Monsieur de Pontaillac?" she demanded at the door.

"Monsieur is having lunch," responded Clement.

"Alone?"

"No, madame."

"Announce the Marquise de Montreu."

Stradowska was dining with Raymond. When Clement announced his visitor, he left the table. Christine followed him, and, face-to-face with her rival, couldn't control herself.

"You're a whore!"

"And you're insolent," snapped Blanche.

Christine wanted to strangle the marquise, but the sight of the two of them, him so anguished, her so desperate, and both so horribly lost, drove the young woman from this house of misery.

Blanche and Raymond exchanged a tender kiss.

"Do you have morphine?" she demanded. "I'm going mad . . . Do you have any?"

"No."

"For pity's sake . . . !"

"No. No."

"Just one injection!"

"Never. Look at me. The poison has devoured me."

Madame de Montreu took no notice. Her hair disordered, her eyes mad, she threw herself on the man, thrusting her fingers into the pockets of his waistcoat, his trousers. Careless of all discretion, she fondled him everywhere, engulfing him with the lust of a courtesan.

At last, with a cry of triumph, she found a Pravaz in his inside pocket. Raymond snatched the needle from her, and crushed it beneath his heel, but, finally, overcome by the tears of his mistress, and her tormented sighs, found another, and himself prepared the solution.

Stretched out on the divan, her clothing disheveled, as if offering all the joys of the flesh, Blanche murmured, "Inject me . . . inject me . . . inject me . . ."

Raymond obeyed. She sighed voluptuously.

"I'm coming back to life. Oh, it's good . . . again? Again? Turn me on . . . Again? Again? . . . I love you! I love you! . . . It's heaven . . . Oh, my savior, I love you!"

Where to run to? Where to hide?

Blanche was too weak to travel far, but Raymond had a villa in the forest of Fontainebleau, and the next night the lovers fled there, with only Clement to accompany them.

The orderly remained in the room below, while Raymond and Blanche locked themselves upstairs. Despite being on the banks of the Seine, they lived not in the sunlight but, night and day, by candlelight. In a room of mourning, of death, they lingered like two people possessed, avoiding the sun—two old people, both gaunt and withered, yet one only thirty-one years old, the other twenty-four!

Thanks to Hornuch, they had all the morphine they could want. Clement was kept busy traveling to Rue de Gomorrhe, and returning with fresh supplies. Otherwise, he left them severely alone, alarmed by the little he glimpsed as they opened the door—their bizarrely flaming eyes, and the mad and menacing babbling that emerged from their lips.

Blanche and Raymond never quite decided that they wished to die together. They simply became aware that it was their fate. Their bodies—their arms, chests, bellies, legs—their entire skin had disappeared under strange arabesques, red as rubies, yellow as topaz. Naked, they would admire one another, their vision supernaturally illuminated, glorying in the way they no longer resembled human beings.

One morning, the captain sent Clement to Paris to fetch his officer's dress uniform. That evening, he ordered the man, "Wake me at five a.m., for the review."

"What review, Captain?"

"Tomorrow's review, imbecile!"

That night, 3 a.m.

In their salon, the lovers embraced until Pontaillac, depressed by his complete impotence, said, "If I die of love, I can't then die for my country."

Then, urged by her lover, Blanche sat at the piano, and accompanied the captain in a battle song.

See how they come, with a flash of steel.
The regiments plunging into the fray.
They've come to die—and to save the day
Giving their blood, to the last hurrah!

Drunk on morphine, his eyes on fire, he slashed his hands to left and right, terrifying Blanche.

"Who's there?" he cried, grabbing her by her hair. "Who's there? In the name of God, who goes there?"

Did he see the angel of death approaching at that moment, to hover above the pale figure of Blanche de Montreu as her young life slipped away?

"Raymond," whispered Blanche in the dark. "I killed our . . . baby. Will you forgive me?"

And she slumped back to the couch, dead.

Slowly, Raymond emerged from his fantasy of the battle-field, and looked down, as if for the first time, at the still, cold, frail figure in his arms—the body of the woman whose life he had blighted.

"I've killed you . . . Oh, darling! I've killed you!"

He would have wailed, had the words not caught in his throat; he would have rung for Clement, had his fingers been able to move. Instead, he fell on his knees by the couch on which lay the corpse of the marquise, and slept.

At 5 a.m., Clement, as ordered, knocked at the door.

"Monsieur, the review!"

Waking, Raymond only gradually came to his senses, and, at first, refused to believe that the motionless figure on the couch was really dead. At the moment of realization, however, the veil of morphine descended again, and the insights that sometimes come at moments of great grief, the sense of looking briefly into an infinite reality, were dissipated, reduced by the drug to nothing but new hallucinations.

5 a.m.

"Your horse is saddled, Captain."
"Very well. I will dress. Help me."

6 a.m.

Captain de Pontaillac, in full uniform, mounted his horse and, turning toward Paris, urged it into a gallop. Dust rose in his wake. In his ears, the trumpets sounded, and, as if in a great painting of a mighty battle, he heard the cannons roar, the rifles crack, and saw the standards snap in the wind of victory . . .

The officers and men of the 15th Cuirassiers, drawn up for morning inspection, were astonished when their former captain, long absent on medical leave, suddenly galloped onto the parade ground in full uniform.

But what a uniform! The plume on his blue steel helmet floated bravely enough, but the face below it was so wasted that the strap swung loose under his chin, and the eyes that glared from the cavernous sockets were mad. His uniform hung on him, sagging over what had once been a powerful and muscular body. His legs were now too wasted to reach the stirrups, and his boots sagged on his bony calves. Pontaillac, once so robust, so handsome, so intelligent, had become a sinister new version of Don Quixote.

Drawing his saber, he turned toward an imaginary enemy.

"Charge—and *vive la France!*"

And at that moment, in the light of the rising sun, in the dawn of spring, he fell. He fell, exhausted but not vanquished. He fell dead, sword in hand, as he had wished to die, at the head of a glorious charge.

See how they come, with a flash of steel . . .

AN IRRESISTIBLE OFFER: GET TWO GREAT BOOKS IN ONE WITH THIS FLIP BOOK!

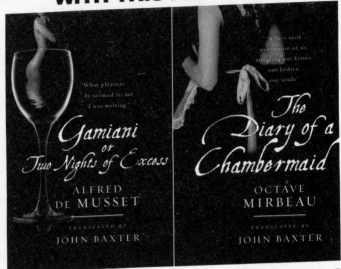

The Diary of a Chambermaid/Gamiani

Octave Mirbeau and Alfred de Musset
Translated and with an introduction by John Baxter

ISBN 978-0-06-196533-3 (paperback)

THE DIARY OF A CHAMBERMAID
Telling the scandalous story of Celestine R., a fisherman's daughter with a taste for men, Mirbeau reveals that "when one tears away the veils and shows them naked, people's souls give off such a pungent smell of decay."

GAMIANI
One man, two women, two unforgettable nights. De Musset allegedly reveals the sexual past of his older (former) lover, the great George Sand. Along the way, he tells a rollicking tale of debauchery.

About the Author

Born in Lyon, France, CLAUDE FARRÈRE (1876–1957) served as an officer in the French navy, stationed in the waters around France's colonies in what would become Vietnam. A prolific writer, he won the first Prix Goncourt ever awarded in 1905 and was elected to the prestigious Académie Française in 1935.

About the Translator

JOHN BAXTER is the author of the memoirs *Immoveable Feast: A Paris Christmas* and *We'll Always Have Paris* and the erotic reference *Carnal Knowledge*. An acclaimed film critic and biographer whose subjects have included Woody Allen, Steven Spielberg, Stanley Kubrick, and Robert De Niro, Baxter is also the co-director of the Paris Writers Workshop. He lives in Paris, France, with his wife and daughter.

MY LADY OPIUM

Selected Works by Claude Farrère

Le cyclone (1902)

Les civilisés (1905)

La maison des hommes vivants (1911)

Croquis d'Extrême-Orient (1921)

Mes voyages: La promenade d'Extrême-Orient (1924)

La quadrille des mers de Chine (1933)

Les forces spirituelles de l'Orient (1937)

Escales d'Asie (1947)

Lyautey créateur (1955)

Also by John Baxter

Carnal Knowledge: Baxter's Concise Encyclopedia of Modern Sex

Immoveable Feast: A Paris Christmas

We'll Always Have Paris: Sex and Love in the City of Light

A Pound of Paper: Confessions of a Book Addict

Science Fiction in the Cinema

The Cinema of Josef von Sternberg

Luis Buñuel

Fellini

Stanley Kubrick

Steven Spielberg

Woody Allen

George Lucas

Robert De Niro

Also Translated by John Baxter

Morphine, by Jean-Louis Dubut de Laforest

The Diary of a Chambermaid, by Octave Mirbeau

Gamiani, or Two Nights of Excess, by Alfred de Musset

MY LADY OPIUM

{ *Opium Fantasies of the Belle Epoque* }

Claude Farrère

Translated by John Baxter

HARPER ⬤ PERENNIAL

NEW YORK • LONDON • TORONTO • /SYDNEY

The photographs that appear on pages xii–xiii and xv are courtesy of the author's collection.

HarperCollins books may be purchased for educational, business, or sales promotional use. For information please write: Special Markets Department, HarperCollins Publishers, 10 East 53rd Street, New York, NY 10022.

FIRST HARPER PERENNIAL EDITION PUBLISHED 2010.

Library of Congress Cataloging-in-Publication Data is available upon request.

ISBN 978-0-06-196534-0

10 11 12 13 14   OV/RRD   10 9 8 7 6 5 4 3 2 1

Common sense tells us that the things of the earth exist only a little, and that true reality is only in dreams.

Charles Baudelaire
Dedication of *Les paradis artificiels* (1860)

CONTENTS

Contents

INTRODUCTION

Kicking the Gong Around: Opium and the Belle Epoque

With the exception of alcohol, no narcotic exercised such a potent influence over European literature of the early twentieth century as opium.

Artists of the Decadent movement found Asia fascinating. France's far eastern provinces of Annam and Cochin, later to become Vietnam, provided painters, writers, and composers with a rich source of inspiration. Monet and Toulouse-Lautrec admired Japanese woodcut prints (which first appeared in Europe as wrapping paper for imported porcelain). The poetry of Charles Baudelaire celebrated the "artificial paradises" offered by drugs, while writers like Pierre Loti and Pierre Louÿs created a vision of China and Japan as cultures of sage philosophers, sexually accomplished courtesans, and opium.

When Thomas de Quincey published his 1821 *Confessions of an English Opium Eater*, the drug was already widely known

A private opium party in a Paris apartment, about 1929. Pipes were prepared by an attractive *congaie*—courtesan—who would also be available for sex.

and abused by European artists. Alfred de Musset smoked it. Lord Byron drank it dissolved in spiced alcohol, as laudanum. In India and China, where it had been used for centuries, the British East India Company enjoyed a monopoly on its trade, even instigating the "Opium Wars" of the 1840s, forcing China to lift import duties on Indian opium, which the British traded for its most precious export, tea.

Laudanum became the preferred remedy of the highly

strung—the Prozac of its day. Though opium's chemically refined forms of morphine and heroin provided a faster, more intense sensation, artists and thinkers preferred the drug raw. Smoking it allowed them to spend an entire evening dream ing of the world transmuted into pure movement and form. To a culture that created the vinelike curlicues of Art Nou veau, Monet's water lilies, and Debussy's evocation in music of fountains, clouds, and the sea, it was the ideal narcotic— organic, transcendent, and ostensibly benign.

Frédéric-Charles Bargone (1876–1957), who wrote as Claude Farrère, was only twenty-eight, and a junior officer in

the French navy, serving on what used to be called the China Station, when he published *Fumee d'opium* in 1904. Literally "Opium Smoke," *Fumee d'opium* isn't a novel but a collection of episodes from different eras and continents, linked only in that they involve the drug. All employ elements of fantasy, horror, or sex. One adds an unexpected postscript to the story of Faust and his deal with the Devil. Others retell Japanese or Chinese legends.

Some stories purport to be based on the writer's own experience. "No one except opium smokers ever will know what a nightmare is," he declared melodramatically. However, there's no reason to believe Farrère, who went on to write dozens of books, and achieve not only best-sellerdom but admission to the prestigious Académie Française, was an addict, or even a regular user. Rather, he knew what readers wanted; in particular, graphic details of how opium was smoked, and what effect it had.

For most people, opium was too expensive and slow-acting. They preferred cheaper alternatives. Patent tonics containing cocaine, heroin, and morphine were freely sold by pharmacies at a time when aspirin—a synthetic drug, and therefore more suspect than "natural" opiates—could be obtained only by doctor's prescription.

To smoke opium was both complex and expensive. Most users did so in smoking parlors known as *fumeries* or, in Anglo-Saxon countries, "opium dens." These provided cots or mats on which the users could recline while they enjoyed the hallucinating effects, and were staffed by *congais*—servants who didn't smoke themselves but refilled pipes, made the smokers comfortable, and, at the luxury end of the business, provided entertainment, including sex.

Fumeries, particularly in private homes, were often sumptuous, as was the intricate paraphernalia needed to enjoy opium.

Opium users regard the pipe not simply as a means of
absorbing the drug but as an object of beauty.

The gum, white when it oozes from the poppy, turns to a dark
brown "jam" on contact with the air. To release its alkaloids,
a pellet is kneaded into shape and "toasted" over a flame at
the end of a long steel needle before being placed in the pipe.
Since each pellet gives only two or three inhalations, a dozen
or more pipes are needed to prolong the experience, which
can last for hours, even days. Each aspect demands expertise
and invites connoisseurship. In that sense, opium is to drugs
what golf is to sports; a pastime that, without the correct
premises, staff, and highly expensive equipment, is impaired,
even ruined.

Farrère drew his readers into the discreet world of the *opiomanes*, normally restricted to the rich and cultivated. He played
on the snobbery of the drug, describing in almost lascivious
detail the gold-inlaid jade pipes, the distinctive glow of the oil
lamp over which the drug is "cooked," and the crackling sound
as the pellet vaporizes in the pipe bowl before being inhaled.

Introduction

Every writer about opium, Farrère included, dwells on its aphrodisiac effects, particularly on women. All the women in *Fumee d'opium* are driven to sexual frenzy by the drug, while men remain aloof, and often impotent. Reliable evidence of this effect is skimpy. Rather, the drug is said by many users not to suppress the sex urge but simply to slow it down, and to prolong orgasm. Certainly its most potent effect is on the sense of duration. All thought of the passing hours disappears. Smokers, in Jean Cocteau's words, "step off the express train of time."

As well as Baudelaire, Loti, and Louys (who contributed an introduction to the first edition of *Fumee d'opium*), Farrère read earlier writers of the fantastic and grotesque like Edgar Allan Poe and Barbey d'Aurevilly, whose 1847 collection *Les Diaboliques* may have inspired the book. Modern readers will be reminded of those American authors of the 1920s who were influenced by the same people—M. R. James, Clark Ashton Smith, August Derleth, and H. P. Lovecraft. Some of these episodes could have appeared in the same pulp magazines that published them, like *Weird Tales*, or even from Derleth's press, Arkham House, had it not been for the sex, which was too frank for American audiences of the time. *Fumee d'opium* wasn't translated into English until 1929, and then only in a limited edition "issued privately for subscribers."

For a modern equivalent of opium, one thinks of mescaline, peyote, and LSD, which attracted the same type of intellectuals and aesthetes hoping for transcendence. Today, we are less likely to be shocked by the sex, or even by opium smoking itself—which won a kind of acceptance when Woody Allen's 1990 comedy *Alice* showed Mia Farrow patronizing a *fumerie* in Manhattan's Chinatown—than by Farrère's casual acceptance of Chinese women whose feet, tightly bandaged since birth, remain at infant size, and his description of a *fumerie* where every surface, including walls and ceiling, is lined with tiger skins.

My Lady Opium reminds us of a time when opium represented a badge of intelligence; the membership of an elite. In the late 1920s, when the Hungarian photographer Gyula Halász, aka Brassaï, created *Paris de Nuit*, his classic documentation of the city's *demi-monde*, his exploration took him to a *fumerie*. Among its clients was a beautiful actress. Brassaï asked to take her picture. Her response condenses vividly the sense of opium smokers as privileged, set apart.

"Of course! And you have my permission to print it. I'm proud to smoke . . . They say that after a while drugs, opium, will destroy you, make you thin, weaken you, ruin your mind, your memory; that it makes you stagger, gives you a yellow complexion, sunken eyes, all of that . . . Rot! Look at me. And tell me frankly, am I not beautiful and desirable? Well, let me tell you, I've smoked opium for ten years, and I'm doing all right . . ."

In translating and adapting *Fumee d'opium*, I've added new material in a few cases and taken other liberties in the interests of greater comprehensibility. Farrère wrote for an audience more anxious for an exotic thrill than a coherent story. He also peppered his narratives with Chinese or Japanese names and terms that have long since passed from general usage. In some cases, I've clarified these, in others removed them.

John Baxter
PARIS
JUNE 2009

MY LADY OPIUM

{ 1 }

In Foochow Road

It has now become my most cherished habit. Each evening, I smoke opium.

Not at home. I don't care to have the paraphernalia of smoking in my house. I live in Shanghai, on the Bund, in the Concession Française. Many people come to see me, and that I like, more than you might think. Don't believe all that nonsense you read about we *opiomanes* shunning company, and living only for the drug. There are so many absurd stories told about smokers!

No, nobody knows of my . . . hobby. In the evening, at an hour when Europeans are dozing in the club or carrying on drawing room flirtations, I adopt a very blasé air so far as fashionable life is concerned, and pretend to go home. But my *jinrikisha*-man, who is waiting at the door, takes me at once, as fast as his sturdy yellow legs can trot, along the deserted streets that lead to the heart of the Concession Internationale.

It is there that I do my smoking, in Foochow Road, Shanghai's street of pleasure. I have no preferred place. *Fumeries* abound, all of them welcoming. Shanghai is the city of festivals, the voluptuous rendezvous of the whole of Yangtze province; imagine Deauville, Biarritz, and Monte Carlo, all in one. And Foochow Road is the Chinese heart of Shanghai. When night comes, the entire street is one red glow of lights. Each door is a den, more or less weird, more or less alluring, but generous in the matter of opium.

I enter, randomly, the first that strikes my fancy. I stretch out near a lamp that is not in use, and immediately, a boy—a brat, but with an old and jaded face—comes up and prepares the pipe. I never tire of looking at these boys.

No matter where, he is the same sweet, prompt being who never smiles and never bestows a glance. He dips the needle into the little jug filled with sticky opium. Then, over the lamp, he proceeds to cook the pearly drop. It swells, becomes yellow, and buds. He kneads and works it against the bowl of the pipe; rolls and stretches it, makes it supple, and finally glues it firmly in the entrance to the bowl. Then he guides the bowl to the glass-enclosed lamp, with its steady flame. The black pill crackles, diminishes, and evaporates. As it vaporizes, I suck in, with long-drawn breath, the tepid smoke.

The first pipe knocks me out and annihilates me. I lie back, incapable of batting an eye. But that lasts one, two, perhaps three *minutes*. The patient boy prepares and offers the second pipe while I continue to relish, minutely, the first fruits of my drunkenness; the distracted wheelings of my brain under the first assault of the divine poison. It is only as the voluptuous vertigo spends itself that I heavily raise my neck and stretch forth my lips for the second pipe.

Though other smokers surround me, I cannot see them clearly, since the *fumerie* is almost in darkness, and we are all

reclining, our figures indistinct against the brown mats. But I can see the glow of lights amid the smoke, hear the crackling of numerous pipes, and am conscious of that indescribable odor. I am aware, likewise, that other, neighboring intelligences are sinking simultaneously into drunkenness; and this fills my soul with fraternal joy and a sense of affectionate security. Opium, in reality, is a homeland, a religion, a secret society that binds people tighter than family. There are Asiatics smoking in Foochow Road to whom I feel closer than certain conventional Frenchmen now vegetating in Paris, where I was born.

Though I always believed a gulf separated our races, I never suspected that we of Europe were the inferiors. But what an abyss yawns between us! To them, we are children, and they the ancients. There is far less difference between the infant in arms and the centenarian, hastening to his grave, than there is between them and us.

I owe this insight to opium, which enables me, in a marvelous manner, to scale that precipice. In its presence, the European and the Asiatic are equal. Races, physiologies, psychologies— all are effaced, replaced by entirely new beings—the Smokers, who, properly speaking, have ceased to be men.

Don't think this is some flight of drugged poetry. I mean it quite literally; we smokers pass over a greater divide than that between the living and the dead. Each evening, in Foochow Road, I and all the other smokers shed our gross humanity, casting it into the street like so many bundles of rags. From then on, our renovated brains make us each other's brothers and sons, able to understand and appreciate one another, and be friends. But intoxication is brief; and in the morning, as I return to home and bed, I abdicate my superiority, and put on those human rags and tatters once more, while the yellow men of that other race become for me books I can neither open nor read.

No matter. Among these same individuals, drunkenness has given me a few friends. For a number of evenings, a youth with piercing eyes has stretched out beside me, in the most gilded of the *fumeries* in Foochow Road; a low-ceilinged room, crowded on every side with grotesque gilded carvings. The young man wears a robe of mauve-colored moire, and his lean fingers roll the opium with marvelous dexterity.

His name is Tcheng-Ta. As his father is a rich merchant, he lives as he likes, in the manner of a prosperous Chinese artist. He has invited me to his own private *fumerie*, on the mezzanine of one of the most labyrinthine homes in Foochow Road. The entrance lies down a very dark alley, from which one has to climb two floors and descend one, all the while negotiating tortuous corridors and crossing narrow courtyards, where one sometimes notices the *strangest* things . . .

The room is very simple, with whitewashed walls, and ample mats and cushions on the floor. While one is smoking, Tcheng-Ta's mistress, Ot-Chen, prepares green tea, or plays the *pipa*, a kind of lute, and sings those Chinese songs that, to the Western ear, sound like a cat meowing plaintively outside a closed door.

We seldom talk, for our thoughts are not of the kind easily exchanged in an unfamiliar tongue. Fortunately the opium spares us the necessity. Our fraternal glances are enough. They make us aware that we share a state of perfect communion.

The other day, my friend intercepted an interested glance I directed at Ot-Chen. Today, he introduced me to Tchen-Hoa, Ot-Chen's sister. They are like a pair of dolls of the pink and white porcelain known as *famille rose*. Their amber-perfumed hands are adorably fine, and their bound feet so tiny that they fit easily into satin slippers the size of two walnuts.

Their hair, black as ebony, is intricately braided and curled,

though one rarely catches more than a glimpse of it, since they hide it under caps of close-crowded pearls. Tchen-Hoa and Ot-Chen are obsessed with jewels. Sixteen bracelets circle each arm, and seven rings each tiny finger. When they present themselves nude for love, they also lay aside their jewelry, but the moment the embrace is over, they scurry to pick up their ornaments before worrying about their scattered clothing.

They smoke opium beside us. They hold the pipes with mannered delicacy, as Western women raise their little fingers when drinking tea, and their lips pout prettily as they arrange them about the bamboo moist from our mouths.

Seized by opium and carried off on its wings, I see Ot-Chen and Tchen-Hoa as two legendary princesses, and myself as a character in a story of ancient times. Tcheng-Ta's den becomes a marble palace. Foochow Road no longer exists. We live instead in the silence of a venerable forest, where imperial *yamens* sleep in the shade of great trees. The smoke from our pipes settles in a fine black dust that masks the brightness of the walls, the mats, and the ceiling, with its enormous red and yellow lantern. Light is veiled and shaded by the dust. Objects take on new and mysterious colors, clothing themselves in bronze, in gold, in ivory, and in lacquer. Queens offer me Yunnan tea in the imperial goblet of green jade, and within my new body I recognize myself as the Emperor Hoang-Ti, the Most Sacred . . .

But here, my memory fails, and I know no more. What century is this, what dynasty?

But then all becomes calm. What I imagined just a moment ago must have been a dream. And so, as if on some nameless, invisible seesaw, the opium rocks me; rocks me between present and past, between man and emperor, between living and dead . . . rocks me to the point of nausea . . .

{ 2 }

The Wisdom of the Emperor

There came a time, when the world was younger, that the Emperor of the Yellow People, Hoang-Ti, led his tribe across the desert.

They were a great multitude, trudging behind the emperor day after day in a dark straggling line, then collapsing at night on the bare ground to sleep. None had horses or camels; few even owned clothing to protect their pallid skins. Only the emperor was yellow. His people were pale, their black hair matted. Low-browed, burned by the sun, they appeared barbarous, with no trace of thought behind their foreheads.

Where had they come from? Nobody knew who saw them, except that they had first been glimpsed among the great solitudes of the glaciers, and that they marched toward the forest—the terrible forest, inhabited, it was said, by dragons, by tigers, and by genii; the guardian forest that, like a bitch set

to protect her master's property, crouched, watchful, before the Promised Empire.

At dusk each day, the servants of Hoang-Ti assembled his tent—a tent of beast skins, sewn together in the form of a house, with a pitched roof. Seeing this, his people turned their eyes to the horizon, where some claimed to make out palaces quite differently constructed—with roofs bent backward, running parallel with the ground.

One evening, Hoang-Ti made camp by a wide river, which ever since has been known as the Yellow River—Hoang-Ho. On the other side lay the forest, the guardian forest. Hoang-Ti stood by the fast-flowing stream and regarded the forest for a long time. From the east, now dark, to the west, made crimson by the setting sun, it spanned the world, without limit, without a break.

It seemed to Hoang-Ti that the forest had awoken at his approach. Lashed by the evening wind, the very leaves appeared to weep; dragons, made apprehensive by the approach of men, hissed in their lairs, while tigers emerged growling into the freshness of the descending night.

The black-haired people huddled behind their emperor, shivering as they sensed the silent gathering of genii in the gloom. In the face of such dangers, many were afraid. Even Hoang-Ti trembled—not, he told himself, at the dangers that faced him, but at the magnitude of the task before him; that of making the Promised Empire his own. But as the west also became dark, and he turned to enter his tent, none of this doubt could be read on his expressionless face.

As the moon rose, his guards brought a stranger into his presence. The stranger's face was deep vermilion, the dusky crimson of red earth. He never ceased to smile. And he had— at least it seemed so to the emperor—six arms.

The emperor, being also a god, decided that his visitor must be similarly endowed, and thus treated as an equal. Dismissing his servants, he gestured for him to take the unoccupied seat next to him on the double throne of ebony, inlaid with mother-of-pearl. For a long time they sat thus, staring at one another, the emperor awaiting the message that brought the visitor to his tent; some helpful piece of advice, perhaps, or offer of an alliance? But in the smile of the creature with the crimson face he could detect no significance at all.

All night they sat thus, in silence. With time to sense the night weighing on the earth, Hoang-Ti noticed that the genii across the yellow river no longer yowled quite so loudly. Were they somehow under the control of his visitor? He was pondering this possibility when, within the ranks of his people, cocks began to announce the imminence of morning.

And at that instant, he of the crimson face lay upon the ground, and puffed loudly three times. From the earth, a bamboo cane erupted, then a crimson poppy, and finally a flame. As the stranger broke off the length of bamboo, it astonished the emperor to see that, by some sorcery he did not understand, the length of wood was now decorated with jade and gold, and that one bud had swelled into a rounded bowl. Gathering from the bulb of the poppy an oozing liquid like honey, the god dripped it into the pipe bowl, held it over the flame—and smoked.

It seemed that the tent trembled, as in astonishment. From the smoldering pipe, a perfume rose like none any person had ever inhaled. It spiraled sluggishly from the bowl, crept along the carpets that covered the floor, rose toward the roof—and reached the nostrils of the Yellow Emperor, who, docile, lay down beside the visitor, facing him, took the pipe when it was relinquished, and smoked.

• • •

In his intoxication, Hoang-Ti experienced a vision.

Through the wall of the tent that now swayed, as transparently as any silk, he sees the forest that lies between him and the empire. And, as though the centuries accelerate, fleeing ahead of his time, he sees his people cross the river and plunge among the trees.

What an assault! Against his force, the forest flings an army of gods and monsters. Clinging together, the trees enmesh themselves with a network of creepers that, even as his people hack through them, grow again. Seeing a clear path, his men plunge into marshes which, as they enter, deepen and widen. Poisonous serpents lurk among the dead leaves. Tigers leap out to slash the throats of their victims, then strike again, as deadly the second time as the first. Most terrifying of all, elephants stampede through the invading army, leaving in their wake trampled bodies, crushed limbs.

Dragons, bloody and voracious, devour the invaders, while lurking genii seize them in a death clutch, from which they escape deathly pale, their teeth chattering, only to die raving of terrifying visions as, overhead, other dragons swoop, then explode in a deadly rain that falls heavily and ceaselessly upon the earth.

And though each step of the emperor, and each advance of his army, costs more in blood than an entire battle—still he advances, and, little by little, mows down the forest . . . until there *is* no more forest.

There is only the plain of the Mid Lands.

Bare, arid, a savannah patched with lakes and marshes, it stretches in every direction, limitless. And his people, lost in this immensity, stare in astonishment at one another at the victory they have accomplished in reaching this place, and the work that remains to be done.

From the summit of the tallest mountain, Hoang-Ti, long

dead, looks down from his tomb—the mighty monument guarded by seven avenues of granite tigers.

Those who have conquered the forest are also dead, as are their sons and their grandsons. It is the fourth generation he sees, laboring to cultivate the plain. The savannah becomes tilled fields, the marshes rice paddies, and a new greenery, obedient to men, clothes the empire.

The few tigers not hunted down retreat to the white-capped mountains. Domesticated, the elephants now draw plows. No dragons of the air survive, and their descendants, the clouds, pour down only a beneficent rain on the fertile earth. As for the people, each night their numbers increase, until it becomes impossible to count them. And the women, gilded by the sun—the yellow women, made in the likeness of their great forebear, Hoang-Ti—are lovely.

Then comes the time of cities.

Along the banks of rivers and lakes, at the intersections of canals and highways, on the shores of bays and estuaries, and in the shadow of mountain valleys, towns begin to appear. At first, just a few timid houses, cowering from the threat of rain, of tempest and thunderbolts; then bolder villages that become cities, proud behind their walls, boastful with palaces. And at last the gigantic capitals, rearing marble towers and cedar-wood pagodas along the lakes of their parks.

No longer does one see flat roofs that run parallel with the ground. Instead, to every horizon, porcelain roofs glisten, all with their corners turned up, in imitation of the tents of older times. And in the countryside between the cities, mulberry trees flourish, to feed the obedient silkworms from which is spun that shining cloth that men prefer above all others.

The emperor and his people have conquered.

Domesticated and resigned, the gods quit their mountain

solitudes and come to dwell in the pagodas where statues of solid gold are erected in their image.

Of the seventeen provinces of the mighty nation, the capital of the seventeenth, spanning a great river, is the richest. Hoang-Ti knows it is not the last city that will stand there. Others will follow. Nothing is eternal. But today, for a moment, she is the empress of cities. Her gray wall encloses a red wall; the red wall a yellow wall; and within that wall lies a palace of violet wherein the emperor dwells.

Hoang-Ti looks down on the man who, after many generations, has succeeded him.

This illustrious being reclines upon a mat, under a parasol sewn with precious stones. Servants travel great distances only to prostrate themselves before him, burning incense held in shells of silver paper.

The emperor holds a pipe. He is smoking . . .

Hoang-Ti recognizes the regal contentment gleaming in those eyes, the inexpressible peace that reigns in the imperial sanctuary.

It is the same peace that he feels now, lying on the carpet of his tent on the banks of the river, next to the six-armed man with the vermilion face.

And now the eyes of Hoang-Ti see further still.

Beyond the violet palace, beyond the walls of yellow, red, and gray, the entire city is smoking; smoking as its emperor smokes. Opium smoke rises in clouds, wreathing the populace in sublime intoxication. No longer low, their lofty foreheads harbor expansive thoughts, magnified by the clairvoyant effects of the drug.

And further still, opium extends its reach, across the savannah, over cities and countryside, and even beyond, spreading everywhere its message of peace, tolerance, and reflection. Universal wisdom and happiness have come at last.

Forgotten is the striving, the sacrifice, the labor that made it possible. Now their victory seems effortless. In the mildness of their repose, basking in the gentle lassitude of their *fumeries*, diverted by the gossamer dreams that float in the dark smoke overhead, their barbarian crudity is tempered, their undisciplined energies curbed, their brutal impulses channeled into the pursuits of civilization . . .

At dawn, the emperor rose. Of the vermilion-faced god with six arms, there was no sign. He had vanished with the fleeing night, leaving behind the pipe, the opium, and the lamp.

Holding these three objects, the emperor stepped outside his tent. His people, wondering at his pale face and eyes like mirrors of bronze, followed him as he walked slowly to the river.

How much he carried in his two hands! It was nothing less than the entire wisdom and happiness of all his people.

At the same time, he beheld the forest, the forest that must be battled through and mowed down before they could reach the plain beyond. It was an abyss ten thousand–fold deep. Yet it was an abyss that his people must conquer.

His people were hard, savage, but effective. A crude tool, and a strong one. Once made sharp, polished, refined, it would no longer be equal to its task, its force transformed into air, into spirals of black smoke . . .

Wading into the shallows, Hoang-Ti held out the pipe, the opium, and the lamp.

"Later," he said, and, opening his hands, let them fall. The stream bore them away.

Those in front were puzzled, but remained silent. Those behind knew nothing of what had taken place. And so it was that, as the sun rose, they quenched the fires of the night, and prepared to cross the river and do battle with the forest that lay, dark and threatening, on the other side.

{ 3 }

Fai-Tsi-Lung, the Pirate, and the Dragon's Daughter

The junk is sleeping in the center of the pearly bay, and Hong-Kop, squatting on his mats, is reading the Philosopher. It is not yet time to smoke.

All around rear the innumerable islands of the Fai-Tsi-Lung; stone monoliths, each like the other, a petrified army. The mystery of their formation is as impenetrable as the Tonkinese fog that, heavy with diffused sunlight, spreads its mystery over the bay; an Asiatic mystery, filled with foreboding and threat.

But Hong-Kop feels no such fear. The labyrinthine Fai-Tsi-Lung and its fog have freed him from the despised domination of Emperor Hoang-Ti, the invader from the north. Under their protection, he is free to maintain his existence as a haughty bird of prey, swooping down upon the timid junks of merchants and fishermen.

Hong-Kop is a pirate. Were you to inquire his reasons for entering this trade, he would explain, with a smile, that he did no more than was urged upon his followers by the Philosopher; to shun degrading toil; to be neither laborer, nor weaver, nor bronze founder, since the mind becomes blunted from repeated contact with the same objects and the same task. One might, of course, speculate that Hong-Kop is a pirate for certain other reasons. For who shall fathom the serene and disdainful soul of a literate leader of men?

As he reads the Philosopher, squatting upon his mat at the rear of the junk, Hong-Kop is, at the same time, alert to those things of which a captain must be aware. The moment, for instance, when the sail overhead, woven of rice straw, bends in the breeze. But there is no breeze. Also any sign that the mist is about to rise. But the wan sky continued to pour over the bay its clammy whiteness.

Putting aside his text, Hong-Kop summons the women, who, prostrate day and night before their master, spy upon his will or his pleasure. One of them opens the parasol of yellow silk above his pensive head. Two of them delicately fan his indecipherable face. A fourth nervously readjusts the long smooth hair, the intricate knot of which seems to be awry. And the other three, pipe and lamp ready in their hands, gaze into his immobile eyes. For often, Hong-Kop, whose heart is always of cold stone, wishes nonetheless to be pleasured while he smokes.

Rising, Hong-Kop, a slender figure in his black robe with the coral clasp, sniffs the heavy air of the south. He glances at the naked, rugged rocks that keep watch over like a regiment of giants. He notes that, in the bow of the junk, at a respectful distance from their leader, his crew chew betel and play *bakouan* with shining silver sapecks; loot from the last capture. Only then, satisfied, does he recline. The lamp is

near at hand, dully glowing under its opium-stained glass. The jade pipe, inherited from his royal ancestors, receives into its gleaming bowl the pill that has been cooked above the flame. The jade bowl tilts above the lamp. The opium bubbles. With one long lingering breath, Hong-Kop draws the whole of the smoke down into his lungs. As his eyes fill with superhuman thoughts, he emits spiral rings from his nostrils, the black smoke of which sinks toward the water in a cloud of mist . . .

And now it is the third pipe . . .

Hong-Kop sees three thousand years into the past. The archipelago of the Fai-Tsi-Lung is as yet but an endless sea of sand. Beyond the horizon, the Dragon King, Hai-Lung-Wang, the Serpent of the Sea, long as thirty pythons, floats indolently in a limitless sea. For seconds at a time, his round head rears, his scales bristle. Soon he will wake, and travel north, into the cold waters of China, where his appearance, once in a century, announces the advent of a new dynasty.

Very occasionally, an emperor resists the rightful succession. One such was the Sun Emperor, Hoang-Ti. Hong-Kop sees him walking rapidly, casting his golden eyes over all the earth. One shaft from his bow strikes home among the scales of the mighty Serpent, who, filled with shame, sinks down into the sea's deepest entrails, the volcanic rocks that obligingly part to let him pass.

One arrow, however, only delays the inevitable end. The hour has already struck for Hoang-Ti. His throat has been slit in the hunt, and a new age is dawning. Impetuously, Hai-Lung-Wang darts forth and bounds above the waters—so quickly that the rocks, swept along in his course, bound with him, and tumble back in a shower of stones. In his wake, an archipelago extends over the Tonkinese sea. The Fai-Tsi-Lung is born.

More opium; more of the brown tear that evaporates upon the jade above the lamp . . .

It is the sixth pipe. Hong-Kop sees three thousand years forward. The Fai-Tsi-Lung lives on, old now, with cascades of leprous green clinging to its rain-drenched rocks. Junks float among the islands. But strange ships, foul with smoke and dust, pursue and shatter them. And thus end those noble hours of piracy, and of wise indolence.

Beyond the horizon, rice fields are about to change masters. Around the cities, chalk-white, walls gleaming green with porcelain tiles, the invaders from the Occident draw closer, laying siege with their cannons. In mighty peals of a new thunder, citadels fall. Dead are the princes clad in embroidered silk, reigning from the heart of palaces inlaid with mother-of-pearl and filled with refreshing shade. Dead are the literate hours of philosophers, the counselors of those who rule. Dead also—who knows?—is Hai-Lung-Wang, buried in the gray ooze.

Three more long pulls on the pipe, which, this time, reach the nerves of the smoker, rendering them enormously delicate and sensitive. It is the ninth pipe . . .

Hong-Kop rises from his mat and turns his eyes toward the east. The opium warns him of a danger that comes drifting over the waters. A junk emerges from between the rocks. Though her sails fill, no breath of breeze disturbs the reflection of the islands on the smooth water. She draws near. The green hull glistens like a shell of jade. A silk awning shelters the poop. Large and gleaming standards stream above the sails, which appear to be of ivory.

The pirates have interrupted their *bakouan* and cluster at the rail. Here is indeed a rich prize; a junk belonging to opulent merchants, or to high and lettered functionaries. Possibly the junk of the viceroy himself, who governs in the name of Hoang-Ti, the usurper.

Hong-Kop watches in silence. He knows the jade junk is no

ordinary vessel. He scents that it is dangerous, freighted with death. But the Philosopher teaches that no person escapes his destiny, neither the ignorant laborer plodding in the mud of the rice field nor the leader of imperial blood, instructed by Kwong-Tsu himself. He regards the approaching junk without desire and without terror.

Under the awning sits a princess, decked in precious stones. Around her feet are many women, singing verses and accompanying themselves with stringed instruments. This creates a harmony that Hong-Kop, himself a skilled musician and gifted poet, at once pronounces perfect. Perfect too is the beauty of the women, who are like queens; perfect the magnificence of their robes, and the splendor of the mats and cushions. Hong-Kop is ravished with admiration.

The astonished pirates exchange questions. Some snatch up their weapons, but pause in the act. Others take their place at the oars, but remain there in suspense, with bent backs, irresolute, regarding their immobile master and wondering at his steady smile. One of his women kneels to offer his great bull's-horn bow. Courteously, he takes the weapon. If this is to be his destiny, then so be it. Stringing an arrow, he lets fly. It speeds true, and nails the princess's hand to the ivory of her throne. A faint melodious cry floats over the water to mingle with the clamor of the pirates.

In an instant, as if lashed by a giant, the water between the two vessels rears into a dense rampart, hiding the jade junk from sight. When the sea subsides, it is not to be seen. Nothing but the Fai-Tsi-Lung and its rocks, drowned in mist.

All that day, Hong-Kop awaits the reappearance of the jade junk, or of some response to the arrow he has sent into the beautiful commander. But nothing disturbs the glassy calm. The sails lie flat; the atmosphere remains heavy and suffocating.

Tired of waiting, immobile, in the center of the scorching bay, Hong-Kop has let down his sampan, the flat-bottomed boat sufficiently light to be handled by a single man with one oar.

Erect, one foot upon the stem, he dips his oar alternately to the right and to the left. It is not the first time he has wandered all alone in the island labyrinth. He has brought nothing with him but the pipe, the lamp, and a day's supply of opium. The Fai-Tsi-Lung is vast. For many seasons, Hong-Kop has traversed it upon his predatory junk, without coming to know its furthermost rocks or the remotest of its grottoes. Round about, there are but steep bare walls, split here and there by narrow passes through which the slender sampan glides. And today, new breaches, never before glimpsed, seem to open in his path, to close again behind him. The rocks that he grazes watch him as he disappears into the warm mist.

Hong-Kop dimly feels that the whole of the Fai-Tsi-Lung, rocks and stones, is a treacherous enemy. He goes on, nevertheless. At each stroke of the oar, his slender torso bends forward, then falls back, his loins curved as in the act of love. His dull skin becomes lightly colored with carmine. Under the silk of his robe, the young and delicately muscled flesh becomes apparent. Hong-Kop is very beautiful.

The rocks become more savage, the water more milky and opaque. Hong-Kop has ceased to row. Reclining on his left side, his head upon the inflated leather cushion, he lights the lamp and takes the opium on the end of his needle in order to toast it. The sampan continues to drift gently among the rocks.

Gently? No, swiftly. As though someone were drawing it with a strong and invisible hand.

And no sooner has the first pipe clarified the smoker's intelligence than Hong-Kop perceives this. But he is preoccupied with something else; there is almost no opium in the porcelain jug, barely three pipefuls. The women have forgot-

ten to replenish his stock. And Hong-Kop, irritated, deliberates whether he shall have one of them put to death upon his return. The least beautiful . . . ?

Too late, he perceives, at the foot of the channel, barring his passage, a gigantic wall, dark, steep, foreboding, its summit utterly lost in the fog. No breach, no crevice. His oar, even though handled by an arm of iron, does nothing to change his implacable course. In truth, the sea sinks before him, and he glides on as down a hill.

Around him, the rocks grin maliciously. The reign of the pirate-king has been abolished; his kingdom is in revolt. Faced with this treason on the part of the long-faithful Fai-Tsi-Lung, one less wise would have grown indignant, would have cursed and struggled. But a vain and ridiculous fight it would have been. Hong-Kop, coldly resigned to the loss which he foresees, rises above it. Though the sampan is about to be shattered against the wall of rock, he scrapes the empty jug with the end of his needle and prepares the third pipe, his last.

But almost on a level with the water, a tunnel opens, and the sampan dives in.

To the right and to the left, down the irregular colonnade formed by the stalactites, other and perpendicular tunnels flash by. The whole mountain must be a labyrinth of subterranean and submarine caverns. He glimpses the inexpressible creatures that inhabit the gloom. In each cranny, weird and petrified sentinels stand guard.

The tunnel diminishes. The only light comes from his tiny opium lamp. He feels rather than sees the moss of the tunnel wall graze his face—and then the sampan, hurled forward as by a sling, emerges from the underground passage—into the open air.

He is in a gigantic circus, a lake encompassed by cliffs; an extinct crater that the sea has filled. Bluffs black and bare rise,

vertical and inaccessible, on every side. Only very high up do they curve back a little into steep slopes to which a meager shrubbery clings. Three hundred feet above the water, large and inquisitive apes venture cautiously as far as the last shrubs overhanging the perpendicular wall. From below, they appear smaller than rats.

Indifferent to his plight, Hong-Kop brings his needle, on which the drop of opium trembles, near the flame. When the drop has been cooked to a golden hue, he fixes it expertly over the jade bowl—but pauses, pipe in hand, as the water opens before him and the King Dragon, Hai-Lung-Wang, long as thirty pythons, rears from the sea his terrifying head.

Hong-Kop has seen him often in opium dreams, but the reality is indescribable. Round about, the water is trembling, as if in terror. The rocks, contracted in horror, ooze cold sweat. In the stupendous silence, Hong-Kop becomes distinctly aware of the panting fever of the entire Fai-Tsi-Lung, appalled in the presence of its creator.

The Smoker and the God are face to face. Those enormous bloody eyes dip into the black eyes which opium bronzes to the point of absolute impassivity.

"Thou hast wounded with thine arrow my sacred daughter, Yu-Tcheng-Hoa," booms the King Dragon. "As punishment, thou shall die here a slow and agonizing death, deprived of rice, deprived of water, deprived of opium."

Hong-Kop disdainfully fixes his gaze upon the Lung. "Many years ago," he remarks, "Kwong-Tsu taught me I am mortal. You tell me nothing I do not know."

His pipe bent low over the lamp, he inhales his third pipeful, the last, speaking no more, and deigning not to notice how, in front of the subterranean outlet, the rocks crumble from the cliff, impenetrably shutting off all retreat.

The sun has set behind the mountain. The bloodshot mist

in the west has tarnished. Then the night envelops it. Hong-Kop's sampan floats sluggishly. Still stretched upon the mat, his head in the cushion, he has placed the empty pipe at his side. He has not suffered, at first. However little opium he may have taken, the kindly drug has mastered his nerves and his blood. It has enabled him to look coldly and with contempt upon death. But as the time for the evening smoke approaches, an uneasiness creeps, for the first time, into his bosom. He has not smoked. He feels a vague discomfort, a muffled pain. Thirst chokes him. The saliva in his mouth is gone. Fatigue stiffens his limbs. And sleep refuses to come.

The evil genii of the night, growing progressively bolder, descend now from the mountain and converge sneeringly on the disarmed Smoker. Their funereal laugh splits their mouths, paved with red teeth. Their nails, adept at ransacking graveyards, claw the night. About the sampan, a macabre ring forms and whirls, accompanied by the gnashing of scale-encrusted wings. Breaths warm with putrefaction mingle near the human mouth. Viscous membranes lash the face and bury it beneath their folds . . .

But in the east, a whiteness suddenly slips down from the mountaintop. And Hong-Kop, rescued from this abominable attack, begins, though bathed in sweat, to stir. Upon the mat defiled by impure contacts, his bruised body gleams through his tattered robe, and his drawn face slowly regains its serene beauty.

The mist grows more iridescent, as the moon's beams begin to silver the waves. Hong-Kop dimly feels that something is watching over his fever, which is no longer so intense; feels it, with odorous breath, moistening his arid mouth and parched veins. It is something very young, very frank, and very delicate, bent pityingly over the agony of the condemned. Hong-Kop whose heavy eyes scrutinize the night, seeks in vain for the reality behind the gentle phantom: his nerves, cut off

from the clairvoyant drug, are no longer able to comprehend the world of the superhuman. And then sleep, sleep so longed for. Eyelids droop over the poor eyes, and the tortured brain slackens and is appeased.

Dreams come, winged with gold, very different from the grimacing specters of but a while ago. Upon the sampan, very near the drowsy Hong-Kop, the liberating splendor comes to rest like a butterfly. And then, punctuating the propitious silence, very slight sounds whisper, clear and condensed: the sound of drops falling, one after another, into the emptied opium jug.

The dawn. Upon the walled lake, there is now nothing but the sampan. The lurid, scorching rays of the sun strike Hong-Kop rudely in the face. He awakes. And immediately, he beholds a miracle. The opium jug is full. Full of real opium, thick and glossy, not very black, but tinted with red gleams—almost, one might say, with blood. But the drops, as they attach themselves to the needle, are as pearly as one could wish, and puff out like fused gold when brought near the flame. The velvety smoke sinks radiantly into the avid breast, expanding, upon its way, in multiple pleasures. In a blink of the eye, all exhaustion, all anguish melts and vanishes.

The hostile rock that imprisons him no longer matters. Nor does the slow death he must undergo, deprived of water and deprived of rice. The consoling opium will soften all that.

The sun mounts to its zenith, then descends the other slope of his course. Hong-Kop still smokes.

And night, once more, succeeds the day. This time, no evil spirits swoop around him. The opium has driven out every impure presence. But he also knows that something else will come—the Protecting Splendor who saved him yesterday. And he waits, respectfully, his eyes fixed upon the east from which she will come.

The moon rises above the rocks; and gliding upon the first beam, the Splendor descends upon the lake. Hong-Kop watches, and his clear eyes recognize her. She has the form of a woman, infinitely delicate and beautiful. Her face, whiter than that of any creature of Laos or of Annam, is deliciously framed in hair finer than wound silk. The neck, flexible as a stem, rises above a pair of radiant shoulders, visible under the robe of precious stones, which is less brilliant than the flesh it veils. And the right arm, extended in a gesture of peace, bleeds from a wound that is still fresh. It is Yu-Tcheng-Hoa, the princess of the jade junk, the daughter of the Dragon King.

She rests upon the stem of the boat a slender slipper of pearls. Hong-Kop hears her holy heart, beating with great fearful beats. She continues to extend, almost imploringly, her poor pierced arm, from which blood continues to drip. And then Hong-Kop understands the miracle. This blood is opium, and it is thus that the empty jug is replenished. The merciful Flower of Jade has willed that her executioner should be watered and nourished with the sap of her own divine veins.

The moon is declining beyond the western mountain. Soon, soon, the dawn will be whitening the east, and enchantments will fly away before the sun. Hong-Kop, becoming more clairvoyant with the Fairy's smile, divines that something irreparable is about to occur, that a sublime door is waiting to be opened—that in a little while there will no longer be time. But uncertainty continues to paralyze his decision—although the desire haunts him, more and more, to place his amorous lips upon the wounded arm, constantly bleeding with opium.

As the moon regretfully declines behind a cliff, Hong-Kop rises and kneels before Yu-Tcheng-Hoa. They remain mute, their lips so close that a kiss would barely bring them closer. And the inexorable dawn coldly rises in the mournful heavens. The Flower of Jade gives a long sigh, tears coating the

purity of her face. Destiny must be obeyed. Already, nascent day is disturbing the phantoms and causing them to pale.

Yu-Tcheng-Hoa flees away over the sea, growing more insubstantial from second to second. Hong-Kop, lucid now, strives, with great strokes of the oar, to follow her, sending the sampan flying over the foam of the waves. But too late, too late. Both are now at the foot of the cliff, at the very entrance to the obstructed passageway. But at the last moment the rocks part in fear: for She is the Dragon's Daughter, and He is beloved of Her.

Another minute, and Hong-Kop is floating free upon the Fai-Tsi-Lung, whence the dragon had exiled him. The verdict is torn up, the sentence of death revoked. But Yu-Tcheng-Hoa, the Exquisite, has been blotted out forever in the mist of the rising sun. And in the metallic eyes of Hong-Kop, who in all his life has never laughed or wept, tears are born, bitter tears.

Hong-Kop, nonetheless, became one of the genii. For such is the fate of those who have loved immortal princesses. Rendered immortal themselves, their life is suspended, limitlessly, between the heaven and the earth.

The life of Hong-Kop is distributed among the rocks of the Fai-Tsi-Lung. In that inextricable labyrinth, he is searching for Yu-Tcheng-Hoa, without ever finding her. And the fishers of Halong and of Kebac are fearful of sighting him, since the sight of him is death. I who write this, I have of a truth seen, in the Tonkinese mist—I have seen, with my own horrified eyes, Hong-Kop, and Hai-Lung-Wang, the Serpent King who pursued him over the sea. But I have survived, for the reason that, on the same day, in the threshold of the Sacred Circus, I have met Yu-Tcheng-Hoa, the Merciful.

And it is since then that I have come to despise all other women.

{ 4 }

The End of Faust

*There is another sort of dream-women known as Fairies, in
Latin called* strigae, *who are nourished on the black poppy,
called opium.*

Jean de Marcouville (1563)

Many years have passed since Dr. Johann Faust signed his
pact with the Devil, transforming the aged savant into
a seductive and attractive man in the prime of life. Even so,
in his sorcerer's cell in the small north German city in the
shadow of the Harz mountains, the doctor has returned to
his studies.

In the fireplace, upon the red coals, retorts are smoking
unpleasantly. Some are of glass and some of sandstone. From
their cracked necks gush varicolored vapors, and a rainbow
from hell streams from his black chimney into the chill night
air. The long table is laden with alembics, globes, and forbid-

den parchments. Upon an easel made of gallows wood, a glass tablet reflects the flame of the retorts, while close at hand, in a jug filled with water, a rod of phosphorus gleams ominously. To the leprous walls, fastened by great rusty nails to beams hung with spiderwebs, cling skeletons that a draft under the door sometimes set to rattling.

In return for his soul, Satan promised Faust thirteen centuries of youth, during which he would be irresistible to all women, but particularly to Marguerite, the virtuous sister of a friend, with whom he had, as an old man, fallen in love.

Satan kept his word. Johann Faust remains twenty, and his doublet shines and glistens in a marvelous manner, under his light gold beard. Since he had his fill of Marguerite and cast her to Satan, the fingers of many women have strayed through that rejuvenated beard, just as the caressing flame of those eyes, revived by the Devil, has set their souls on fire. And the list is not yet closed.

Outside, the chill breeze from the Brocken sets weather vanes whirling upon the gables of the Gothic houses. All the same, a woman, half naked under her hooded mantle, has ventured through the empty streets, and now stands knocking on the door. She is young and fair, and her eyes glow with a tender light. But the door does not open, and the cold lock resists her passionately obstinate fists. Too many women have crossed that threshold before her. Johann Faust is tired of caresses. For him, a blond head resting timidly on his shoulder offers no pleasure, nor does watching maidenly modesty surrendering to pleasure. Johann Faust, who damned his soul for love and youth, is now satiated with youth and with love.

And the fair visitor, weeping in shame and despair, flees in the direction of the consoling river.

The doctor, indifferent, does not even hear the plaintive footfalls as they die away. His eyes red, his manner weary,

he has closed his vain conjurer's tome. Behold him now as he sits staring, by the gleam of the pitch candles, at the empty armchair where Satan sat as they concluded their bargain, the leather still bearing the scorch marks of the Evil One.

The fire in the grate grows green and vacillating. The smoking retorts give forth black fumes. A faint odor of sulphur exudes from somewhere or other. And in an instant, a *being* occupies the armchair; someone clad in red, whose viper's-tail beard periodically glows, like a cluster of burning branches fanned by the draft. Someone who has materialized there before. Someone whose clawed hand envelops the pommel of a rapier, and whose skinny legs, nonchalantly crossed, end in a pair of split hooves.

"Good day, Doctor," the Devil has just remarked.

But there is no reply from the doctor.

"Exquisite weather," the guest continues. "Upon my word, it is really quite cool in the street. By the way, I just met, a couple of steps from here, the prettiest lass in Germany, making for the river—wanted to take a bath, perhaps; who knows? If I had had my way, I should have plucked her mad little soul as I went. But I did not have the time. Plenty of business, Doctor, when one is in your service—as, need I remember, I am, for the time you inhabit the earth. Just as you will become my servant when you pass to my realm. I have not forgotten, you see, that the mark of my claw appears at the bottom of our contract."

A heavy, breast-heaving sigh from Faust; no other answer.

"Melancholy? Ah! Of what are you thinking, then? You still have a few thousand years ahead of you. Sir, enjoy what is left. There you are, still fresh and rosy, and your doublet is new, as it was that famous evening on Marguerite's balcony when you achieved your heart's desire. The pretty and despairing one whom I came near plucking just now is proof of the esteem in

which young ladies continue to hold you. And who, for that matter, could doubt it—a fine-looking man like yourself?"

Johann Faust glares at the chatterer. "Flattery? Please! Don't insult my intelligence."

Satan shrugs. "Then you had better tell me, my master, what it is that you wish."

"I wish," slowly enunciates the doctor, "for the opposite of what I have wished for up to now. When I signed your parchment, I was not very wise. In those days, I was already old—bald, tottering, knock-kneed, and humped of spine. In my withered brain, exhausted by all the stupidities which you see here"—pointing to the rubbish on the table; retorts, crucibles, and parchments—"in my arid and unhealthy brain, one single idea sprouted—one single mania, rather—a mania for living on and on, and for becoming frantically inebriated with this life I was about to leave behind me.

"Accordingly, I sought to become young again. I regret that. You have crowned my futile desire beyond all that I dreamed. You have made the cup from which I wanted to drink so large that I have drowned myself in it. And as for this youth, over centuries upon centuries I have been surfeited with it, without ever once finding rest."

"If it's rest that you wish," says the Devil, "there's nothing simpler. Why have you not mentioned it before? So, my dear doctor, too many pretties have played with your mustache, too many balconies have let down a ladder for you by night; and, it may be, too many jealous ones have caused your path to bristle with annoying sword blades and with daggers that were skeletons at the feast! Though love notes make pleasant reading, they are very much alike. And duels are a kingly sport, but one grows tired at last even of ushering one's enemies to the cemetery. So true is this that I find no difficulty

whatsoever in understanding this latest fancy of yours. Well, then, you wish to grow old again!"

"No," says Faust.

"No?" The Devil frowns. "Well, there are other remedies. If you wish pretty girls to be a rarity at your door, this is easily achieved. In the blink of an eye, I can make you as ugly as the Minotaur or as poor as Job. Ugliness or misery, which do you choose?"

"Neither," says Faust.

"By Jove," says Satan, "but you are in a contrary mood. You have need of rest, and yet, you must keep intact your youth, your good looks, and the ability to transform lead into gold that I, in the old days, tacked on to our contract. Anyone but myself would tell you it is impossible. But that's a word my grammarians have erased from my dictionaries. There is still one way left, the surest one, and one which, undoubtedly, you will find to your taste. Dissolve the pact we signed. I promised thirteen centuries of youth, but if that is too much to suit your appetite, very well! Strike out the clause, and follow me without delay."

"No!" cries Faust, turning pale.

"No again?" sneers Satan. "I have my share of trouble with you, sir, I must say. But very well; do what you like! I shall not insist any further. Keep what you have, then, and do not bother my head anymore."

"Stay," says the doctor. "Listen. I know that I am asking a miracle; but it is for miracles that the devout beseech the Other. And so, master, lacking His aid, it is to thee that I make my request." He paused to collect his thoughts. "I desire to drink without vomiting, to eat without ceasing to be hungry, to love without becoming surfeited with love—in short, to live without boredom, disgust, or fatigue. I wish to remain young,

and never to grow tired of my youth. That is my prayer! And passionately, without hate or rancor, I lay it at thy feet!"

"By the Almighty!" cries the Devil, "are you mad with pride, my master? There are no prayers whatsoever that will open such a door. I have no such spell to give you. Search for it alone, or go beg it of others, if any others there be who know it."

Silently, from the vase filled with water, the doctor takes a phosphorus pencil, and writes with it, upon the glass tablet, a mysterious pentagram, which flames in the shadows. And the Devil recoils.

In the bewitched room, the two damned ones remain together, mute. Gradually, the fire-image is extinguished upon the pane of glass. And the Devil ventures to speak, very low.

"You have not lost your skills, sir! Very well! You remind me that, of the two of us, it is you who are the master here on earth. Give your orders. I am not in possession of the secret of which you stand in need. Where would you go to look for it?"

Faust spreads his cloak upon the floor. "I would go," he says, "to visit those who are beyond your empire."

"Very good," says Satan, "I know the road."

Together, they take their places upon the cloak. It lifts, and soon they are flying away through space.

"Let us look first," suggests Faust, "among those magician races that have thrown off your yoke."

"There is no such *race*," replies Satan, peevishly. "Just a few men and women of mystery, scattered here and there throughout the world. Scholars armed with the rites that I fear; exorcists, who write with letters of fire upon the walls."

"The latter," replies the doctor, "are the Magi, whom I know. They taught me that sign which compels you to obey. But there is yet another race."

"You speak, I suppose, of those weird individuals, men and women, who live in dreams, where I am denied admission. They despise the earth, and laugh at me when I offer them its delights."

"Then it is perhaps with them," murmurs the doctor, "that I shall find the secret you do not possess, and the peace that I seek."

Under them as they fly, the earth thickens its veil of night. Cities sleep in the embrace of their walls, and curfew chains are spread in the streets, while peasants in the deserted countryside cross themselves at the shuddering of the poplars, grazed by Satan.

Farther on, the bald mountains set a boundary to the habitable land. A terrible plain, black with dried blood and white with old bones, stretches beyond. The cloak on which they travel shivers as in a tempest, and Satan smiles.

Upon the horizon, a red fire surges up, sending twisted flames to the heavens. Closer, Faust beholds women laughing about a furnace. Some straddle broomsticks, or flail the air like demented birds on wings of flaming brands. Others hang lasciviously from the horns of a he-goat.

"These," Satan explains, "are Italians. French sorceresses come to the Sabbat without broom or mount; a little magic goes a long way with them, and magic of the grossest sort. What is more, all of them are in my hands, and I rule them as I will, through desire, through pride, through wrath, and above all, through lust."

The women continue their sport, mingling together in obscene groups. Faust perceives with disgust that they are but withered and tottering hags.

Flakes of fire fly upward. Satan reaches out and touches one, which flees back magically into the ring, transformed into a slim and seductive boy, with young and naked flesh. Instantly,

two sorceresses throw themselves upon him and, rivals for his favors, fall to beating each other in a blind fury. As the Sabbat roisters around them, hair and blood are scattered and torn out by red nails, as teeth bite and gnash in a mad rage.

"All are mine," says Satan in satisfaction, and the cloak bears them away into the ensorcelled night.

They pass above a public square.

"Below us," says the Devil temptingly, "lies the City of the Astrologers and the Magi, who know all things."

"Their science is hollow," says Faust. "I found it barely powerful enough to enchain and constrain you."

The Devil doesn't argue. Instead, he points to a glow in the sky ahead. "We are coming to the fairies and the vampires, who know nothing of science or of exorcism, who know only how to dream. They can be of no interest to you."

Something in Satan's tone alerts Faust. "It may be," he remarks, "that they have discovered how man can free himself from this bad dream that we know as life. Let us descend."

A peaceful moon reigns over a softened landscape, the lines of which roll themselves up into dreamy curves. The atmosphere, transparent as on a mountaintop, offers no barrier to the moon's illumination, so that the night resembles a sunless but indescribably gentle day.

On the shores of the lake, a small temple shines, its columns opaline, and crowned with pediments of moonstone. Beyond it rises, in calming slopes, a landscape where nothing either smiles or weeps.

By the lake, the travelers pause, as Satan sullenly indicates the portico.

"This is a poor place. I could show you a thousand palaces more vast and sumptuous, not five minutes' flight from here. Let us press on."

But Faust is intrigued. "Come," he says, strolling toward the steps that lead to the colonnade.

"No! No!" vigorously protests the Devil. "Go alone, if the excursion tempts you. A certain odor reigns there which displeases my delicate nostrils. Go, Doctor, and I shall have, nonetheless, the honor of awaiting your return, here upon the shore. May I see you soon, and may the spirits treat you kindly."

He sits down beside the lake and brushes the water with his forked foot. It at once begins to boil.

Faust climbs the temple steps. Above the door, a carved motto reads, "Neither God Nor Devil." For a second, he hesitates.

Then he pushes the door, which offers no resistance.

In the temple, there is no altar nor statue nor anything of mystery. Those present are not decked in precious stones, and carry no wands or distaffs.

They are simple women, or at least appear so. Their supple bodies are scattered over the couches in an abandonment of repose. Their serene mouths smile toward the invisible, and their clear eyes follow, without seeing, the energetic flight of dreams, hovering under the sacred vault.

Between the flagstones of flaxen-colored shell, singular plants take root—a bizarre flora that blooms throughout the temple, thick as ripe wheat in a field. Tall stalks sway, weighted with long, wide leaves, and flowers, deep as cups, and black.

Sometimes, with a slow gesture, one of the vampires stretches forth her bare arm and plucks the nearest flower. She breathes in its fragrance, then lifts it to her lips and sucks the black nectar that pearls upon the edge of each petal.

In his instant of recognition, Faust has exclaimed: "I am here!" But they have not heard him, nor gazed in his direc-

tion. They are dreaming, and eating the flowers of the black poppy.

An imperceptible drunkenness worms its way through his nostrils and glides to his brain.

The vault, assuredly, is empty. What appeared to be a veiled ceiling is but vapors floating along the frieze and spreading out in intermingled scrolls. But how strangely those scrolls coil. They are iridescent, with a multitude of colors. They clothe themselves with singular forms, by turns indefinite and precise. And these phantoms, never before seen, begin to move and to take on life.

Dream scenes are written and effaced within the period of a sigh, and are reborn, and metamorphose. Scenes light and fugitive, then clearer. A mist dream—then limpid, then real— as real as the reality of life, or even more so. Faust, dazzled, looks on.

Near his lips, a large flower has bloomed, temptingly. A potent odor rises from the opened corolla. Faust, with the slow gesture of the vampires, pulls off the first petal—and, little by little, brings it nearer his opened mouth . . .

It is a thousand years since Dr. Faust entered the temple. On the shore of the parched lake, the Devil is waiting still.

The pact is long overdue. From the height of the firmament, the ironic moon draws long horns behind Satan's shadow. The Devil, in a rage, occasionally approaches the portico. But each time, he recoils. At the threshold, his power expires. Nothing within belongs to him. And he returns to his seat upon the bluff of the lake. His goat feet have hollowed red holes in the soil, and glowing coals shoot forth about him.

He will very soon fall back, all alone, into Hell.

{ 5 }

The Vermin

The palace of Tong-Doc is on the edge of a far eastern city, capital of a nation where a lank, brown people, mixing every race from Mongolian to Malay, bend under the yoke of barbarous white masters from the West.

Don't imagine that Tong-Doc's palace is one of those structures beloved of conquerors, bristling with turrets and ringed with colonnades. The old prince, a willing traitor, has tossed to the dogs all his honor as a patriot and his loyalty as a subject, not to mention the ancestral belief that dignifies his race with its skeptic philosophy, and openly proclaimed himself a European, a democrat, and a Catholic.

It is a foolish turncoat, however, who entirely discards his old wardrobe, and the prince, not without a number of polite excuses, has discreetly retained some reminder of his race and its distinctive art. Surrounding Tong-Doc's palace is a park, rendered somber by great cedars, where slumber five scattered

yamens—guesthouses; offices; retreats for reflection, hospitality, or what you will. Each is ringed by a wide terrace, affording shade and discretion. Their floors are of marble and the partitions of ebony, while the roofs are of gleaming tile, and the furnishings inlaid with mother-of-pearl. Under the trees, streams trickle. The wind brings its coolness to the depths of the innermost courts, while the sun never once has trespassed into these buildings, not even onto the terraces.

In the *yamen* reserved for her personal use, as the rhythmic wing beats of white-silk *punkas* fan and cool the air, Tong-Doc's daughter, who in former times would have been addressed as Princess, takes her afternoon siesta.

True to his policy of accommodating his foreign masters, Tong-Doc calls her Anna, like a child of Europe. No one ever uses her true name—that perilous name which is, yet, murmured each evening, with regret and with desire, in certain dark quarters on the fringes of the city, where it meets the surrounding rice field. She is Anna, likewise, to the lieutenants and naval ensigns who visit the palace to play tennis, and to receive, afterward, from her lithe brown hand, a cup of tea, sugared after the English manner, along with cream, and cakes. (For tea in the style of her forefathers, a faintly scented infusion of tepid water, Mademoiselle Anna professes amused contempt.)

Mademoiselle Anna, convent-educated, can curtsy with the easy grace of a London debutante. Mademoiselle Anna forms an admirable team at doubles with her partner, the young wife of the viceroy. And Mademoiselle Anna, lastly, flirts—flirts a great deal, and with so knowing a degree of coquettishness that two of the governor's aides-de-camp are beginning, it is said, to be a bit unnerved by the pastime.

All in all, Mademoiselle Anna differs little from any "Mademoiselle Anna" of Paris or of London. And yet, one would

be wrong to overlook the Oriental costume, the sober sheath of black silk, buckled with gold, and the Annamite sandals, revealing an irreproachably Asiatic foot—in overlooking, above all, her differing type of beauty, finer and less lurid, more deeply rooted in race. Mysterious . . .

But enough of such idle speculation. The daughter of Tong-Doc has obviously forgotten her race, and no longer concerns herself with the destiny she might have expected in earlier centuries. The old language of the empire means so little to her that when she speaks of those who would, in former times, have been her subjects, it is as "the natives."

It is four o'clock. Today, they are not playing tennis. But two colonels with bristling white mustaches have come to pay Tong-Doc a friendly visit.

As her father's hostess, Mademoiselle Anna gives her orders to the servants: tea will not be served.

"No tea, mademoiselle?" inquire the officers. "Surely you are not serving alcohol?"

"Oh, I thought I could, Colonel. In your honor. A cocktail I invented myself. You take a finger of maraschino, a drop of Scotch whisky . . ."

Sweating under his uniform, the second colonel says hopefully, "And a lot of ice?"

"Heaps of ice! Whole icebergs. Floes of it!"

Loud foreign laughter shakes the humid air under the ancient and unremembering cedars.

It is five o'clock, the excursion hour. Clad in a heavily embroidered green robe—never yellow, never purple, colors forbidden to all but the emperor—Tong-Doc's daughter climbs into a carriage for her evening drive. Her preferred vehicle is also the fashionable choice—a victoria. Open, though with a folding roof in case of rain, it is of German construction but French design, and pulled by two Australians, of that superb

breed that lives but a year under the sun of Indo-China. Her
driver and footman wear discreet black, without gold cock-
ades, while the black varnish of the carriage shows no armo-
rial bearings of any sort. In all the city, there is no turnout
more elegant, more Parisian.

The fashionable drive is just over a mile long, a straight
path covered with red sand. Along this path, Asiatic Nature
displays her melancholy splendors: rice fields green as lawns,
shrubbery-muffled rivulets, tall thickets of graceful bamboo,
forests of hardy cabbage palms. And the sun, fatal to European
skulls, embroiders with rubies and emeralds all the shimmer-
ing substance of this humid greenery. For centuries, cultivated emperors, invisible behind the curtains of their golden
palanquins, have aired their disdainful indolence amid these
preferred shades.

Tong-Doc's victoria mingles with the other carriages along
the drive. There are two lines, one going up, the other coming
down the lane, with occasional single men mounted on high-
stepping hacks. The light-colored dresses, the gay umbrellas,
the bare half-gloved white arms—and the sun at the horizon's edge, grown less brutal with its declining rays—all this
is a glimpse of Europe, a reminder of Armenonville or Hyde
Park.

The green robe, embroidered with hieratic leaf work—
tone laid over tone—barely makes a discreetly exotic splash;
barely: Mademoiselle Anna sits negligently under her parasol
and glances at the attentive cavaliers who greet her in passing. Here and there, hands move, and good-evenings are exchanged on the wing, in the cool tones of young girls' voices.
The evening is already hastening on, streaking with brown
like a tiger's fur the deepening yellow of the sky. The victorias
speed back to the city like swallows to their nests, but Tong-
Doc's daughter stays till the last. Those who glimpse her note

her smile—an extremely distant smile, certainly, and one that has in it something of the ineffable sneer found, in the pagodas, on the grimacing faces of the empire's forgotten idols.

Ten o'clock, the theater hour. The stage is banked with a harvest of roses. Tong-Doc's daughter, reclining, in a half-meditative mood, pays little attention to the touring company's performance of *Samson et Dalila*. Her mother-of-pearl opera glasses occasionally skim the tenor or the contralto, but more often search out the boxes and take minute note of the gowns to be glimpsed there.

At the door of the box, two discreet knocks signal a visit from two of the aides-de-camp with whom Tong-Doc's daughter carries on a continuing flirtation. Compliments, bows, kissing of fingers. For the time, Saint-Saëns has the worst of it. They sit down, make themselves comfortable, and chatter, the music forgotten—just as it is at Paris.

And now, it is late night—an Indo-Chinese night, warm as a summer's day. Through the exhausted city, Tong-Doc's daughter returns to her *yamen*. In the silent avenues, there is no longer anyone to gaze upon one of the many innovations of the foreign masters—electric street lighting, the violet-colored bulbs veiled by a curtain of green trees.

Beyond the wide avenue begins another world. *Fumeries*— "opium dens" to the tourist—glow a smoky red in the night. Low doors open into wretched, dimly lighted rooms, with a floor of trampled earth, walls of botched plaster, rafters caving in, and rotting mats. Large oil lamps befoul the stale air, and closed booths with flapping wickets give shelter to lubricious couples. On the floor, lamp, pipe, and needle await the smoker. But there are no smokers tonight. Only a few drunken sailors and, occasionally, some merrymaking crowd, slumming.

Far away, behind Tong-Doc's palace, an armed sentinel, flat cap planted upon his correct topknot and rifle resting against

his right forearm, stands guard at the small rear gate—where, this night, light footfalls crunch the sand, and the gate silently swings open on its hinges. A brown figure passes through, a woman slipping out of the palace, confident that the sentinel, alert only for interlopers who might wish to enter the palace grounds, will see nothing of a person leaving.

At the farthest edge of the city, the remotest of the opium dens opens its wan mouth. Three wrinkled prostitutes—young or old, it would be hard to say—squat with a boy of raddled and spoiled beauty. All are drunk on rice brandy, which they swill from cups without handles. In the corner, a teapot steams.

The worm-eaten door opens, and someone enters; a woman, young, beautiful, and elegant despite the mean simplicity of her brown robe. And then, an altogether weird thing happens. The prostitutes, ordinarily lacking in courtesy and slow to return greetings, hastily rise, join their hands, and bow in profound respect. Phrases are exchanged in the purest Annam dialect, the hosts stammering humble professions of homage and offers of service. Quickly, the brandy is put aside, the lamp lighted, and the pipe heated in its flame. One of the prostitutes, upon her knees, proffers the first cup of tea—the green tea of Yunnan, of which the barbarians know nothing—and the opium, above the lamp, begins its mysterious crackling.

But at this moment, the door opens with a hubbub, and a noisy band bursts headlong in, a crazy band of merrymakers, returning from a supper party and looking for debauchery. Officers, civil servants, a magistrate, they are a perfect picture of the invading Occident, the very essence of Europe, and its gross and busy barbarism.

"How terrible! What a stench!"

The woman visitor, stretched out on the mat beside the

lamp, the bamboo pipe in her slim hand, keeps her head turned away.

"It takes some nerve to lie down there!" says the magistrate. "And take a look at the vermin, will you! They're swarming this evening."

"The vermin?"

"Yes." He points to the corners, beyond the guttering light of the lamp. "Cockroaches, moths, ants, spiders, millipedes, scorpions even. This is their kingdom; they're in full sway here. Occasionally some case brings me into these places. I've seen the mats black with them."

One of the other men belatedly notices the girl. "Y'know, this one isn't half bad." He stoops for a better look. "Hey, girlie! You talkee?"

Italian and French at the same time, poet, doctor, and soldier, he's seen as the harmonious embodiment of the refinement and wit of the two peoples, as well as of the pride and wisdom of three castes. In fact, in the presence of such complexity, he is like a child confronting a puzzle far beyond his capacity.

"Talkee French?" he inquires, as to a coolie, or a child. "Talkee Ingles? What your name?"

Impassively, the smoker draws on the pipe, her eyes fixed on nothingness. Possibly, he decides, she does not understand.

He prods her shoulder. She looks at him, coldly. A sense of strangeness deepens between them.

"So you haven't anything to say?"

"Forget it," says one of the men uneasily. "She doesn't speak French. She's a little savage."

But the master of the universe is determined. "Come on," he says, "let's have a look at your breasts."

"Now look, old man . . ." begins one of his companions. But the magistrate shushes him. "Oh, that's quite all right, in a

place like this. All these women are whores. She'll do it, right enough."

Yanking apart her plain robe, the man exposes small pointed breasts, with nipples the color of corroded silver.

"A nice pair! What about the rest of you?"

But the woman is disinclined, shrugs him off, and turns away.

"Ah, no? No further than that? Have it your own way, my dear." He straightens up. "I suppose you realize that you've got a very pretty figure?"

He tilts the lamp closer, so that light falls across her face.

"You know," he says to his friends, "I've just noticed. Isn't she the very picture of Tong-Doc's daughter, Anna?"

The magistrate peers. "My word, there is a slight . . . But still, not quite so fine-featured. Something more common. A good deal above the average, though."

The man leans closer, and murmurs a question in the ear of the magistrate, who raises his eyebrows, but nevertheless turns to the Asian women huddling in the corner.

"Who's your new boarder, *baba?*"

The oldest of the prostitutes laughs, her big obscene mouth split back over black teeth. A brawling, stupid laugh, underneath which no outsider would suspect that a fierce mockery lies concealed. And then, with jabbering words, she explains. "She arrived yesterday; she comes from down there . . ." An indeterminate place in the countryside, a vague gesture. "She says her name is Thi-Nam . . ." A very common name.

"Is she . . . ?" He rubs his fingertips together in the international gesture.

A mad laugh, growing more brawling and stupid. The three prostitutes bend double, writhing with mirth. No, such a thing cannot be; it is the most impossible thing in the world. Thi-Nam is inviolable, in the most literal sense of the word.

Why? His honor would like to know? *Ah, gods!* Because—an obscene gesture—Thi-Nam is sick, with the worst dose of syphilis in the whole country. Just so: those coral lips, those black eyes with the silver gleams, that throat, so proud and so pure, those breasts—all that is rotten!

"Ha! There's realism for you, old man," says the magistrate. "She's got the pox. After this, beware of little girls who look too good to be true, because they invariably are, no matter whether French or Italian or Chinese."

"And look at the little one, will you?" says another of the group. "It's all the same to her, this public revelation! A white woman would die of shame; but the women here don't care. They're no better than animals."

"Come on," says the master of the universe. "There's nothing doing in this mud hole. Shall we go?"

They leave. The magistrate pauses upon the threshold for a backward look. He has a dim intimation that there are many mysterious things between those four walls, many enigmas behind those brown foreheads; minds that think other and different thoughts than the thoughts of the Occident. Nevertheless, he leaves, after a moment's hesitation. And no suspicion comes to him of the improbable truth.

As the door closes, bolts grind in their sockets, sealing it tight. At the same time, the unaccommodating proprietor falls to her knees and touches her head to the mats. The Holy Princess, Suzeraine of the City, the One Set Apart, by right of race, for the Imperial Couch, the daughter of Tong-Doc, who formerly was the seventh in the empire, the irreproachable Virgin, will she grant pardon, will she pardon the most worthless of her slaves, vile as the excrement of toads, for the blasphemy which has been uttered? Will she show mercy to the criminal creature who, in order to ward off barbarian outrage, has dared defile the princess with her, the slave's

own, vile ignominy? The prostitutes and the catamite tremble, their hands joined and their foreheads in the dirt. Gone
the hypocritical grimace that serves to mock the oppressors'
brutality; bitter tears are flowing now, hot with terror and
with indignation.

Impassive, Tong-Doc's daughter gazes upon her subjects
and does not speak. Only an impatient clack of the tongue
escapes her: the pipe is empty. Timidly, the women come to
the rescue. Once again, the fumes rise and fall in the silent
smoking room. The magical odor expands and hovers. The
mats become impregnated with it, then the earth of the floor,
and the walls, and the rafters of the ceiling.

Mysteriously drawn, the numberless hordes of vermin
emerge from every cranny and hole, and make their way, little
by little, toward the lamp.

For the kindly drug spreads its mantle of royalty to cover
all beings. Nothing living is beyond reach of its scepter; and in
the presence of those potent atoms with which it saturates the
dens, the woodlouse's instinct sways like human reason—that
same reason that leads a fallen princess to come here to forget
a throne that is no more.

The vermin slowly converge on the smoker, without daring
to touch her body, which smells of opium. Between the mats,
the interstices of earth cease to be visible, since they now
heave with brown bodies.

Over several generations, myriads of insects have penetrated the worm-eaten planks, and nested in the damp, warm
earthen floor. In the corners of the gaping roof, hairy spiders
have spun their webs. Along the bamboos that serve as beams,
and between the crossed laths which comprise the ceiling,
brown cockroaches toddle and sometimes clumsily drop
from their perches. Others, very big and black, spread their
lazy wings and launch themselves, randomly, from one wall

to the other, only to tumble back, half dead from the impact. Down below is the realm of the ants, millipedes, scorpions, and earwigs. All run busily over the mats, chasing and evading each other, colliding and fighting, loving and devouring, in accordance with the laws of race and of sex. On the walls, tiny lizards emerge from the plaster crevices and leap from one chink to another, with abrupt, timid stops. In the center of the room, finally, in the tepid, moldy atmosphere, the moths dance their sarabands as they assail the oil lamp, only to fall, one after another, into the flame.

And now the smoke is having its effect on all this confusion of furtive life forms. Little by little, the buzzings and the cracklings fade away. The vermin have not fallen asleep; but their troubled instincts are calmed, as gleams of intelligence—a calm and sanguine intelligence—dawn within their rudimentary brains.

Taken by surprise at first, but soon growing avid, the flying insects turn their thin breasts toward the wisdom-conferring and peace-giving spirals of smoke. Abandoning their random movements, they form concentric circles that hover above the smoker, orbiting her in a subtle shifting aureole.

She, the uncrowned queen, has not deigned to look upon her lowly, docile subjects. She abandons her relaxed body to the respectful mats, and smokes. In the wink of an eye, the Occidental varnish vanishes. There are no more tyrants here to flatter. The soul of the Far East may now rear itself, sovereignly, above the barbaric mummeries of a conquering race. And the smile that parts the thin opium-blackened lips now resembles, resembles more and more, the smile of those imperial idols that rest forgotten in their crumbling pagodas.

The daughter of Tong-Doc dreams.

She dreams dreams unknown to the Occident; dreams filled with a philosophy that is too arduous for the intelligence

of young races. In the setting of her dream, there hover, undoubtedly, *yamens* which the barbarians have not yet polluted, *yamens* furnished with virgin smoking rooms, where the dangerous genii of feverish forests are proud to serve, on bended knee, the princess of the sacred blood. But as for the dream itself, its color, and its outline, and its soul, the gods themselves would not be able to discover anything upon that immobile brow, or in those dark eyes metalized by the drug.

Now, however, the princess lays aside the bamboo pipe. She casts a look upon the vermin population, curdled with ecstasy amid the spirals rolling upward from the ground. Is she thinking the Virgin Widow of the Emperors, of a treacherous Destiny, that has robbed her of the obeisance of another people—more numerous—a human population like the insect populace in its immovable respect and in its petrified adoration? Is she weeping, solely, with these sobs of rage, for a dead empire and a scepter metamorphosed into a yoke?

Once more, the pipe bends over the lamp, and the sweet mouth breathes on the bamboo. The compassionate drug is one that can heal all sorrows. And so it is with opium that Tong-Doc's daughter sustains her bleeding pride, her tragic pride in a dynasty that is sixty times a hundred years old.

{ 6 }

The Pipes

In my *fumerie*, I have five pipes—one for each of the essential virtues honored in China, the source of opium.

My first pipe is of brown tortoiseshell, with a black earthenware bowl and two mouthpieces of light-colored shell.

It is old and precious.

The stem is thick, and opaque or translucent according to the marbling of the shell. The knob, with which one holds the pipe while smoking, is of amber, finely carved in the form of a tiny fox.

The bowl is hexagonal, and secured in the middle by a silver fang. Its walls are coated with the coagulated tar that accumulates in any pipe, no matter what one smokes in it. In these tiny beads—the dross of opium, bitter, and rich in morphine—resides the accumulated memory of bygone pipefuls, the soul of dead intoxications. And the shell, progres-

sively penetrated by the drug, retains among its molecules the vestiges of years gone by.

Those are Japanese years. For my first pipe was in Kyushu, the island of turtles. And in the convex mirror of the wide stem, I see the whole of Japan reflected.

The Japanese call the fox *kitsune*, and believe it can change its shape at will. I never fail, as I take the shell pipe in my hands, to examine the knob, in case it may, mysteriously, have changed form. If it were to undergo such a change, I should not be greatly surprised. The *kitsune* of my pipe must indeed be a famous beast to have been selected as a model by the artist who did this carving. Perhaps he was the very *kitsune* who, in former times, misled the heroine Sidzuka in the mountains of Yosino.

Sidzuka was a Japanese lady of noble race, whom the hero Yoshitsune loved. Yoshitsune lived in Nippon, many centuries ago. A brother of Prince Yoritomo the Terrible, it was he who assured his brother's triumph over the rival clans of Taïra. But his enthusiastic supporters were too loud in proclaiming him the bravest of his race, and the jealous Yoritomo condemned him to die.

The fugitive Yoshitsune wandered for a long time, far from cities, in the solitude of the violet mountains, where only wild boars climb. Nevertheless, this perilous exile was sweet to him, for the reason that Sidzuka, the sweetest of all, had followed him in his disgrace, and shared his hardships.

The moss-covered cedars of the forest provided dubious protection. The moon, all too white, dangerously silvered the pools of light and the bark of the birch trees. But at these anxious moments, Sidzuka would dance voluptuously for her lover, and the enchanted hero would forget his sorrow, would forget the unrelenting pursuit of the tyrant's soldiery, bent upon hunting him down.

This lasted till the day of grief, when, with the enemy tight-

ening his death circle, Yoshitsune sent his mistress away, preparing to face his destiny alone. Then, before she departed, guided by a faithful samurai, the hero presented his loved one, in token of his tender gratitude, with the tambourine that had served as accompaniment to her nocturnal dance, in the wooded solitudes of the mountains of Yosino.

Her eyes blurred with tears, Sidzuka departed. But the samurai, for some mysterious reason, failed to keep faith with her. The path on which he led her plunged into a strange and fearful region of jagged peaks and abysses. The terrified lady no longer recognized the way. And as she paused, overcome with fear, the guide, casting off his two swords and suddenly shedding his human form, became visible, in the silver rays of the moon, for what he was—a long-tailed *kitsune*, howling fantastically at the betrayed princess as he performed the *kitsunes'* supernatural dance.

With furtive steps, the shape-shifter approached his victim, and Yoshitsune's tambourine at once flew from her hands to his. For that had been the cause of all the trouble. The *kitsune* had recognized the membrane as fox skin, taken from a slain companion who, in dying, bewitched the instrument. Freed of the cursed object, Sidzuka regained the path and, guided by the blue-eyed moon, found her way to the convent chosen as the place to weep for her beloved.

The shell pipe knows many such stories, and sometimes tells them to me in a low voice, during the winter evenings, while the opium is budding and crackling above the lamp.

My second pipe is wholly of silver, with a bowl of white porcelain. It is old and precious, with a long and fragile stem, in order that the pipe may not be too heavy in the smoker's hands. The knob is of solid silver, molded in the form of a rat. And the bowl, carefully polished, is as round as a little snowball.

The whole length of the pipe has been engraved by the artist with marvelous Chinese ornaments. For my second pipe is Cantonese. It speaks to me of southern China, where I passed some very charming years.

Coiled about the silver pipe are flowers, leaves, and grasses. The flowers are the beautiful hibiscus in bloom; the leaves are leaves of wild mint; and the grasses are rice stalks. Everything exhales a delicious odor of the China of Kwang-tung, with its cool lanes, its fertile rice fields, and its pretty villages squatting in groves of trees.

Coiled about the silver pipe are men and women. The men are, alternately, laborers and pirates; and both groups are courteous and impassive. The women are the daughters of Pak-Hoi, of Now-Chow, or of Hainan. Their soft skin gleams like amber-colored satin. Their hands and feet would make the most noble of our marquises jealous. Ot-Chen, my mistress, where are you? It is your memory that haunts me now, the memory of your fingers so expert in handling the needle, as I dream on amid the black smoke, the silver pipe resting in my hands.

My third pipe is of ivory, with a white-jade bowl and two mouthpieces of green jade. It is older and more precious than either of the others. Carved in the form of an elephant's tusk, it is very thick, and so heavy that one guesses it to have been made for the men of old, who were more robust than we. The knot is of bark, and carved in the form of an ape. The square jade bowl gleams like milk to which a little pistachio essence has been added to turn it green, while opaque serpentine veins twine about the middle of the transparent stone.

The ivory was once as white as the Western race that conquered the elephants beyond the mountains. But the accumulated residues of opium turned it yellow, then brown, until it is today like the opium-smoking Oriental race. Thus, the souls of the two rival races mingle—in the ivory pipe.

Fertile India, swarming from the Ganges to the Deccan; wise Tibet, crouched upon her snowy steppes; nomadic Mongolia, where the gawky camels trot; China, incomprehensibly huge and divine, China, imperial and philosophic: the ivory pipe mysteriously evokes the whole of Asia.

For it is old, older than many civilizations. I happen to know that, thirty centuries ago, an Occidental queen— Persian, Tartar, Scythian?—presented it, one historic day, to the Chinese emperor who had come to visit her. I used to know the name of the queen and the name of the emperor, but opium has swept them from my memory. All I can remember is the noble and peace-inspiring tale of those great rulers who, each hastening to anticipate the other, traveled across the breadth of their empires, to exchange, over their frontier, treaties of mutual accord that were partly vows of love. Thirty times a hundred years . . . Ivory pipe, to how many imperial mouths have you been pressed since that time? How many rulers, clad in yellow silk, have sought forgetfulness of their sorrows and of their cares in your cradling kiss? Forgetfulness of the ruin and injuries that, growing each day more bitter, befell the Sacred Empire of the Hoang-Tis. And if I behold you now tarnished and blackened, is that merely the mourning you wear—mourning for all the wise centuries that have died in order to make way for this century of ours, so trivial and frivolous?

I do not know of what my fourth pipe is made. It is my father's pipe, and it killed him.

It is a funereal pipe. Wholly black, on account of the dross, and decorated with gold chasings, which shine like coffin trappings, it is darkened by the opium residues that saturate every pore. Ten deadly poisons—morphine, codeine, noscapine; what others?—lurk in ambush within the black cylinder, which is like the trunk of a venomous cobra. My father died

from having smoked too much, and the opium, evaporating in the pipe bowl, retains the mysterious odor of death. I dare not bring it near my mouth—not yet. But often, I gaze upon it—as one gazes upon a tomb that stands ajar, with desire and with vertigo.

My father died from having smoked it—my father, whom I loved. He chose a serene death of marvelous intoxications to a life of ugliness and futility. One day, I shall do the same. And when I do, it shall be upon the black gold-chased pipe, marked with the cold taste of paternal lips.

And now the lamp is lighted, the mats are laid out, and green tea is steaming in the cups without handles.

And here is my fifth pipe, all ready for me. It is not old, nor is it precious. The coffin maker, who is skillful with all woods, sold it to me for six taels. It is of plain brown bamboo, with a terra-cotta bowl. A bamboo knob gives sufficient grip to the fingers.

It has no gold, nor jade, nor ivory. No prince, no queen has smoked it. It does not evoke, in magic fashion, poetically distant provinces or centuries of past glory.

But all the same, it is the one I prefer above all the others. For it is this one that I smoke. Not the others; they are too sacred. It is this one which, each evening, pours an intoxicating draft for me, opening for me the dazzling door to clear-headed pleasures, bearing me triumphantly away, out of life and to those subtle spheres that only opium smokers know: those philosophic and beneficent spheres where dwell Hoang-Ti, the Sun Emperor; Kwong-Tsu, the Perfectly Wise; and the God without a Name who was the first of smokers.

{ 7 }

The Tigers

My *fumerie* is not upholstered with mats. I despise the rattan from Hong Kong and the bamboo from Foochow. Nor are the walls hung with *kakemono* scrolls showing horned gods grinning from pagoda-studded landscapes.

Rather, from the floor, where the dim opium lamp keeps watch, to the ceiling, normally reached only by the highest-soaring smoke from our pipes, the entire room is upholstered with the skins of tigers; tawny yellow skins, striped with black, with, at each extremity, a thicket of claws.

As well as their claws, the hides have retained their heads—glaring visages, brought back to life with eyes of green enamel. Some of the heads provide pillows for smokers' necks. Others, ranged in a circle, closely observe our intoxications and monitor our dreams. Surrounded by this ferocious coterie, I enjoy greater peace and a deeper repose.

I was not always so preoccupied with peace. In that part

of China where I first became acquainted with the mellow quality of pipes, I believed a bizarre or sumptuous setting improved the effects of the kindly drug. For a while, I frequented the dives of Canton, until a tendency on the part of certain patrons to knife strangers came near to making the peace of the pipe permanent. After that, the *yamens* of Pekin, where the beautiful *congais*, dressed as idols, mingled soothing songs and voluptuous dances with the charms of opium, occupied me for a time. I chose those polished, courteous places frequented by the finest minds, where my enjoyment was seasoned by the subtle salt of philosophic discussions. When this palled, I drifted to certain lewd resorts where opium is but a pretext for vice and for crazed expressions of revolt that find their final satisfaction in Satanism.

But today, opium has washed me clean of that restless inquisitiveness. I no longer need to decorate the experience with an intricate setting, lascivious women, or eloquent philosophers. I smoke alone, surrounded by my striped bodyguards, their gleaming fangs on every side to protect me. An empty room would give me much the same sensation, but my tigers' fur keeps out the cold of chill mornings. And if I'm honest, I do love, in my drunkenness, to rest my eyes upon the black and yellow geometry with which they zebra-stripe my walls.

At one time, I would dream, as I looked upon them, of those barbaric forests they had once tyrannized. I dreamed of red afternoons rudely swooping down upon the jungles, of sudden sunsets timidly lighting the striped hunter's awakening, of his deep yawn, and the famished stretching of his claws. I dreamed of his penetrating roar, once heard in the Tonkin night; a roar that throws the cattle in the pens into an uproar. But my tigers no longer summon up for me the phantasmagoria of old and distant visions. I have been a smoker for too

long. The world of men and of things, the world of life itself, is too far removed from me. There is nothing in common between that world and my present thought. My tigers please me merely because their skins are soft, and supply me with a diverting *bizarrie*.

I no longer worry about anything. I no longer have any business, any friends. Instead, I smoke. Day by day, opium plunges me deeper within myself. And I find it sufficiently interesting to enable me to forget all that is outside.

There was a time when I permitted myself to be seduced by the sorcery of opium. The drug works a metamorphosis among its most faithful followers, and it seemed a wonderful thing to have a part in that; to submit my body to its transforming power of fantasy. I relished the ravishing sensation of becoming another animal, with senses atrophied or multiplied. The exhilaration of no longer seeing as well, but of hearing better, of no longer tasting, but of feeling more deeply those base instincts of hunger and fear. Even the atrophy of the sense of touch or the torpor of my sexual organs held a perverse attraction. But these trifles have ceased to amuse me, since the opium has penetrated my brain sufficiently to make possible, at last, a revelation of the true wisdom.

The mere physical pleasure of the pipes—which, admittedly, my body finds indispensable—now constitutes only a small fraction of the delight I find in opium. No spasm of the heart or marrow is comparable to the radiant rape of the lungs by that black smoke. And each day makes me more adept, as I breathlessly accept the gentle, treacherous kiss of the drug. I am skillful in becoming tipsy with its warm odor, in enjoying, to the utmost, the multiple itching that riddles my arms and my belly with tiny pinpricks. Mostly, however, I am skillful in the anxious watch I keep for that fatal torpor that, with

each passing day, squeezes my neck more tightly, and which is slowly but inexorably destroying my muscles and my bodily members.

Yet with this obsessive preoccupation with the flesh goes a new relish for the ecstatic joy of thought.

Oh, to feel one's self becoming, from second to second, less carnal, less human, and more a creature of pure spirit; to experience the free flight of the mind escaping from matter, the soul unfettered from the lobes of the brain; to marvel at the mysterious multiplication of noble faculties; intelligence, memory, a sense of the beautiful; to become, in the course of a few pipefuls, the true equal of heroes, of apostles, of gods; to understand, effortlessly, the thought of a Newton, to share the genius of a Napoleon, to correct the artistic faults of a Praxiteles; to bring together, finally, within one heart, which has become too vast, all virtues, all goodness, all tenderness; to love beyond measure the whole of heaven and the whole of earth, to blend in one gentle fragrance enemies and friends, good and evil, happy and sad—surely, neither the Olympus of the Greeks nor the paradise of Christians offers such an overflowing store of beatitude. And yet, such are my blessings!

In truth, the religions on which, from the heights of Nietzsche's philosophy, I used to look down with such contempt now seem to me by no means wrong in exalting charity and mercy above justice and pride. For my joy in surpassing all men in my genius yields, strangely enough now, to my joy in being the best of all men. Out of this superiority of my own heart over all other hearts is born a warmly felt and inexpressible satisfaction. Generous souls, tormented with the ideal and the hereafter, frequently know the bitter pain of life, for the reason that life appears to them vile and ugly, blackened with evil.

But I, who sees more clearly, have ceased to notice the evil. From the fifteenth pipe on, evil disappears. At a single glance, I comprehend every action in both cause and effect, each gesture in all its motions, each crime in all its motivations. So numerous are the actions and reactions, the causes and excuses, and so clearheaded am I in judging them that I never can bring myself either to condemn or to curse—but only to absolve, to commiserate, and to love. From the Olympian heights of my opium-inspired justice, Cain, Judas, or Brutus is no more guilty than Caesar or Kwong-Tsu.

And now that I reflect upon it, *that* is why I have decorated my den with tiger skins. These tigers, ferocious, treacherous, sacrilegious, are my Cains, my Judases, and my Brutuses. Their snouts, ill-cleansed of blood, their skulls low-browed over rudimentary brains, and the treacherous suppleness of the spines over which I run my fingers—everything about them speaks to me of the deplorable imperfection of this world, a world that is, as yet, all too excusable, even in its worst mistakes, for me ever to dare condemn it.

And I have no ill feelings whatsoever against my tigers for having, in their jungles of old, defiled with blood those blue light pools where the moon stooped to meet Endymion's lips.

{ 8 }

Interlude

When the last thrill seekers had departed and the door swung shut on the hostile darkness of the corridor, the *fumerie* was left to us; we three men, and the woman—the true initiates.

Shadows danced on the ceiling, only to melt in a swirl of dark gold. From the lamp on which we toasted the paste, thick smoke rose, annihilating every other perfume. We no longer noticed the tang of Turkish tobacco from the cigarettes smoked between pipes. Gone was the citrus scent of Guerlain's Jicky, which we trickled, drop by drop, from its crystal *flacon* to clean hands blackened by the drug. Even the scent, gentle yet lingering, that rose from the half-nude body of the woman seemed less insistent—the body that, wet with licking, perfumed the air as does incense smoldering in a hot brass bowl.

Comfortable in our friendship, we entwined and huddled more closely upon the straw mats where we reclined while

drowsy with the drug. In warm drunkenness, the hours slid by so softly we heard not a sound.

At last, Itala lifted his head from where it rested on the woman's body.

"I loved you a great deal," he told her serenely. "I still love you, painfully, and desire you, even though you've taken a new lover. And I don't mind that you've chosen this occasion to demonstrate the fact, by letting him caress you. Because the kindly drug allows me, whenever I wish, to remember those times when your body was mine alone. And it also enables me to look forward to that moment when, tired and sad, you return to my loving arms. I can enjoy your sighs of pleasure today because I remember the same sighs from the past, and look forward to them in the future. So I'm not the least bitter—thanks to opium."

The woman, without relaxing the thighs with which she clamped the head of her new lover, turned her lips from the pipe and gave them to Itala in a kiss.

"Women," said Timur from the darkness. "They tell you they 'aren't like the rest.' But really they are all exactly the same."

Itala hadn't noticed Timur observing them. In the gloom, his Tartar profile was almost invisible against the brown silk of the cushion that supported his head.

"During my affair with Laurence de Trailles," he continued, "she didn't love me, nor I her."

Itala was surprised to hear him speak so frankly, since he was normally reticent, even secretive.

"All I did was turn her silly little head," he went on, "and she came running to me, just as I knew she would. It's the same with all convent girls; they're incapable of any emotion beyond a false and childish sentimentality. She knew I felt nothing for her, but it didn't concern her in the least. I remember her laughing, and saying, 'It's just sport for you, isn't it?'

"But she enjoyed the game; it excited her, and she wanted to be excited. She *liked* the fact that we felt nothing for one another; the emotional aridity, the perversity of it, the taste of new kisses . . .

"And yet . . . she never stopped sleeping with her husband. Poor devil. Loved her, of course—and *jealous!* Uncomplicated chap—but, for her, a kind of refuge; the quiet harbor where you dock after visiting all the more sensual ports of call. Even after our most . . . sporting days together, she never failed to go home and offer her lips to her husband—just as our friend here just offered her lips to you. Because you, as her sometime lover, are like a kind of husband."

The third man, Aneyr—the lover for whom the woman had abandoned Itala, and whom she had imprisoned between her legs—might have commented, had she not, at that moment, wearied of opium. Grabbing his hair, she pulled him up her body and kissed him so hungrily that he could not speak.

"Trailles was your friend," said Itala. "Yet you slept with his wife, even though you didn't love her. You felt no remorse?"

"No. If he was foolish enough to attach any value to sexual fidelity, he deserved everything he got. Anyway, you might say I was acting in the best interests of the race. Had he and Laurence produced children, his stupidity and her empty-headedness could only have resulted in idiots. Whereas any child from our liaison would have the blood of nomadic conquerors running in its veins."

Aneyr detached his mouth from the woman's voracious lips. "Don't bring logic into it. The pleasure you gave and received is justification enough. As usual, the Prophet was right. 'Each cry of joy from your wives opens wider for you the gates of Paradise.'"

"Perhaps that would mean something to a Mohammedan," said Timur, "but I don't qualify. For a start, I don't believe in

paradise. But you're right. I shouldn't have offered justification for an act that needs none. Hypocritical old maids or castrated Protestants are the only people in the world who would cite the prior existence of a wife or husband as a good reason for two like-minded people not to make love. Imagine trying to justify that in logic! A woman has the right to present her cheek or her hand to be kissed by whomsoever she pleases, but not her mouth or vagina? Ridiculous!"

They fell silent. Itala smoked pipe after pipe. Aneyr, while his lover slithered down to occupy herself with the lower half of his body, rolled the pills of opium and spiked them on the long needle to toast over the lamp flame. Once they began to bubble and fume, he transferred the drug to the pipe.

From time to time, one of the three men let the pipe drop and, resting his head back on the cushions, drifted enraptured in the pleasure of intoxication. Already silent, the room became also motionless. No expression disturbed the pensive, lucid faces; no movement deformed the clarity of line.

"A *fumerie*," observed Timur after one such timeless interval, "is as beautiful as a fragment of ancient Greece."

Weary of flesh, the woman brought the pipe to her mouth; then, having breathed in the smoke, stretched herself like a cat, and, also like that animal, began to prowl the room on hands and knees. Unclasped, her Japanese robe trailed across the naked bodies of the men. In that confusion of limbs, she found no clear space. But since opium arouses feminine nerves to lust, the woman was not looking for a place to rest. She hesitated, examining the three men. Their bodies were as supple as one another, their strength as great . . . But it was Timur who, eyes closed, first knew of her choice when two soft arms slipped around his shoulders and a wet mouth sucked violently at his tongue.

From the start, he let her do what she wanted, knowing he

Claude Farrère

would feel nothing. Opium, while appeasing every desire in a man, erases his virility. Closing his eyes, he thought of Laurence de Trailles doing the same things . . . His mind wandered.

Aneyr stood, and lit a cigarette at the lamp. Itala joined him. Neither seemed much interested in the woman, or what she was doing to their companion.

How much time passed? Minutes? Hours? Long enough, anyway, for the effect of the last pipe to pass, since Timur, to his surprise, felt the first stirrings of desire.

"Aneyr, go to sleep," he said. "I want her. Don't look."

Aneyr, voice heavy with black smoke, replied, "Wait till I finish my cigarette."

Hearing the voice of the one she truly desired, the woman abruptly disentangled herself from Timur and flung herself on Aneyr, twining herself around him—so greedily that, surprised, he reeled back, and fell with her onto the convenient divan.

Itala passed Timur the pipe he had just prepared, and they shared it, indifferent to the groaning of the hard-pressed divan and the frustrated cries of the woman as in vain she tried to excite her impotent lover.

"Timur," murmured Itala, "you are the most perfect of us all. Such men do not come about by accident. Surely your mother selected some splendidly auspicious night for your conception. Like that one in the poem perhaps—'a milky, violet night, like a silver vase among diamonds.'"

"They've forgotten," said Timur. "Even gods forget. Did Alcmene and Zeus remember the instant they came together to make Hercules?"

A sob of exasperated desire interrupted their rambling. Eyes closed, they heard the woman's naked feet trampling the mats. A few moments later, she passed them again. Sleepily, they barely noticed the small flask she now carried.

A few moments later, the struggle on the divan began again, this time with more success.

Competing with the drug, a new odor crept into the room. The musk of lust? None of them was sure, since opium smoke still ruled their senses.

But then the pipe slipped from Itala's hands. And Timur too sat up, nails clawing at the mat. Their eyes, abruptly sober, met over the brass tray on which the implements of smoking were scattered.

"You smell that?"

"Yes . . ."

Above their heads, just below the ceiling, the smoke swirled, like a living thing, distracted. Terrifyingly, into the opium-saturated den, plunging among the atoms so peacefully and decorously distributed to every corner of the room, other atoms burst tumultuously. Terror and death invaded. Overpowering the friendly odor of the poppy, redolent of plants and flowers, a pungent, choking chemical stink pervaded the air, and the perfume of opium was diluted, eroded, killed.

Ether . . .

Glacial ether, cousin to madness and hypnosis . . .

It was not sex in which the woman had found satiety for her painful libido but in ether. And now the flask, upset, spilled its fuming stink into the room, and, with it, the truth.

"Never, never again," babbled the woman. "Not him. Oh no, not him! I don't want to. It's too late . . . too late . . ."

Sober now, Itala and Timur were on their feet.

"Was I telling you that I loved her?" muttered Itala. "I lied! I don't—not anymore."

And Timur . . . not imperious now; no descendant of Asiatic conquerors, but pathetic, whining, "Laurence . . . I didn't speak your name, did I? Tell me I didn't speak it! It's not true, it's not true . . ."

{ 9 }

The Sixth Sense

Sixteen, seventeen, eighteen? I no longer know. Have you noticed what an impossible thing it is to keep count of one's pipes? I don't have the faintest idea how many I have smoked . . .

Let's see. My brain feels agile and alert, while my forehead has become transparent . . .

This could be the twentieth, then.

My veins feel as though they were filled with an astonishingly light and effervescent fluid that is certainly not blood. But that makes sense, since my blood would no longer be the thick red blood of humankind, anyway—because, from the first puffs, I become the superior of men—to tell the truth, more like a god.

I'm almost sure this pipe is the twentieth, since the burden of that damned sixth sense weighs me down less heavily now.

Once it's gone, I shall be the absolute equal of God—pure intelligence.

How I hunger to materialize all the marvels which my brain incessantly creates. But I cannot, since my spirit simply won't take flight and rise from these mats. It's quite silly, really; on the one hand, an extreme lightness of body that transcends all the physical senses, but on the other this paralysis of the flesh that anchors one to the earth! The effect of the drug, of course— though I know some effects far weirder than that . . .

"Mowg, will you smoke this? The next is mine."

No, the sixth sense is not yet absolutely atrophied. I shall need more opium before it disappears for the night. How do I know? Because, as I watch Mowghi turning her throat toward me, and see her hips become visible under the silk of her kimono, a temptation still comes to me to enjoy that flesh . . .

Four pipes . . . yes, four more pipes will do it. Y'see, it's not enough simply to suppress desire. You must suppress even the *appreciation* of desire; you must be able to look at the act of copulation free of all those emotional filters, and simply say to yourself, *What on earth is my wife doing with those people?* To see it for what it is, a ridiculous bit of clowning. Once I reach that stage, the quintessence of my intoxication, those sighs of pleasure from the mats around me just won't mean a thing.

"You've finished? Give me the pipe, and I'll scrape it out. This opium is too strong, I think. They should have mixed the Benares with the Yunnan."

Who are the smokers this evening? The lamplight is so dim, and I've stared too long into the flame that I can't make out faces.

"Mowg, dear, see to it that each one has his mat and his cushion, with a lamp and a pipe not too far away."

. . . but reserve for my neck alone the soft pillow of your belly . . .

Now, you see! It still hasn't gone. That sixth sense continues to gnaw at me.

Give, Mowghi, give to whomever you like your body and that flower of yours—since I no longer can make use of it; but save for me only your conjugal soul, your soul which is a twin to mine, brought up like mine on opium.

We go back a long way, you and I. Here I am, thirty, and you twenty-seven; and never a cross word—isn't that right, Mowg?—since our first kiss.

And how long ago was that? To tell the truth, I have almost no sense of the time we've been married, it's been so incredible.

It's especially hard to remember when I remember the years that went before, of the time when I was a mere lad, eager to live, and bent upon squandering my father's millions in the pursuit of pleasure. That was also me—that boy who rode steeplechases on the fillies from my own stable; who sailed the bay of Cowes on my yacht; who fought on the Grande Jatte for Cendrelli's lips—she who was so beautiful in *Isolde*, and to whom I gave a thousand louis each month.

And here is something that is odder still: it is I who am in love with the Miss Mowghi who is over there, whom I impetuously married, giving up all pomps and all the works of the devil, dreaming of nothing but her ingenuous mouth and the chaste embrace of her cool arms. Miss Mowghi (we selected between us that pretty, savage name, and I afterward forgot your real one). Miss Mowghi, daughter of the old admiral, the victor of Formosa; the barbaric little lass, barely out of her convent, whose clear-seeing eyes seemed beyond the reach of the whirlpools of sensuality. I remember our first modest nights, and the supreme intoxication of kisses timidly given.

We traveled at first. Sailor ancestors undoubtedly had

given my loved one dimly sensed desires in this direction. For one whole year, Japan held us under her spell; and I can recall yet—even now—I can recall with gentle fervor the silent ecstasies of her twilights, as our yacht crossed Simonoseki in the light of the setting sun. Yes, really, happiness was achievable then—even for those who do not smoke.

Mowghi, little loved one, do not turn away just yet. Being careful not to blacken your lovely white fingers, prepare me up a pipe. Make me ripe for your next treason. Your faithful soul can hide nothing from me. I know you are merely restraining your desire until the moment, soon to come, when I shall be free of churlish jealousy, and no longer care what you do, or who with.

It was later, in China, that the two of us smoked for the first time. In Shanghai, in Foochow Road. Oh! how clear it all is in my head! The sixth of October, 1899—eleven o'clock at night. We had dined at a Chinese merchant's by the name of Tcheng-Ta. When the singers had done with their meowing, Tcheng-Ta suggested that, out of curiosity, we try smoking a pipe in his *fumerie*.

Tcheng-Ta's den, in the body of the building, looked out upon an inner court. On the walls were four very obscene *kakemonos*, which raised Mowghi's eyebrows. But no sooner had I smoked a second pipe than I forgot everything. I no longer perceived anything except a miracle, mysteriously worked, and which I always had believed to be impossible. The clear eyes, the virgin eyes of the companion of my journeyings grew large and hollow, then filled with giddiness and sensual anxiety, as if gazing into the depths of an abyss. And that evening, Mowghi, blunt and sweet, sought my caress and breathed it in harshly between her closed teeth.

Mystery. The sixth sense awoke in her, at the same time that it became extinguished in me.

After that, we smoked every day. Naturally. Young, almost obscenely rich, eager for any sensation that would make us feel more alive, we would have been fools, indeed, to refuse so rich an opportunity as opium. Our souls, always very intimate, always sisters, always wed, at once came to understand each other better.

And now, on these nights with other lovers of the divine drug, our love is at its apogee. Our thoughts are identical, simultaneous. We smile, dream, and weep at the same instants, for the same reasons.

But there is something more! While her body abandons itself to indifferent kisses, there, near me, in the *fumerie*, I *know* that her soul detaches itself to come and embrace my own: *the sixth sense awakens in her flesh at the same time that it goes to sleep in my own.*

You find this irrational, abnormal? Not at all—though I can see how, to someone who has not known opium, it may be incomprehensible. For that is the capricious—no, the wise!—opium's sport. In women, who are creatures made for love, it provokes and increases amorous ardor; while in men, who are creatures made for thought, it suppresses that sixth sense, which is coarsely opposed to cerebral speculations. Opium causes this to come about—and opium knows best. Opium is always right.

Another pipe.

In stripping me of my virility, opium has delivered me from that sexual obsession that is such a weight for proud spirits and those truly eager for liberty. At first, fool that I was, I resisted; I rebelled like the slave who, set free, pines for the food and shelter of servitude. I blasphemed against the opium's wise law, calling it absurd and unjust for desire to cease in me just as it swelled in the flesh of my companion. Stupidly, comically, I wanted to go back upstream; I declined to abdicate my

lover's role—until that wiser day when opium unsealed my eyes, and her eyes too; until the day when our bodies became divorced in order to permit our souls to share a more amorous marriage—in opium.

One more pipe. Mowg, dear, patient one, it is the last. I am free now. And I can feel your soul coquettishly wheedling, beginning to skim my own with its provocative kisses. Let your flesh do as it wishes. Untie, unwrap your smarting body, hungry for carnal satisfaction; direct your fingers, offer your throat, your belly to the nearest male, forgetful of all futile modesty. Opium elevates us above the earth. I see only the black smoke that swirls magnificently about the lamp. A thousand marvelous harmonies mask for me your sighs of joy, your cries of pleasure. Go on, laugh and weep, twine tonight's lover in your arms, clutch him between your lascivious legs; feed on him with your lips, your teeth, your sinuous tongue; crush your quivering breasts upon his chest. But as you do so, enjoy with me the communion, a thousand times more intimate, of our blended souls, along with a limitless wealth of ineffable caresses, of unspeakable passions. And not for a moment do I doubt that, if it were not for opium, it would be *my* arms, my tongue, and my bosom now reveling in the possession of you . . .

What's that?

Why are you all laughing?

What name do you call me, imbeciles?

Well, how can I expect you . . . nothing but barnyard animals . . . how can I expect *you* to understand . . . ?

{ 10 }

The Events in the House on Boulevard Thiers

Don't ask me what took place in the house on the Boulevard Thiers. And if I write down here what happened, it is against my better judgment. Because so-called reasonable individuals will laugh, while others, of whom I am one, will find nothing in the narrative to convince them they aren't crazy.

I'm describing it here, nevertheless, because it's true.

It happened the first of May, last year, in a city which I won't name—out of prudence. Specifically, the events took place on the fourth floor of a house that is neither old nor haunted by mystery, but newly built, ugly and unpretentious. But the Boulevard Thiers is impregnated with the odor of lurking vice. Until the city reduced it to rubble, the area where the house stood was disreputable, even notorious. Where a

wide boulevard now overlooks the river, hovels, with shut-
ters permanently closed, had clung to the slopes of the cliff.
Whatever air of respectability the new quarter may have, it is
undermined by the old stones of its foundations, grown corrupt from the vice they had witnessed.

The house bears the number seven. The building is given
over to furnished lodgings. We occupied one whole floor—
eight or ten friends. I never was sure how many, or who
the other tenants were. At the center of our apartment was
the *fumerie*, surrounded by bedrooms, but we never slept in
them, since everyone preferred to smoke and talk until dawn,
stretched out upon the rice mats. Opium extinguishes many
of our animal needs, including that for sleep.

Some days, we amused ourselves with holding spiritual-
ist seances. One of the tricks of the so-called mediums is to
have everyone present apply the pressure of one finger under
the tabletop, and make it rise in the air. It's not hard to do,
once you know the secret, and we played at it a lot, without
feeling we were in touch with "unknown forces." One young
chap, Hartus, with a boyish face and long flowing black hair,
would turn up in a blue and yellow clown's costume, which
he claimed was particularly suited to spirit-world experiences.
That will give some idea of how seriously we took it.

There were always plenty of women around the house on
the Boulevard Thiers. Once word got about that we were
smoking opium, they all wanted a taste, and didn't care what
we did with them afterward. Opium dulls their senses so much
that any number of men can fuck them any way they like, and
as often as they want, and it all seems like a cuddle with their
best girlfriend.

On the evening I'm writing about, a girl of twenty had
turned up. We called her Ether, since she doted on the stuff.
Each time, she arrived with a full flask of sulphuric ether, and

didn't leave until it was gone. That didn't prevent her from smoking her fifteen pipes afterward. On this evening, she was doubly drunk, and was sleeping, nude. One of the men was halfheartedly fingering her. The rest of us lay about in the half light of the lamp, talking about who-knows-what.

I've no idea why we suddenly decided to try table turning. The first I knew was when Hartus, the blue and yellow clown with woman's hair, called for us to help him carry the table into one of the bedrooms. Supposedly, the trick won't work in the presence of opium; the spirits didn't like the smell, or something.

I was slow in getting up, so he started to carry the table into the next room all by himself. For a minute, I remained stretched on the mat, sulky at having to leave the gentle torpor of my sixth pipe. To my right, Ether, stirred out of her doze by my friend's fingers, was now holding his head with both hands as he explored her with his tongue. The sight didn't particularly excite me, so I rose and followed Hartus.

The bedroom, which got little use, felt damp, almost clammy. He'd lit a candle, and the flame, as it wavered in the draft, sent shadows dancing across the walls and ceiling in a saraband. Outside the window, the moon had frosted the roofs of the town with white.

One by one, the others wandered in and took their seats. At the direction of Hartus, we placed our hands on the table and concentrated. But something had gone wrong, since the table remained motionless. It didn't even creak—you know, those weird dry sounds that tell you a thing is about to move? No, something had gone wrong. Maybe it was because we had all smoked quite a few pipes of some rather good Yunnan. That may have been the cause of it.

Eventually I got up and, with the idea of letting some air into the room, opened the window. It really was a beauti-

ful night; the roofs drowned in whiteness, the river starred with reflections. A gentle breeze half opened my pajamas and brushed my chest. It was so quiet that I heard Hartus behind me blow out the candle.

And then the inexplicable thing began to happen.

The breeze playing over my flesh seemed suddenly cold, very cold, as though the thermometer had dropped a dozen degrees. There was a noise behind me as if the table had been jolted into the air, and fallen back. In the darkness, I imagined Hartus had bumped against it and overturned it. But then he yelled for me "not to make so much noise," and I realized that I was alone in the room, and that *none of us had touched the table.*

With an effort of will, I unclamped my fingers from the windowsill and turned. The table was motionless now. I detoured around it, giving it a wide berth, and returned to the room with the mats.

Nothing looked different. Our friend was still browsing on Ether's nude body, and she showed no signs of disliking it. The moonlit bedroom seemed to belong in another world. Maybe I had imagined the whole thing . . .

At that moment, Ether pushed her lover's head away and rose to her feet. Backing away, she leaned against the wall, her hands at her throat. This surprised me, for the moment before, ether and opium had held her completely paralyzed. *But she was no longer drunk.* I could see her clear eyes. Her slender nudity impressed me as having grown and changed. The soft shoulders, the small rigid breasts, the narrow, feverish head remained the same. But the harmony of the whole was different. No longer Ether, the whore, illiterate daughter of a washerwoman, but the daughter of a great house, chaste and haughty, with noble blood in her veins and rare thoughts in her brain.

Belatedly, her lover realized she'd gone, and called lazily for her to return.

She didn't move; only spoke, in a slow-cadenced voice.

"Mundi amorem noxium horresco."

Naturally, I thought I had imagined it. I'd never heard Ether say anything except in the execrable local French, riddled with Breton slang. And I knew she'd never learned to read, let alone to read Latin.

I pushed my drugged brain into translating what she had said.

Unclean love makes me shudder.

She continued, without interruption, in the same austere tone of voice, the voice of a nun or an abbess. *"Jejuniis carnem domans, dulcique mentem pabulo nutriens orationis, coeli gaudiis potiar."*

A couple of the men looked at me inquiringly. "She says something like, 'It is by conquering my flesh through fasting, and nourishing my soul on the gentle food of prayer, that I shall finally attain the joys of heaven.'"

But the others didn't seem particularly interested. To their opium-degraded intellects, this transformation appeared perfectly natural. Of all people, Hartus, the clown, was the only one who shared my astonishment. And to *my* surprise, he started speaking to her in very good Latin, and as politely as if she was not the little whore we called Ether, but the dignified woman of the new voice and manner.

"Don't remain standing," he said. "You must be tired."

Ether, still with her back flat against the wall, subsided into a crouch. *"Fiat voluntas Dei!"* she—or, rather, the spirit within her—said. *"Iter arduum peregi, et affligit me lassitudo. Sed Dominus est praesidium."* May God's will be done! I have traveled a hard path, and I am very tired. But God is my refuge and my strength.

"Where are you from?" Hartus demanded.

"A terra Britannica. Ibi sacrifico sacrificium justitiae, quia nimis peccavi, cogitatione, verbo, et opere. Mea maxima culpa." I come from Britain. There I offer just sacrifices, for the reason that I have

sinned much, in thought, word, and deed. The great fault is mine.

"In what way did you sin?"

I distinctly saw her blush.

"Cogitatione, verbo, et opere. De viro ex me filius natus est." In thought, word, and deed. By man, of me a son is born.

She and Hartus went on, speaking always Latin, a medieval Latin, a Latin of the convent and of the missal, which I understood only by snatches. Ironically, the smell of opium, so related to that of ecclesiastical incense, stimulated my memories of childhood catechism classes. During pauses, I heard the crackling of opium as our friends, oblivious of the drama taking place in the corner of the room, rotated their needles in the flame. The very ordinariness of it all was the only thing that tempered my fear.

Hartus, emboldened by the pipes he had smoked and complete master of his nerves, continued speaking without any show of doubt. It's a picture so etched on my retina that nothing will ever efface it. He, the blue and yellow man, crouched upon the mats, one hand upon the floor, as the lamp at times turned his flowing black hair to blond. She, the strange woman, nude, her back to the wall, her elbows crosswise, her fingers interlaced under her throat. Words came and went between them with a lively seesaw verve, as the room became more and more impregnated with the atmosphere of the beyond. Her voice preserved the monastic timbre, but strengthened, as if the spirit that spoke through Ether was coming closer.

At first, mere phrases, desultory and brief; phrases uttered in haste, as by a traveler who is in a hurry, who has no time to talk. Then more detailed, descriptive, rhetorical, in Latin far beyond my meager comprehension.

I have preserved only the memory of that voice, that Latin voice, gravely intoning what sounded like liturgical re-

sponses. I caught certain words on the fly, the names of men or of countries, or ecclesiastical terms, *Astrolabius, Albanasius, Sens, Argenteuil, excommunitio, concilium, monasterium.* The voice grew animated and louder. Two words, out of all the drift of phrases, remained floating upon the surface, two words ten times repeated, with vehemence and with fury at first, afterward in a tone of grief and contrition. *"Panem supersubstantialem."* And then the voice paused, saddened, infinitely saddened.

"The sin of lust?" Hartus said. "What was God's punishment?"

The white face of the girl flushed red, and the voice dropped an octave to an urgent whisper, such as is heard in a confessional, and a few words barely reached my ears, with strange and repellent accents. I understood *"modo bestiarum—copulatione—membris asinorum erectis."* Like animals— copulation—that huge cock erect.

And violently uttered, as though vomited forth in disgust, was the word *"castratus."*

Having become calm once again, the voice slackened, to such an extent that the last phrase fixed itself in my memory. *"Fuit ille sacerdos et pontifex, et beatificus post mortem. Nunc Angelorum Chorus illi obsequantem concinit laudem celebresque palmas. Gloria Patri per omne saeculum."* He was priest and pontiff, and blessed after his death. The Angelic Choir is now singing his praises with palms. Glory be to the Father forever.

"And you?" asked Hartus.

"Dominus Omnipotens et Misericors Deus debita mea remisit. Virgo ego fatua. Sed dimissis peccatis meis, nunc ego sum nihil." The Almighty and Merciful God has forgiven my sins. I was a foolish virgin. But now, my sins have been forgiven, and I am as nothing.

She repeated, three times, the word *"nihil."* And it seemed as though, of a sudden, she was speaking from a long way off. The last *"nihil"* was no more than a breath of sound.

The blue and yellow clown strode up to her, close enough to reach out and touch her; and then, fastening his gaze upon those unflinching eyes, he said,

"Héloïse?"

The eyes closed in affirmation.

He took her breasts in his hands and blew some opium into her face. She was motionless. But gradually, her muscles relaxed, and I could see tremors appearing upon her pallid face. A minute more, and the eyes opened and rolled to their whites, the head and shoulders drooped, and upon the mats there remained now only a flaccid, lifeless form.

Then her body slowly stirred, and from her mouth, that same mouth, there came another stammering voice, drowning in drunkenness.

"Fuck me, it's cold!"

It was true. The room was chill as a cellar.

"Gimme a pipe, will ya? And a blanket! I'm fucking freezing here!"

One of the smokers thrust a brown ball of opium into the pipe bowl and handed it to her. Had he heard the conversation?

Possibly.

Had I heard?

Sometimes I wonder . . .

Later, I questioned Hartus, of course. But he didn't answer. He prefers not to speak of that night.

Later, feeling a bit ridiculous, I looked it up. Just to confirm that I hadn't dreamed that part, that the whole thing wasn't a piece of opium madness.

Peter Abelard (1079–1142), the most renowned philosopher and logician of his time, met Héloïse (1101–1164) when she was fifteen. She became his student, and the

couple began a passionate relationship both intellectual and sexual. Héloïse soon became pregnant, and Abelard took her back to his family in Brittany, where they married, though in secret, to protect his reputation. After their son was born, Héloïse's uncle tried to make the marriage public, but Abelard removed her to a convent. Believing he was attempting to renounce her, the uncle had him castrated. Abelard ultimately retreated to the monastery of Saint Denis, where he became a monk. Héloïse, unwilling to repudiate their marriage, became a nun.

Did we intercept the lonely spirit of Héloïse, forever flying from her guilt? Who knows? Anyone who's tried opium will tell you—it can induce the strangest visions.

{ II }

The Cyclone

I know this story is true, because the man who told me is a fellow sailor, and a smoker.

So while it may sound strange to you, if you're not a smoker (or a sailor), it would appear to those who *do* smoke—and whose intelligence has therefore been sharpened by opium—to be a simple and normal occurrence.

Do *I* smoke? No, I don't anymore, as a matter of fact. I promised someone . . . but that's another story. I do hang out at a seamen's *fumerie*, however, sometimes for the whole night, talking all night, and only going to sleep as they open the sky-light at dawn and let in some fresh air. And yes, maybe a little of the smoke does penetrate my brain, but that doesn't cloud my perception; just introduces a little clarity and honesty.

On that evening, a group of us were lying on the mats as usual. Not alone, for opium loves company. There were two women upon the mats. One of them, I can't mention her name.

Her husband has a steamer run, and the moment he's upped anchor, she's down to the *fumerie* for a pipe, and whatever else may be on offer.

The other one we call Toytoy, because, once she's had a few pipes, she lets the men use her as a plaything, and do anything they like. In the street, these two women, from completely different levels of society, would cut one another dead. But opium is the great leveler, and so they're friends as long as the lamp is lit. I've often seen them drifting off to sleep naked in each other's arms.

That night, three young fellows had dropped in to flirt with opium. They smoked a few pipes, but spent most of their time with the women. I could just make out their intertwined bodies by the dim glow of the lamp. They didn't hear the story I heard—and even if they had, who knows if they'd remember? Kids like that think with their dicks.

This man I told you about—the truth is, I know almost nothing about him, not even his age or what he looks like, since when I saw him, he was always reclining upon the mats, and the lamplight was very dim. His beard, however, was silver and his eyes were of a metallic green.

He stood out because he preferred to make up his own pipes, which he did very expertly. Someone told me he was captain of a fighting ship, but I am not sure; what takes place outside the *fumerie* is no concern of mine. Around the place, he was just known as Silent, since he never spoke after the third pipe. Up to then, however, he was full of stories. There were few countries he hadn't visited, and opium made it possible for him to understand them. This, then, is what he told me, one night when we had spoken for a long time of visions and of phantoms.

"The most sinister ghosts aren't those that lurk in cemeteries, or so-called haunted houses, and jump out to scare the unsuspecting. We all have seen that sort, we smokers. They

don't dare raise a hand against us, because they know that opium, by separating mind from body, makes smokers a bit like ghosts themselves—fluid and immaterial. We scent them in the night more quickly than they can scent us.

"But there is another kind of ghost, a sort that isn't concerned with the living. Their business as phantoms weighs too heavily and too terribly upon them.

"Tell me, do you, by any chance, remember the *Renard*? No? That happened many years ago, in the days when seven good-sized pipes were enough to make me drunk. These days, I need forty. This shit they keep sending us . . . Anyway, the *Renard* was a cruiser. Three-master. Lovely lines. The hull seemed scarcely to be resting on the water. I can see her now, just skimming over the black waves.

"Well, the *Renard* put out, one fine calm day, and was never seen again. Though that's not precisely true—but I'm getting ahead of my story . . .

"That was the year a cyclone completely devastated the China coast. All right, you'll say that we have cyclones every year, and you'd be right. But this one was different. Now you know that the winds of a cyclone spiral inward, and that in the northern hemisphere those winds rotate counterclockwise but in the southern hemisphere they move clockwise.

"But this cyclone was not like other Chinese cyclones; it whirled from right to left, whereas its brothers of the Indian Ocean invariably whirl from left to right. That always impressed me as being a weird sort of thing; but I thought no more of it at the time. Except that one day, in a Tonkinese *fumerie*, a Dutchman assured me that there was such a thing as a special kind of tempest—living tempests, which were to be recognized by the fact that they violated all natural laws, blowing from the north, when they should blow from the south, going to the right when one expected them on the

left—doing everything, in short, upside down. Those tempests, he explained to me, are caused by evil and occult spirits, and they are the most dangerous of all for ships. And he had a variety of stories to tell me on that score . . .

"You hear a lot of nonsense on the mats, but in this case the Dutchman seemed to be talking sense. I fell to wondering how a ship would perform in a storm like that. During a cyclone, it doesn't take much to sink even a big three-master if the captain or the first mate makes a few mistakes. By the time I left that place, I'd decided the *Renard* had gone down in just such a storm.

"But I didn't give the matter much thought, otherwise. For one thing, no one was any longer concerned with the *Renard*. A year or two had gone by. The widows had finished mourning and packed up their black dresses and crepe veils. A few had even remarried. In short, the years had slipped by. How many, I no longer know; for the pipes prevent one from taking note of the flight of time . . .

"I say, would you mind lowering the lamp a little; the flame has scorched this pipeful . . ."

He was silent as I adjusted the wick. A gentle, panting wail reached my ears from the mats.

"Oblige me, sir," said Silent, "if you would, and push my jar a little closer . . ."

He teased another pill of deep brown jam and toasted it over the flame with the familiar crackling. While he took a couple of hits and let them rise to his head, I watched two of the young chaps giving Toytoy a workout. One of them, a young lascar, black as ebony, had a dick on him . . . Well, I'll just say that more than Toytoy's eyes were wide open.

But that sort of thing doesn't interest me much. I preferred to watch how the drug grew yellow and puffed up as Silent rotated it in the flame.

He went on, his voice underscored by Toytoy's moans of . . . well, I suppose it was pleasure; rather the way that a singer with a soft voice will accompany himself with the quiet chords of a guitar.

"Yes, everyone had forgotten the *Renard*. There was only one proof that the ship had been lost, but that pretty definite sort: a shattered plank that a tea clipper, racing to England with her holds filled with the first picking, had snatched up in passing. More than a plank, actually; it was half of the name board. The letters 'RENA' could still be distinguished. After that, nobody was in any doubt.

"And then, one day, I took it into my head to go to China, since, as I don't have to tell you, the opium the druggists sell here is worthless. I signed on the crew of the packet carrying mail to Shanghai. I won't name the ship, since she brought me bad luck.

"Two days out, a cyclone swooped down upon us. They'd cabled a warning, but you know those packet captains; the mail must go through, and so on. As an old sailor who knew those waters well, I'd been assigned to calculate the track of the storm, which, as you know, is not difficult. I made my observations, drew up my figures, and turned in my papers on the evening of the second day out. Having done this, I retired to my cabin and, after carefully locking the door, lit my opium lamp.

"I smoked quite contentedly until nightfall. More and more of a sea was coming up all the while, but on my mat, I hardly noticed the motion of the boat. As night fell, I felt, all of a sudden, that something abnormal was happening. What? I had no idea. But I scented something of the unknown, of the supernatural, and *that something was coming nearer to us*.

"At that moment, the taste of the opium appeared to me to undergo a change. You know how, sometimes, the smoke seems almost like a living thing? With a mind of its own? I

got that feeling then—that the smoke was as troubled and disturbed as I. However, I kept on smoking, as the night all the while grew blacker.

"And then, suddenly, a horrible thing happened; for absolutely no reason at all, my lamp went out. In the darkness, I could hear the cabin furniture groaning as every plank of the ship strained and twisted in the tempest. Even the straw fibers of my mat crackled, as if with fright.

"The howling of the wind pierced the walls and swept over me, bringing an even more precise sensation of peril. First, I had a sense that we faced *a double danger.* Why double? I couldn't say; only that two equally mortal perils were bearing down implacably upon us. I understood, very clearly, that this was no natural wind, no simple, more or less furious displacement of air, but rather, a living thing, one capable of calculation and thought, and which, at that very moment, was asking itself whether or not to shatter into pieces the little nutshell in its teeth.

"But then came the second realization. I felt that the storm was rotating *from right to left.* My calculations, in that case, had been wrong.

"I put aside my pipe, got dressed, and headed for the bridge to try to correct things before it was too late. Except part of me knew that my calculations were of small importance, because we were not dealing with any ordinary cyclone.

"All the same, and even though I was dizzy with opium, and my legs shook under me, I staggered out of the cabin, and, clinging to every rail, made my way up on deck.

"The wind was so strong that I scarcely could hold on. But just as I reached the top of the companionway, it died away. You'd think the voice of Christ had stilled the waves as he did for his apostles on the sea of Galilee. But I knew the explanation was simpler than that.

MY LADY OPIUM

"We were in the center of the storm—what they call the eye. Less than a kilometer away, a wall of windswept cloud showed where the storm continued to whirl, giddily clockwise, against all the logic of my years in these seas. I looked around for the captain or any of the officers, to explain how I'd been mistaken, but the deck was empty.

"What with the rush of cold air into my lungs and the sudden stillness of the ship, I had a chance to get my sea legs and reach the rail. And it was then that I saw the vision.

"On the surface of the eerily phosphorescent water, which was like a shroud sewn with an infinite number of silver brilliants, a ship rode beside us. A long, slender ship, whose hull seemed scarcely to rest upon the sea, and whose three very tall masts appeared to be fleeing the world of the living. They shimmered, those masts, as reflections shimmer upon the water, and their tops were lost in the sky like smoke. The hull, on the other hand, was outlined with extraordinary precision, more precisely than any hull of wood and steel. And upon the deck, men were distinguishable, with blanched faces, and gold braid glowing on their uniforms. All these objects, however, were quite transparent, and through planks and men I could still make out the sea and the wall of the storm beyond.

"The phantom vessel passed without a sound. As it glided by, I saw the name board, from which one plank was missing; two letters of the ship's name alone remained—'RD.'

"It disappeared, then, in the distance. The wind began howling again, more violently than ever, and I saw nothing more. Evidently, the center of the living cyclone was dragging with it, into infinity and into eternity, the ghost of the dead ship.

"So . . . what happened then?" I asked.

"Oh, I went below and lit my smoking lamp again," said Silent. "But the opium had no more savor than milk, and the

{ 85 }

pipes all tasted stale. It was as if all the goodness in the opium had been sucked out by . . . other mouths. And that was what frightened me the most. On the *Renard*, there must have been smokers. Maybe one of them was my opposite number—the navigator, ordered to track the path of the storm—and who, like me, didn't expect a phantom cyclone that spun clockwise, not counterclockwise. He could even have been smoking, as I had been, when he realized the horrible truth. If there was such a man, and he and his friends had shared my opium that night, it could account for our ship being spared . . . Pass me the sponge, will you? My bowl is all dirty."

I wet the sponge from the carafe and passed it over.

In the silence, the other noises of the room became more audible. Toytoy and her friend of the mats were both naked now and crouched on hands and knees, tits and asses swinging, sobbing with pleasure as two of the young guys slammed into them from behind while the third leaned against the wall and jerked off in their eager faces.

But I was content merely to watch the pipe as its metal surface began to gleam anew under the friction of the moist sponge.

{ 12 }

Out of the Silence

No, it is not yet night. I had thought it was night. But not yet. Fact is, I don't see so well anymore. As soon as the smoke gets to my brain, it's like a mist falls in front of my eyes, a brown, wavering veil. I can't make things out, and sometimes they seem to change shape. It's very funny. I keep on smoking, and the smoke from the pipes expands enormously and becomes opaque, exactly like the foul smoke from steamer stacks—the disgusting smoke of the boat that carried me away from my beloved Tonkin . . .

Crap! I don't even think of that anymore.

No, it's not night. Well, that's something at least! Another hour yet, maybe, an hour to go on living, satisfied and reassured by the solitude, and the noise. You wouldn't think so, but even here there's noise—up here in the bloody Cevennes, this godforsaken region of mountains and sheep, even in the absolute isolation of my *fumerie*, in the absolute isolation of my

own house, in the absolute isolation of my graveyard, far from village and from farm, far from the last human hovel.

The people here don't come near the graveyard. They're afraid of it. Nobody was willing to be the sexton, and so they had to come looking for me; the old sergeant of the Foreign Legion, wounded in action, scraping by on a pension, and dying of hunger on the streets of Paris. It was years since I left the village to join the Legion, but someone remembered me. I was glad of the job. I'm not afraid of the graveyard. I'm not afraid of anything.

Is that dusk? No, it must be the smoke from this pipe. Hell of a pipe! There's too much dross in it; the bamboo is all black . . . Wish I had one of those metal jobs. Silver-inlaid. Maybe gold. Or jade . . . a jade pipe. Jesus, that'd be a smoke you'd remember.

Still maybe an hour of daylight to go. Just the same, I'm going to shut the gates this minute . . . I prefer to go down there before nightfall. Before twilight, even.

I *am* going down there.

There, I've locked up. God, what a racket in this sunny graveyard! I'm deaf with it. There are bees and dragonflies, buzzing and humming. Crickets and grasshoppers. Birds too, with their calls and twitterings. And then the trees, and the wind that rustles their leaves. That's not counting the more distant noises. It's surprising how sound carries up here. I hear cows lowing; the occasional motor; even the workshop in the next village, though that's ten miles away at least.

Not that I mind all this noise. Because it drowns out other sounds . . . Faint, murmuring, low-voiced noises—the noises of the night, awaiting their turn . . . but it's not yet night, eh?

I never used to hear so many sounds. It's the opium. It's as though I had wax in my ears, and the warm smoke melted it.

All this began at Tonkin, when I first started smoking. I remember my arrival, on the deck of the transport. We had

put in at Saigon; and in the evening, those of who had leave were turned loose in the city. Like the others, I thought only of getting a decent feed, getting drunk, and getting laid—not necessarily in that order.

But no sooner had I left the gangplank than I stopped short before a large wall that skirted the first street. From behind it came an aroma I never smelled before, a gentle and disturbing odor—an odor that, from the very first, made its way through my nostrils to my soul.

I didn't smoke anything that time. My first pipe came at Pak-Nah, in the mountains. It was a tiny post, surrounded by a forest filled with dead and rotting vegetation; with fever and madness. We smoked a lot down there. That's when I really began to *listen*. At night, we could hear the roving tigers, even though they trod as lightly as house cats. It was rather amusing at first, those imperceptible noises which we, nonetheless, infallibly detected.

One night, a bandit from Doc-Theu's gang came to spy on the post. He slipped in along the palisades without any more noise than an adder, but we heard him all the same, and our hearing was so precise that, just as he went to climb the bamboos, our corporal gut-shot him, by guesswork, without even seeing his man. Another night, the alarm bell started to clang. Everyone was up and grabbing for their rifles when I caught the sound of our pet goat's hooves. She'd broken her tether, ducked her head, and run full-tilt against the bell rope.

Yes, back then, it was useful to have good hearing. I don't find it so useful now.

From the day of my arrival back in Paris after being invalided out, it proved to be a curse. The little *pension* where I took a room, for instance. I could hear every movement in all the rooms: the guy who snored, the couple who fucked all the time, and the one who left the water running in his washbasin.

I moved to the other end of Montparnasse, away from the boulevard. Nobody else in the building—but that just made it worse! Because now I could hear what went on in the streets around. All the prowlers, the forced locks, the fences that were scaled. It was like at Pak-Nah, when I had heard the bandit legging it over the palisade. And I'd dig my fingernails into my bedclothes, constantly expecting to see my door open and some brigand busting in.

So I moved again, this time to the busiest place I could find, in the heart of Paris, the Faubourg Saint Antoine. The racket was such—day and night—that I couldn't tell one noise from another. It was like a full orchestra with all the instruments howling and screeching in unison.

Since I couldn't sleep, I started using opium more—no friend of sleep, opium! But this caused another problem. My supply was already running low. I'd brought with me from Tonkin all that I was able to carry; but to begin with, those dirty customs officers stole a box from me; and in the second place, I had figured that I would smoke less in France than I had down there, whereas the contrary was the case. I found an obliging druggist in Paris, but the stuff he carried was nothing but rubbish, and what's more, my pension money was going fast.

I'd been advised to put in for a license to run a little *tabac;* veterans with disabilities were supposed to get preference, and I limp a little, ever since my wound at Son-Tay, but as usual it went to some priest's bastard. That's when I got this job as sexton of the graveyard in my old village.

There you are; it's night now. I can hear the bats . . . that odd muffled sound their wings make. And there's the birds, sounding a retreat. And now the wind has dropped. That caps the climax.

About this is when I start to hear those other sounds . . . Not so clear, not so simple, not so innocent as the noises of

day—but more dangerous to listen to, more agonizing, more
torturing. At first, I thought it was the dead slipping out of
their sepulchers to do a skeleton dance in the moonlight. But
no, it is not that. The dead are dead, and do not come back.
Or if they do come back, it is with footsteps so furtive that I
do not hear them—not even I!—not yet . . .

No, I cannot hear the skeleton dance. I hear something else.

I hear forbidden sounds, sounds which no one has ever
heard; the pallid and macabre sounds which lie stagnating at
the feet of cypress trees and of mausoleums, those nocturnal
sounds that shun the sun, the living breeze and the birdsong;
cold sounds that freeze the flesh of men and cause the hair to
bristle on the backs of their necks.

My opium lamp alone is left to yellow my walls. Not a single
reflection of twilight any longer enters my shutterless window.

Down there, I can hear the will-o'-the-wisps grazing the
yews. It is night, black night.

Hey, is that the coffins moaning? Do you hear them?

I hear the creaking and moaning of coffin wood as it warps
in the rain-soaked earth. I hear metal caskets, too heavy for
their graves, gradually sinking into the slimy mud, sinking
eternally. I hear rotten flesh swarming with nimble vermin,
and the clattering of dried bones as they subside, one after
another, upon the cloth of winding sheets. And from this
square-walled enclosure where fifteen hundred corpses have
come to sleep, one after another, fifteen hundred terrifying
noises escape from it and come gliding, every night, to my
too-finely-attuned ears. Fifteen hundred groans from the
beyond, each one of which insinuates its seed of madness into
my ruined brain.

My God, I wish I could leave this tumultuous graveyard.
But I cannot. Where would I find opium; the opium that keeps
me alive; magic opium, which intoxicates me with delicious

illusions; faithful opium, which supports me here, trembling but true to my post, in defiance of vagrant madness? Where?

Because there's something I haven't told you.

The poppy is a hardy flower. It grows anywhere, and needs almost no cultivation. Only the black poppy of Yunnan and India produces opium, but some old friends kindly sent me some seeds of the Tonkinese poppy. Planted in the corpse-fattened grave-yard, they flourished marvelously. The moment I make an incision in the sugar-swollen heads, white drops pearl out to my heart's content, and when I roll all the drops into one big ball, dissolve them in warm water, then filter the water and reduce it—ah, then my smooth black opium is worth all the drugs of Benares and of China. And it is the graveyard which has worked the miracle. So, you can see plainly enough that I am in no position to leave.

Hey! I heard . . . No, maybe not.

I did not hear. It is not true that a louder creaking is audible, working its way up through the mortuary soil. It is not true that a coffin has vibrated in its bed.

Because if it were true, that would be the sixth one buried alive to agonize in my graveyard—the sixth one this year. The sixth to whose groans and death rattle I have had to listen. The sixth grad-ually to expend his or her failing strength against the wooden so-lidity of his casket. The sixth whom I have heard mangling feeble hands, even teeth, and dying, dying of fear and of despair.

Yes, I have undergone this atrocity five times within a year . . . and I shall have to endure it one time more, for the reason that—of what use to lie? It is true—the one buried alive is stirring, and I can hear his anguished sigh, close neighbor as yet to the lethargic sleep from which he is waking.

Ah, yes? So, you think, my good folks, that this does not happen, that it is a pure invention on the part of the madman or the novelist, that tombs are always peaceful, and that there is no such thing as persons buried alive? You foolishly believe,

upon the word of solemn undertakers, that medicine never makes a mistake, and that it never buries any but corpses? Keep counting on that, and sleep in peace, *you who can*. As for me, to whom opium has given ears with which to hear, I hear. And I tell you plainly that, out of every ten who are buried, there is one who *is not dead*. And I also know that this one's agony—his second agony—surpasses in horror all that your poor obtuse brain could possibly imagine.

Perhaps you believe another fantasy of the funeralmongers; that even if some old bloke is buried alive, he would just half wake up, six feet under, look around, shrug, and quietly fade away with a sigh. You really believe that, having miraculously regained both sense and breath, he would relinquish them again without a struggle? Then you do not know what life is, and with what claws a dying man clings to it, when he feels it escaping him.

At Tonkin, in the old days, I used to hunt deer—big, tawny deer, with tapering legs. Well, one day, I put two shots from my 8mm Lebel rifle into a poor doe. She went down in an instant, her whole rib cage torn open. I easily could have shoved my two fists into the hole. I came up to her and placed my foot upon the red carcass—and the carcass rose and trotted off, dragging after it bowels, heart, and lungs!

They are like that, these ones I am telling you of, who are buried alive. Very nearly as dead as their neighbors, they still howl at the top of their voices, and keep turning over to strain their backs against the lid! Listen, listen, do you hear that creaking? Fortunately, the earth is heavy above him. He won't get out, the bugger! I shall never see him, all pale and smeared with thick mud, lurching toward me from between the tombstones, feet crushing the poppies that bind me to this place with cables woven from dreams . . .

Another pipe! Good God, how long the night is!

{ 13 }

The Red Palace

One thing is certain: I am no longer a man, no longer a man at all.

Of that, there can be no doubt. There is no longer anything in common between myself and the human race—neither sense nor thought. It is clear that whatever force powers me differs completely from that which motivates others, and is altogether novel and superior.

I am, then, no longer a man. But—and this is surely a unique circumstance!—*I have not become anything else.* Neither corpse nor ghost—nothing at all.

My body is there. I look upon it, and I touch it. It is the body of a man, no doubt about that. Apparently there was no need of my sense and thoughts to leave that body during the process of transformation. I even look the same. Anybody seeing me would have no idea that I have broken with the earth, and am heading for the Beyond.

What has happened is, simply, this: my spirit has ripened too quickly, in advance of its proper season. One springtime, I remember seeing a barn on fire in the middle of an orchard. From evening to morning, the peaches and the apricots grew heavy and vermilion, having been ripened by the fire; and yet, they did not fall, because the branches that bore them had remained green.

And so it is with my body, which has remained alive about me, even though I'm technically dead; or at least gone on to a superior life.

But when one reflects upon it, what reason is there for an obligatory simultaneity in the death of the two, the death of the Being and the death of the . . . well, call it the Wrapper? None whatsoever. Any accident is sufficient to bring such a thing to pass: that fire which ripened the peaches, for instance. In my case, I believe it's the opium that, patiently, pipeful by pipeful, I have come to substitute for the blood in my veins. *For I have smoked my weight in opium in the course of my life.*

It stands to reason that, if you smoke that much opium— opium the immaterial, opium the prodigious—it might very well—might it not?—raise a man above all other men, and absolutely disengage him from his grosser substance.

That is somewhat the case with me. My body is living, yes, though not completely intact. Opium has been able to emaciate it and attenuate it sufficiently to prevent it encumbering me further. Flagellants and hermits achieve the same effect by depriving the body of food, or punishing it with hair shirts, whips, and so on. Barbaric and puerile methods, compared to smoking a few hundred pipes.

And so I float, between body and soul, earth and heaven, the past and the great Beyond . . .

And, to speak simply of my body at this particular moment, on a stretch of dark water under a sky scattered with stars.

I am still sufficiently tethered to my body to be aware of that sky, of the salt water of the Golden Horn of Constantinople that splashes against the side of my boat, and the spray from the oars that makes me shiver with the cold. I can hear the boatman singing, and his song, melodious to human ears, is not displeasing to my own. It really would seem that I am a man still.

There's the bank, and the stone steps leading to the quay. Behind me, the waters of the Boghasi indulge in their nightly plaint, and gnaw tirelessly at the two continents they separate.

In front of me, the Red Palace, deserted and in ruins, cuts off the horizon with its bloodred bulk.

At the gate, the sentinel leans heavily on his musket, the red of his fez blending with the wall. One does not enter here, under pain of death. But I have given the sentinel—who is a smoker—some opium, and the freemasonry of the drug is a bond between us. He pointedly turns his back and stares into the dark as I pass. Here I am in the antechamber, under the great beams which, gnawed through by age, will soon come tumbling down; now on the stair covered with mats so ancient they have turned to dust; now in the high-ceilinged rooms, from which one perceives, at the rear, a park in the form of an amphitheater; and now under the roof, where my *fumerie* is.

It's not much of a *fumerie*. Just a carpet in an empty room. An old Bokhara carpet, it's true. On it sits a smooth copper tray, a black bamboo pipe, and a lamp that smokes, because its glass is cracked, and crudely mended.

The walls are bare wood, and the paint on the rafters is peeling. But through the window, which has no glass, the park, forty times a hundred years old, spreads in all its formidable majesty.

And no sound comes, save the sighing of the wind through the pointed branches of the dead trees.

Here I am now, reclining upon my left side, as I prepare my first pipe. The Red Palace is an ancient dwelling, built by nobody-knows-whom. Many masters have inhabited it, and nearly all of them have died there by violence. An evil destiny hovers within its walls and lurks near the gates, within the thick foliage of the park.

A prince once made it his residence; a Greek prince, celebrated in history, whose name signifies treason.

In those days, luxury and magnificence filled the Red Palace. Slaves of all races scurried along its halls, and nobility that came there to visit its master arrived on admirals' barges with fourteen rowers each.

The prince was old and powerful. Age and pride had forged for him a heart of steel. Frequently, for slight cause, he would condemn servants and eunuchs to the most extreme punishments. Heads fell under the scimitar until the terrace of the park became soaked in blood.

And I happen to know that this blood was there mingled with vestiges of other and more ancient blood, a horrible blood that had been spilled upon this same terrace so many centuries before that no one any longer was able to remember.

One evening, certain mutes crossed the threshold. They were under the command of one who bore a green parchment, at the sight of which all genuflected. The prince, rudely seized in his own room, offered no resistance, and even kissed the august signature. And there, to that hook in the rafter above me, a rope was fastened, and the prince was hanged.

When the violet-colored tongue had slipped out from between the bloodless lips, when the great toes ceased their

convulsions, the executioners cut the rope, and then severed the head to bear proof to their sovereign.

For three days, the decapitated body remained unburied— here, upon this very floor. The slaves, frightened out of their wits, had fled. And it was a woman, whom nobody knew, who furtively buried it, down there in the park, at the foot of the big spindle wood tree.

Since then, the Red Palace has known other masters. But not one slept without fear, and misfortune came to many. The sovereign himself, whose seal upon a piece of green parchment had brought about the death of the prince, was deposed in turn by his own people, and died strangled in a dungeon. His empire, for centuries brilliant and glorious, foundered in shame and in blood. Warlike peoples battered it from all sides, and princes claiming the halo of Destiny shared their spoils. Now, the Imperial Standard, a pathetic rag, feebly waves over a few uncultivated fields, some sand dunes, a handful of crumbling forts—scraps with which the conquerors couldn't be bothered.

And the Red Palace, also crumbling and empty, awaits only the empire's last agony before sinking at last into dust.

So as I explained, I am no longer a man, no longer a man at all. But I have not yet become anything else.

I am, thus, in the middle of the bridge, equidistant, like this city, from one bank and from the other. But nobody can live in the middle of a bridge. One must go on, or go back.

To go back, to become a man once more? Impossible. Since I'm already dead, I would have to be resurrected. Which is clearly impossible.

But since I'm still uncertain, the better course is, I've decided, to wait, even though the waiting be extremely difficult and fatiguing; to wait—and to smoke.

And so, if I am here in the Red Palace on this evening, following so many other evenings, it is not with any purpose of
unraveling the Gordian knot that holds me bound, since I am
not yet able to unravel that knot, and since I dare not cut it.
No, it is merely to wait, and to smoke.

Opium, moreover, is the only sedative my anxiety knows,
since it alone is able to bring men near to phantoms, and to
lift that veil separating the Here from the Hereafter. Up to
this moment, it has not seen fit to undo the knot for me—to
make me a phantom. But every night, it renders visible and
intangible, to those new senses which it has given me, beings
of the other world, of that world to which I soon shall belong.
Thanks to opium, I taste the exile's melancholy joy as he con-
templates from the altitudes of his island the shoreline of his
fatherland.

This pipe is my thirtieth, as nearly as I can tell. That is
sufficient to unseal my eyes. And now, as I look out into the
park, I begin to see less clearly the bushes, the clusters of foliage and the lindens on the terrace, which stretch out their
branches like writhing serpents toward the black sky.

Less clear are the vague, discolored, and wavering forms
that glide here and there through the night mist.

Opium does not call up phantoms. On the contrary, its
dark and sovereign power frightens them away. I know that
the black smoke now spreading over my rug is sufficient to
protect me from any supernatural attack. The frail appari-
tions that prowl the park would never dare cross this windowsill. But, thanks to opium, the intrepid and the clairvoyant,
I can see them, and so am able to stroll freely through my
fatherland-to-be.

And that is why I have chosen the Red Palace as an asylum.
That is why, each evening, I drag my tired limbs here, the
tired and complaining limbs of a smoker who is never satis-

fied. Where better than in this blood-bespattered dwelling to encounter those beings who will soon be my compatriots in the land of the dead? As phantoms are in the habit of wandering near those places where their cadavers have reposed, the Red Palace swarms with pale and weeping ghosts.

This is my sixtieth pipe. This evening, I have smoked more than usual. And I shall, accordingly, behold more phantoms than usual.

They arrive in order of their dissolution. I have, just this moment, happened upon some recent ghosts. They are decent, and more sad than strange or terrible. Their skeletons clatter lightly in the breeze, while the tatters of their shrouds and funeral vestments still flutter about them.

But now they scurry back to their tombs, alarmed by specters from the century earlier, who always arrive at the fiftieth pipe. A dismal band of barely perceptible beings emerges from the cypresses, trailing after them the instruments of their death—ropes, scimitars, bowstrings. Slaves, eunuchs, and faithless wives, they were executed at the sovereign's whim. Their insubstantial bones no longer make any noise, and I am scarcely able to distinguish the effaced outlines of their former bodies. Nevertheless, suffering and fear are upon their faces, and they are careful to skirt the terrace with the big lindens; careful, also, to avoid the dark lane that leads to the funereal spindle tree. Throughout all eternity, the executioner's victims continue to fear him and to flee his terrible shade.

More, more opium. I wish, today, to go all the way to that frontier that separates drunkenness from death.

I have smoked a hundred pipes, all of them heaping ones, and my opium is a powerful mixture of Yunnan and Benares. Those ties which, until recently, bound me to my fleshly rags

and tatters, are stretched tight as a bowstring; and in that flesh there remains barely the power to lift the bamboo and to cook the drug over the flame.

My immaterial soul is almost free, and wanders, vagabond-like and at will, across the overgrown greenery of the park. I hover at the tomb of the decapitated Greek prince, and see why it is the branches and the leaves of the trees are shuddering so. It is his tall figure that brings terror to the trembling cypresses. Behold him rising from his grave, blood still streaming from his severed neck. His robes, embroidered in gold, gleam brilliantly, despite the putrescence of the dank soil, as his decapitated head grinds its teeth beside him.

He is walking now. In terror, lesser phantoms flee back to nothingness.

After him, by the hair, he drags his head, the stubble of his beard catching on the brambles of the path. Red drops coagulate upon the sand, and a skeleton dog sneaks up to sniff them.

He has taken the center path, the one that leads to the Red Palace. But at the door, the odor of the drug stands guard. Instead, without pausing, he ascends the marble stairs to the terrace with the big lindens; the terrace soaked in blood, in ancient blood.

He mounts with exceedingly slow steps, with the gait of a prince and of a master. In the light of the stars, his hands may be seen gleaming with rings, and occasionally, he lays one of his hands, imperiously, upon a plinth or balustrade. The dog trots after him, at a distance, and sometimes pauses, irresolute.

In the shadows at the top of the steep flight, the Red Palace is barely distinguishable, and nothing is to be perceived except the sea, beating dolefully at the foot of the walls. From above,

the terrace resembles a scaffold. The lindens cover it with a veil of black leaves, and leprous mosses creep about its base like a funeral garment.

The headless silhouette has reached the last of the steps. I now can see it pulling up short, as in front of a precipice, as the skeleton dog, trembling with fright, turns and flees, with fantastic leaps and bounds, through the thicket. The severed head upon the ground gives a weird start, each of its hairs bristling with horror.

As I approach, anxious to discover the cause of all this terror, the phantom wavers and becomes a discolored apparition. I already can see through it; it is no more than a gray vapor, with a few scraps of gilt still gleaming here and there, and with some tinsel of embroidery and jewels. Gradually, all becomes attenuated and effaced, blending with the darkness. The severed head remains behind for a few seconds, the gleam of its white eyes surviving the loss of bodily contours. Then, all disappears, and nothing is left but the night.

The terrace is absolutely dark. The terrified will-o'-the-wisps have retired underground. The dead trunks of the lindens shiver with fright, and fragments of bark slip from them, to hide under the moss.

One by one, the minor phantoms creep back into sight, looking around fearfully in case the decapitated prince should choose to return. I can see the bodies of two slaughtered infants, silently weeping. Others have less form. That one there is dragging itself along on the ground; that one is groveling in the red slime; it is, in short, a horrible pulp of amputated members, bloodless heads, and hearts snatched from their bosoms. Unspeakable crimes emerge from the earth.

And now, I know, I know . . . I have gone down the whole course of the centuries. And here comes, from out the ancient mist, a creature spilling all its blood.

Like a giant bat, a female bat, grazing the trees in its shaggy flight. I can make out the mortal beauty of its love-inspiring face, and the opulence of that somber hair, strewn with venomous serpents.

I recognize her. Her name is Medea. Medea the sorceress, wife of Jason, victor of the Golden Fleece. When he abandoned her for another woman, in vengeful fury she poisoned his new wife and slaughtered her own children.

It is here that Medea gathers her poisons. It is here that the blond hero, the golden-haired conqueror, throws her, palpitating, upon the amorous grass. It is here that she takes vengeance upon the flesh of her flesh, and pays each stolen kiss with an infant's corpse.

She comes, I think, for me.

Can it be that my body, down there in the *fumerie* of the Red Palace, is now at last wholly dead?

{ 14 }

The Nightmare

It is the end, the end of everything.

It has been eight . . . nine . . . no, more than that . . . forty days? that I have had nothing to eat, or drink. My throat no longer accepts even tea. Something on the threshold stops it, something like dross, like opium, something . . . I do not know what. It has been forty days, or forty months, that I have had no tea to drink, and nothing else whatsoever, naturally—and how many years since I last slept?

I do not know. I know nothing anymore. Nothing anymore. Good heavens! In order to know, to reckon, to attain some sort of certitude concerning anything, it would be necessary—would it not?—to see, to hear, to feel—to make use, in short, of what men call their senses, their five senses? Five? Are there five? It makes little difference, after all. Yes, it would be necessary to do all that. But I have no more senses. It has been a long time, indeed, since I had any. I cannot see.

I have looked too long at the lamp, and at the yellow opium, budding and crackling above the lamp. I have looked too long into the night, opening wide my horrified eyes in an effort to compel them to see what men do not see, the beyond, the pale and terrifying world of phantoms. My eyes have seen them, and that is why, now, they no longer see anything, except the lamp, the opium lamp.

Yes, the phantoms . . . As a matter of fact, that is not true; there are no phantoms, since I have ceased to see them. A hallucination, a hallucination which has disappeared, that is all. I am well enough aware that there are no phantoms. Alas! There is nothing.

There is Nothingness.

I can no longer hear, either. I have listened too intently to the sounds out of the silence, sounds which no one ever heard except myself, who am about to die; sounds made by the motionless air, and by the earth in repose, and by the infinite little beings that live and die upon the earth. And the buzzing that comes from it all has embedded itself so formidably into my ears that I no longer have any eardrums left. And now, no sound from outside breaches my solitude. My solitary brain clamors and howls in the middle of my cranium, so loudly that all within me is shattered, as my bones crumble to dust; that dust which I so soon shall be.

Tell me, do you think that the dust will smell of opium? No? And yet, I have smoked much. Three, four, a hundred pipes a day—or more, even, who knows?

I no longer see, and I no longer hear. And so it is with everything. There is not one human sensation left me, not one human action of which I am capable. Not one, not one.

Nothing.

Ah! yes, one thing, a verb: to suffer.

Oh, the suffering that I endure! Oh, the fire which rends and

devastates my entrails, reddening them to a white heat! Inside me, there is a flaming wound, a wound that begins at my throat and ends lower down than my ankles; a wound that spares nothing, neither vein nor bowel, a wound that is perpetually spouting flames. The rivers, lakes, the sea and all the oceans might roll over those flames without extinguishing them. And it is forever, forever, with no pause, no respite, no sleep. All the way to nothingness, a more terrifying nothingness.

Upon my skin, the opium's itch has bitten in so deeply that I no longer have any epidermis left. My fingernails have torn it all away.

And if that were all! If there were nothing more!

There is the hunger and thirst after opium. Days and days without eating or drinking? All that is nothing, less than nothing: a pleasure. But an hour without opium, that . . . that is the terrible, the unutterable thing, the one disease for which there is no cure. It cannot be cured, for the reason that satiety itself does not extinguish such a thirst. Before smoking, I am dying from need of opium, and I die again afterward, and while I am smoking, and always. My body is in agony from the moment I abandon the pipe. I am that damned one who, in seeking comfort from burning coals, finds only molten lead.

At first—how long a time ago it was!—I had only brief sleeping spells, prostrations lasting a few hours, a few minutes, between two intoxications; a deadening slumber, utterly enervating, from which I arose more fatigued than by the most violent of love embraces; but real sleep, nonetheless, free of phantasmagoric images, closed to the terrors of the world without. Then day would come, with its feverish lethargies and its deliriums, filled with bewilderments, atrocities, and apocalypses.

And it was then that a sort of dismaying proportion was set up: to the degree to which opium abbreviated, cut short my moments of repose—for it was still repose, almost, in a cor-

responding degree—that same opium began filling, heaping, and cramming those moments with more bewilderments, with more atrocities and with more apocalypses. Until the super-human limit of this series, which no mathematician ever will be able to add up, was reached at last: that limit where sleep is reduced to zero and nightmare is raised to a corresponding and inverse power—one divided by zero equals: infinity.

I do not sleep anymore.

And nightmare, overstepping the too-restricted confines of my slumber, now has spread over all my day. I dream all the time, and that is vastly more atrocious.

Nightmare.

No one except opium smokers ever will know what a nightmare is.

I have heard people say, "Last night, I had a *frightful* dream: the walls came together and crushed me."

Or maybe, "I fell down a precipice." Or, perhaps, "I saw my wife and children being tortured, without being able to rescue them."

And those persons will raise their hands to their eyes and remark with horror, "What a nightmare!"

In my own nightmare, there is neither precipice, nor wall, nor wife, nor children. There is the void, nothingness, and the night. There is the awful reality of death, so near, so near, that the condemned man waiting for the guillotine never glimpses eternity so close up as I. Death, round about me, roves and stagnates. It blocks door and window; it crawls across the mat; it flowers into atmospheric molecules; it enters my lungs along with the black smoke; and when I emit the smoke, it does not come forth.

Here is a chap who is already dead, like myself. They have tossed him into a well.

But wait, where is that well, in reality? That makes no dif-

ference. They have tossed him into a well. There is an eel at the bottom of the well.

An eel, or a water snake? Or a water snake! Do you hear?

The snake has bitten the corpse. It, in turn, is dead—naturally. They fished it up because it was an eel! And the cat has bitten the eel. The cat! Do you hear? It is here, the cat. Big as a tiger, naturally. But with the head of a very small kitten. It is dying. It whirls about the lamp. I whirl, too, in an opposite direction. We are going to meet . . . we are going to meet . . .

Ha! ha! ha! Help . . .